D1545823

Dark Diamond Reel

Sequel to Constancy's Waltz

Dark Diamond Reel
Copyright © 2005 Donna Parker
All rights reserved.

Cover Art
Copyright 2005 © Lee Emory
All rights reserved.

WhoooDoo Mysteries
A division of
Treble Heart Books
1284 Overlook Dr.
Sierra Vista, AZ 85635-5512
http://www.trebleheartbooks.com

Published and printed in U.S.A.

The characters and events in this book are fictional, and any resemblance to persons, whether living or dead, is strictly coincidental.

All rights reserved. No part of this book may be reproduced or transmitted in any form by any means, electronic or mechanical, including photocopying, recording, scanning to a computer disk, or by any informational storage and retrieval system, without express permission in writing from the publisher.

ISBN: 1-932695-08-7

Other Books by Donna Parker

Constancy's Waltz

Dark Diamond Reel

Donna Parker

Treble Heart Books

Dedication

For Neal, my real-life hero

Chapter 1

*A*spirin. *I need aspirin.* Or something more potent. I lay in bed a moment longer, willing my head to stop pounding.

It didn't work.

This flu, or whatever it was, had got much worse overnight. Yesterday it was nausea. This morning, my head. I had to get something to ease it.

I crawled out of bed and wobbled into the kitchen for some water to go with my aspirin.

It was automatic to turn a light on in a dark room. Sometimes it's a mistake.

What was that at my kitchen table?

No!

Not again! Oh, please, not another *dead body.*

I stared at the dead man with eyes that couldn't quite focus. Maybe I was still asleep. Maybe he would soon vanish like bodies did sometimes in my nightmares.

I should have known it wouldn't be that easy.

The whole thing was absurd, insane, unfair. Again.

I wanted to scream. Too bad I never could do it on demand. Couldn't last time, couldn't now.

Who is he? How did he get here? Why me?

I wasn't ready to play the role of chief suspect in a murder investigation again. Why did some dead guy have to appear in my kitchen?

I didn't even know this man. I didn't know how he'd died. I didn't know what to do next.

One thing I did know. I was in trouble.

Deep, deep trouble.

Again.

At least my finding this corpse can't harm Gram.

If that thought was supposed to be sent as a consolation, it was bittersweet at best.

I clenched my jaw against the familiar, crushing flood of grief and defied those ever-lurking tears one more time. I couldn't fight them off forever. I knew that, but a crying fit now wouldn't help anything. Gram herself would've said so.

What *should* I do, Gram?

How many times had I asked her that question? As many times as I asked, she always answered the same way. *Just calm down and use the good sense God gave you. Take a deep breath.* Well, why not? It worked when I was a kid. Maybe it would work now. I took a slow, deep breath. Despite the hammering inside it, my brain began to function a little better.

Things actually didn't look so awful this time: No sprays of blood on my walls. No dark crimson puddles on my beige tile floor. No gory scissors lying around. This body was, as far as I could see, undamaged. I had no reason to assume he was dead, except that his eyes were open and staring, and empty of anything that remotely resembled life.

I hurriedly turned my eyes in another direction. Everything else in the kitchen seemed normal. Gram's ivy plant looked thirsty, though. In all yesterday's excitement, I'd forgotten to give it its weekly drink of water. Mustn't neglect that. Gram had loved that ivy plant. She made its crazy pig pot in her own backyard workshop years before I was born.

What was I doing? A dead man was sitting in my kitchen, and I was halfway to the sink with a glass in my hand? How could I be interested in watering plants? Even precious ones.

I put the glass down with a shaking hand and took another deep breath. It had hit me that way the other time, too. My first concern then was for the poster board I'd promised to collect for one of my fellow teachers.

Not to worry, Danny assured me. (He was still being kind at that point.) The reaction was merely an escape mechanism. Plain, average Constancy Grace Stafford involved in somebody's violent death was unthinkable. So I thought of other things until I could begin to cope. As a permanent escape, it was worth nothing, and no matter how fervently I wished that today's body could be only a figment of my over-worked nerves, it wasn't.

But maybe, maybe this one wasn't really dead. Maybe he was only in the throes of some kind of fit. How could I really know? I swallowed hard, approached him warily, on tiptoe for some idiotic reason, and fumbled for a pulse.

The phrase "stone cold dead" took on deep, new shades of meaning.

I backed out of the kitchen into the living room, made a dive for the telephone.

A moment later I returned the receiver, unused, to its cradle. Who was I going to phone? 911 would roll a fire truck, an ambulance and a police car. Neither the corpse nor I needed a fire truck. An ambulance would come too late for him, too soon for me.

That left the police. Sure. Some suspicious officer, probably Lon Tirso, would demand to know what I was doing with a corpse in my kitchen. Another corpse.

Oh mercy! I couldn't face a re-run of that last horrifying episode. This one would be a million times worse than the original. Most of Fraserton's small police force knew me on sight. Some of them had been my high school classmates. They wouldn't have forgotten that business in May. Suspicious deaths were rare in Fraserton. Or they had been. How could I be involved with a second less than half a year later, and this time in my own apartment?

Even phoning Zared was out of the question. His engagement ring felt more foreign now than it had when he'd put it on my finger yesterday. Such base things as the discovery of dead bodies surely couldn't happen to outstanding citizens like Zared Fraser, or presumably to his new fiancée. Yet here stood his fiancée with her second find. The Triumvirate would not be happy.

Maybe Danny Egan would. Danny Egan. He'd said more than once that I attracted trouble like carrion attracts crows. Danny did so enjoy being right.

His beautiful, sardonic face perched like one of those waiting crows in the corner of my mind. If I could connect with the policeman instead of the civilian that lived in Danny's skin, he might help me. He wouldn't necessarily want the job, but he wouldn't come in a screaming squad car greedy for an instant arrest like Lon Tirso would. On the other hand, if Officer Egan weren't on duty, darlin' Danny might not come at all.

We hadn't parted on the best of terms, though I honestly hadn't meant to trip him. I didn't intend to crack his ribs or give him concussion. Or that black eye. He, however, chose to take it personally. As a result, our paths hadn't crossed in all of five and a half months. Please God he was healed by now and had forgiven me for the injuries, and for some other, even more stupid, mistakes I'd made.

Whether he had or hadn't, though, I needed his help. Danny would have to put personal feelings aside and be professional. Wasn't assisting endangered people, like them or not, the first item on the list of police priorities?

I still had Danny's unlisted phone number in my book. With a little luck he hadn't changed it for fear of me. While I punched in the seven precious digits, I prayed as fervently as I knew how that Brendan Egan didn't hold long grudges.

The phone rang four times before he answered. "Egan here." Barely awake. More than a little annoyed by the interruption of his sleep. No wonder. It was still dark outside.

"Danny?" I couldn't project much more than a whisper.

He let only a second of silence go by before his computer-brain came awake and effortlessly retrieved the necessary information. "Heaven preserve us," he said, in his most aggravating Irish-cop caricature. "It's the banshee of Holly Court, is it?"

Banshee was one of the nicer titles he'd bestowed on me after I'd landed him in the hospital. "A banshee," he had explained with malice in his swollen and blackened eye, "is a fairy woman who flits about announcing grave tidings. You should take that literally. It's a death she gives voice over. Like you, Constancy. Now you've nearly finished me as well. Get out of my sight!"

"Constancy? It is you?"

"Y-yes." A plague on my shaky voice.

"To what do I owe this interruption of my hard-earned rest?"

"I—" Stress made me inarticulate. Danny sometimes had the same effect.

"Well?"

I cleared my throat and tried again. "I have a problem."

A groan. "Ah, love, you're not going to tell me you've found yet another corpse? Not at this unearthly hour of the morning?"

The endearment meant nothing. That kind of thing rolled off his tongue with the inevitability and velocity of water over Niagara Falls. "Not exactly," I said. "It found me this time."

"'And there is no end of their corpses; they stumble over their corpses.'"

"What?"

"I found that in the Bible not long ago. Book of Nahum, if

you're interested. Unpleasant, isn't it? It reminded me of you, somehow."

Why did I ever think his penchant for quoting Bible passages was an endearing quality? "I didn't stumble over the one this morning."

"This is, I assume, a joke. We are not amused."

"How could you think it's a joke? The man's in my kitchen. He's sitting at the table like he's fallen asleep over breakfast, except his eyes are open."

The silence at the other end seemed to stretch on forever. Some detached, adolescent part of my psyche registered pure glee. Danny Egan wasn't easily shocked into even temporary silence.

"What shall I do?" I asked.

"There truly is a body?"

"Yes, yes, yes."

"Then phone the police, darlin'."

"What are you, the milkman?"

I thought he never would speak. When he finally did, his voice was all silky warning. "Why did you not phone the station or 911?"

"I have this unnatural aversion to Lon Tirso and that police station." My voice kept catching in my throat as if I were near tears. I would not cry. "Last time you believed I was innocent."

"I paid dearly enough for it."

A hint of amusement there, after all. Not exactly what I'd hoped for, but better than what I'd feared.

"You know I didn't mean to trip you."

"I know that. You're still in your apartment?" Deep weariness saturated his words, but it was his working voice now. Thank goodness!

"Yes, I'm in the apartment."

"Alone?"

"Except for the body."

"You needn't count the deceased as company, but I want to be certain there's nobody else with you who shouldn't be."

"As in murderer?"

"As in murderer. If your man was murdered. Given your talent for finding trouble, he'd about have to be."

"The apartment's not big enough to hide in. I could see if anybody else were here, and he's not my man."

"All right. Constancy, are you altogether sure he is dead?"

"I couldn't feel a pulse."

"Any obvious wounds to account for it?"

"No. He doesn't look murdered, just dead. Maybe he had a heart attack or something, I don't know."

"Was he a friend of yours?"

"No!"

"Then why is he there?"

"I have no idea why. I have no idea how or when he got in here. I just know I don't want him here."

"Are the doors and windows of your apartment locked?"

"They should be."

"Check the locks. Don't touch, just look."

"Now?" I didn't want to put down the phone. That fragile line to the outside represented great safety. Or was it Danny who made me feel safe?

"I'll wait."

Everything was locked.

"All right," Danny said. "Now make the both of us a cup of tea, if you can do it without smashing the pot or scalding your hand. Make it strong and sweet. I'll be there by the time it's brewed. Can you manage that, do you think?"

"I'm perfectly capable of making tea."

"See and don't over-brew it, then."

He hung up before I could add that I wasn't about to make him his precious tea in a kitchen full of corpse. What had happened to "don't touch"?

I dressed as quickly as I could. At least he hadn't rejected my plea for help. I should be thankful for that much and take the rest as it came. I could manage as long as he stayed professional. Sadly, Danny didn't come with that kind of guarantee.

On official records, he was Brendan Conor Aengus Egan. All those glorious mythical names to choose from and he called himself Danny. That was the only simple thing about him. He was a dark-haired, dark-hearted, cinema-faced charmer who loved flaunting his native Irishness, especially when he suspected it would irritate.

He hadn't lost the accent. It could be delightful or devastating as the mood struck him, and his tongue needed to be registered as a lethal weapon. If one escaped drowning from the buckets of blarney, he might easily be cut down by the stabbing, slashing sarcasm the man could deliver with equal ease and sometimes in the same breath. I was, during those few days of our unavoidable close association, imperiled by both.

Yet, there was another facet to Danny. He could also be a nearly ideal policeman: careful, thorough and dedicated to finding the truth. He could even be kind and compassionate when it suited him. On that awful day in May, he had banished the demon of the arrogant, bullying Lon Tirso, and, with a subversive smile and a voice as soft and gentle as Irish mist, had spoken away the worst of my terror. Then he had applied his talents to ferreting out the real murderer. That was the Danny that mattered, the one I needed now.

Not even for that Danny, though, would I stay another minute in the same apartment as an unknown corpse. I pulled on a coat, locked my door and escaped down the outside staircase to wait on the front porch swing.

My breath fogged in the apple-scented air. As cold as it was in the October pre-dawn darkness, and even with the possibility of a murderer lurking in the vicinity, I preferred sitting in the open to keeping company with the dead stranger.

People consumed with self-pity never got much sympathy from me, but as I huddled there shivering and waiting, I began to develop a bad case of it myself.

My apartment was on the second floor of a comfortable old house on a beautiful, quiet street. I'd moved in a little over a year ago when I came home to Fraserton to take charge of my first kindergarten class. I wanted to teach here to be close to my great-grandmother, Amanda Casey.

I rarely ever saw my landlady. She wasn't home much, so I had the place mostly to myself. I had enjoyed my cozy, peaceful nest. *Would it ever seem peaceful again?*

Maybe I wouldn't need an apartment now, anyway. Maybe this time I would go straight to jail. Do not pass go. Do not collect two hundred dollars.

Since the end of May, my life had become a real parade of horrors. The first body, Danny, the loss of a job I loved and my inability to find another like it, my great-grandmother's death three weeks ago. Now this.

Zared Fraser was the only bright spot. He seemed to want me when nobody else did. Would he wait and marry an ex-con? The media would love that. The other Frasers would have conniptions.

If only Gram were still with me. But she wasn't. She never would be again. As much as I wanted to, I couldn't even quite believe, like she had, in a benevolent and caring God. I was on my own. Except maybe for Danny.

The eastern sky turned from cold gray to pale lemon and a chilly-sounding bird chirped a few rusty notes. Too bad I hadn't taken that aspirin. But I wasn't going back for it now. Not until Danny came. I pulled my coat collar up around my ears.

Somewhere in the neighborhood one early riser, then another, started a vehicle and drove away. As the sound of the second faded, Danny's car shuddered to a stop at the curb.

I fought it. I truly did. I'd fought it since the first moment I knew I had to phone him. But the instant I saw him again, the old feeling exploded inside me like somebody had torched a major fireworks factory in the vicinity of my solar plexus. I didn't want that. Didn't need it. I couldn't afford to feel anything for Danny Egan. It hurt too much.

"I suppose your sitting out here means no tea," he said as he waded through the frosty grass toward the porch.

The grim turn of his mouth confirmed that he wasn't any happier about our reunion than I was, but he had come. At least he had come.

The weird, lemony light revealed new, deep lines etched into his forehead and a few silver hairs glinting among the black. Dressed in ragged jeans and only a light jacket, his shoulders hunched against the cold, he seemed to have aged years since I last saw him. He looked thinner, too, and exhausted. Totally, utterly exhausted.

I fingered the diamond solitaire on my left hand, brought Zared forcibly to mind and took refuge in attempted sarcasm. "I've seen enough television to know not to touch anything."

"Television doesn't always get it right."

"You didn't really expect me to stay up there with him, did you?"

"Not at all. Ordering you into the kitchen was the surest way to keep you out of it. Did they not teach you reverse psychology in your education courses? It works especially well with pets and young children."

Good. Good! Danny hadn't changed on the inside. That would be a great help in squashing whatever silly, lingering attraction I thought I was feeling.

"Come along now and let's see this corpse," he said.

"You can look without me."

He grasped my icy hand firmly and pulled me up from the swing. Zared's diamond, sliding sideways, bit into my finger. "Be brave now, *a chuisle*. The man could hardly be harming you, could he?"

"Not unless you count his causing me to be a murder suspect again, and don't spout those stupid Irish endearments at me." I jerked my hand free. It was trembling.

Danny put on his best martyred-saint face. It should have warned me what was coming. "Constancy Grace," he crooned. "What a shame it is that a mother can't foresee the future when she puts a name on an infant. I've never known one less appropriately named than you. Grace. I ask you!"

With great effort, I kept silent. Arguing only prolonged it.

"There's no need your getting upset over the Irish. A chuisle merely means—"

Enough was enough. "It doesn't mean anything when you say it to me. All I am to you is a super pain." I was shivering with cold and fright, sick of being insulted, and my head hurt worse than it ever had in my life. Knowing that I sounded like a spoiled five-year-old didn't improve my temper, either.

"You underestimate your attraction." Danny's voice was solemn. "You are a fascinating diversion, a morbid and dangerous entertainment akin to keeping a plague rat as a pet or carrying an armed atomic weapon during a ski-jump competition."

I had never in all my adult life slapped anybody, but such was the state of my nerves that I took a serious swing at Danny then.

Emerald eyes glinting, he neatly caught my wrist. "Feeling better now, are you? A bit more steady?"

Nobody should have eyes that vivid shade of green. It wasn't fair. With some difficulty, I transferred my gaze to my hand, which was no longer shaking, and once more snatched it free from his grip. Maybe Lon Tirso and jail would have been better in the long run. "I wish I had never called you."

"On that point we're in perfect agreement, but you've done it now, so let's have a bit of co-operation, shall we?"

I turned my back on him and marched up the stairs. Even though my hands had stopped shaking, I still fumbled over the key.

With an exasperated sigh, Danny tweaked it from my fingers. Even in his frustration, he looked carefully before using it and herding me inside. "We'll get it right over," he said. "Where is he?"

"Through there. Danny, I don't want to see him again."

"Did you know him?"

"I told you I didn't know him."

"You told me he wasn't a friend. There are other things he might have been to you. Did you know him at all?"

"No. I never saw him before in my life."

"What's that door?" he asked, nodding toward the far corner of my living room.

"It goes to Mrs. Jamison's part of the house. It's always locked. I don't have a key."

Danny inspected the door. "Someone must have had a key, then, to this door or the other. I see no signs of forced entry."

"I don't give out keys to my apartment."

"Was I saying you did? He, or whoever put him here, could have got it any number of ways. We'll be having a chat with Mrs. Jamison about putting a bolt on this side."

"She's never home."

"Is she not? Then we'll just see what's in the kitchen."

"Danny, I'd rather not."

"You needn't go. Wait here, if you like."

I liked it better than the alternative. I planted myself in my rocking chair, the chair farthest from the kitchen, and sat staring out the window. Though there was a pleasant view from that window, I could see nothing but a dead man's soul-empty eyes.

How had he got into my kitchen? Did he come in and then die? Why had he been here in the first place? Or had he been brought in already dead? If that were the case, who put him there? Why? In either case, why? Even if my head had felt perfectly normal, I was sure the situation wouldn't have made any sense to me.

Only a moment passed before Danny was back, his hand very gentle on my shoulder. "Constancy?"

Not love or darling or even one of his meaningless Irish endearments. Just Constancy. "Um?"

"What are you playing at?"

Danny had been angry with me the last time I saw him, but this wasn't the quick, hot anger I'd experienced then. I'd heard this exquisitely controlled note in his voice only once before. It wasn't directed at me that time, and if the man on the receiving end of it hadn't been fully deserving, I would have felt sorry for him.

I looked at Danny, then quickly away. I couldn't bear that icy, merciless expression.

"I'm not playing at anything. What have I done now?"

"That's what I'm asking you. Come with me."

Nobody defied Danny when he sounded like that. He headed for the kitchen and I followed. "Where is this body you were so upset at seeing?" he asked.

"What are you talking about? He's sitting there in plain sight."

Naturally he wasn't. The chair was empty, tucked neatly under the table as if it had never been disturbed.

Chapter 2

"Why didn't the man have the decency to vanish before I had to phone you?"

"If he ever was here."

Danny, you can't believe I'd make up something like that. Why would I? He was here. I t-touched him." I quickly dropped the hand I'd held out toward Danny. He couldn't see the impression of cold death that felt as if it would be imprinted forever on my fingers.

His expression thawed slightly. "Tell me exactly what you saw."

"He was sitting in that chair, slumped over the table. His face was turned toward me when I came in. He was thin. He had greasy blonde hair that looked like it was growing out from a bad cut. He was wearing a dark sweater and jeans, I think. They looked sloppy, way too big." I swallowed hard. "Danny, his eyes were so blank."

"Well done. Can you guess at an age and his height?"

"I don't know. Forty, maybe. I couldn't tell how tall, either. Average or a little above."

"Any distinguishing features?"

"Only that he was dead."

The last bits of Danny's cold policeman mask melted into a worried frown. "Then he can't have gone far. Were you waiting the whole time in your swing?"

"Yes. I couldn't bear to stay in here with him. If I had, I suppose he would still be here. I'm sorry."

"No need to be. It's just as well you went out. If you hadn't, you'd likely have been in the way of the person who moved him. Being in the way of a murderer, or even an accomplice to murder, is not a safe thing. However, if the body had come down the outside stairs, you'd not have missed him. Did you hear anything unusual?"

"I don't know. I didn't hear much of anything, really. Just a couple of neighbors somewhere leaving for work."

He wandered back into the living room and returned his attention to the locked door in the corner. "I'd guess your visitors came in and went out this way. Probably with a key, but not necessarily."

"Do you think they're still in that part of the house?"

"Most likely one of the vehicles you heard was the body being taken away, or at least the murderer going." Danny bent down and peered at the old-fashioned lock.

"What are you doing?"

"Considering a safari. Just in case." He pulled a key ring from his jacket, selected an old-fashioned black skeleton key with an ornate top and jabbed it experimentally into the lock.

"Isn't that breaking and entering? Don't you need a search warrant?"

He ignored me and turned the key. The lock clicked open. "There. Care to join me?"

"You can forget your reverse psychology."

"Fine. Keep a few steps behind me. You know the rules."

I knew his rules from previous experience. I was to

stay out of the line of fire until Danny had, dramatically, concluded any given room was clear, and I wasn't, *ever*, to get in front of him.

"We won't take any unnecessary chances," he said, and pulled a pistol from under his jacket.

"Going into that part of the house isn't?"

But there was no discouraging Danny from something he'd already decided to do.

The connecting door opened into a hall. There were three other doors on the landing, all of them open. Danny edged up beside the first door, took a deep breath and flung himself through it, gun leveled and steady in both hands. He repeated the action with the other doors.

"Nothing here," he whispered.

Nothing was right. Mrs. Jamison certainly hadn't stashed any bodies in her attic. She hadn't kept any odd bits of broken furniture or outgrown toys. No boxes of mementoes. No racks of clothing waiting the pendulum swing of style. Not a cobweb. Not even one visible speck of dust. It was as unlike Gram's attic as it could be.

"Swept clean." Danny was still whispering.

"This is not natural." The whispering was contagious. "Who'd have an empty attic? A clean, empty attic?"

"All the better to prevent foot prints, my dear, if one is criminal-minded."

"Mrs. Jamison?"

"You never know. Let's go down."

The stairs were in the center hall of the house. The rooms formed a kind of rough circle around the hall. We looked into three bedrooms, a bath, the kitchen, the dining room and the living room with all their attendant closets. No dead body. No living one, and not much else, either.

"Were you ever in here before now, Constancy?"

"No. The only time I've seen Mrs. Jamison face-to-face was

when I signed the lease and we did that in the apartment upstairs. I pay my rent by slipping the envelope through the mail slot. Once in awhile I hear her down here, but we don't visit."

"Would you recognize her if you saw her in a different context?"

"I don't know that I would. She's not a Fraserton native, but she's lived here for years."

"Does this look as if she's lived here for years? You'd think she'd at least have a jar of instant coffee and a cup in the kitchen, and maybe even a bed and a few extra clothes. She doesn't."

Only the living room had furniture and not much of it. The ragged sofa, chair, table, lamp looked lonely and forsaken. "Maybe she sleeps on the couch," I said, "but it doesn't look lived in."

"It's like a badly designed stage set. I'm beginning to wonder about your Mrs. J." He glanced at his watch. "Isn't it time you were away to school?"

So he hadn't heard. Why should he? I didn't bother to fight the decision. Even the gossip column that masqueraded as our hometown newspaper didn't print that snippet of news. "I don't have a school to go to, thanks to the first corpse. People suspected of murder in May don't come back to school as kindergarten teachers in August."

"You were altogether cleared." Danny sounded almost indignant. "There's no doubt at all who the murderer was. None. Nobody in his right mind could possibly still suspect you."

"Protective parents of five-year-olds take a lot of convincing. I'd probably feel the same if my child were involved. The 'what ifs' can't ever be wholly erased. They can't quite forget all the rumors they heard." *Including rumors that featured Danny instead of the murder.*

Danny glanced at me thoughtfully as we climbed the stairs. Not all the rumors about you were directly related to the murder, were they?"

I sighed. "Fraserton's still a very conservative community.

Most of the time that's fine with me, but they should base their conservative decisions on facts, not rumors."

"I'm truly sorry about that. Forgive my asking," he said, "but I won't have my friends starving. Are you okay financially?"

So I counted as a friend now, did I? Well, it was nice of him to be concerned. Thanks to Gram, I wouldn't starve if I didn't get work immediately, maybe if I never got work again. Danny couldn't know that, of course. He didn't know about Zared yet, either. Zared was fully capable of supporting me, as Gram might have said, in a manner far above that to which I was accustomed. "I'm fine, thanks for asking. What now?"

"I'll get some equipment from the car, then I want another look at your kitchen. Go sit in your rocking chair and stay out of my way." He re-locked the door to Mrs. Jamison's attic, ducked outside for a few minutes, returned with a briefcase.

He was in the kitchen a long time. I listened to stretches of silence interspersed with bouts of noise: things banging, water running, Danny whistling some slow, sad Gaelic lament. Eventually he returned to the living room, pushed a mug of steaming liquid into my hand. Coffee. I accepted it gratefully and swallowed three scalding gulps before I realized it wasn't normal coffee.

Gasping for air, I thrust the mug back at him. "This could have r-resurrected the dead guy if he'd stayed."

"It's medicinal strength," he said quietly. "You're too pale by half. Just hold the cup and warm your hands if you don't fancy drinking the stuff. Constancy, I'm sorry I doubted you. You've cracked my bones, dented my skull and blacked my eye. One way and another, you've caused me more suffering than any criminal I've encountered in all my years on the force, but you've not lied to me ever." A wry face. "Not even when it might have been better for you if you had." He sighed. "It's been a terrible, long night and a ridiculous morning. I'd only just got to sleep when you phoned. Forgive me?"

Danny asking forgiveness? Wonders never cease. I took one

final, tiny sip of his filthy brew to show I held no hard feelings. "I'm just glad you came. What did you find in the kitchen?"

"Nothing. Nothing at all on the chair you pointed out, nor on that bit of the table."

"Great."

"It is, in its way. No matter how good a housekeeper you are, you see, there should have been smudges from your own hand, an occasional settling of dust, the usual residue of everyday life. The rest of the chairs had it in normal amounts, but that chair, that one chair and the corresponding bit of table and floor, were all wiped very, very clean. He was here, certainly, but there's nothing to explain why, or who the man was, or where he's gone."

"So what do I do now?"

"Interesting ring." He caught up my hand and twisted it slightly, gently playing the light from the front window against the facets of the stone.

Interesting? Zared's ring was a full three carats of brilliant cut diamond in an antique gold setting. Not a common clear stone, either, but a rare golden brown, the color of imperial topaz shot through with diamond fire. Needless to say, it was a piece of the lauded Fraser Collection. I hadn't chosen it as an engagement ring. Zared had. "What about it?"

Danny kept his eyes on the ring. "It's no piece of costume jewelry, is it? The thing sparkles like diamond, though I've never seen one this color. I assume it's an engagement ring, given it's on that finger. Besides, it looks rather shockingly grand for an unemployed school teacher to be buying for herself."

"Oh, it's diamond, and for now it's an engagement ring. If I were buying jewelry for myself, I wouldn't buy diamonds, and I sure wouldn't buy anything so big and expensive. Look, this ring has nothing to do with the vanishing body."

Danny wasn't ready to get back to the subject of the body. "I had no idea diamonds came in such an incredible color."

"You haven't seen the rest of the Fraser Collection, have you? It's mostly dark diamonds. At least that's what I call them. 'Fancies' is the more technical name. They can come in almost any color and intensity, although some are considerably more rare than others."

The most minute pause. "So this is from the Fraser Collection. How long have you had it?"

"Since yesterday. Aren't you going to congratulate me?"

"I'm not sure it's congratulations you need. Which one of them are you marrying?"

"It won't be officially announced until Friday night. You can read all about it on the front page of our Gossip Gazette on Saturday, probably."

"Which Fraser?"

"Zared."

He dropped my hand as if it had stung him. "I don't think I care to see more of the Fraser Collection if they're all as gaudy as this."

"Gaudy!" But hadn't that been my own first impression when Zared put it on my finger? The ferocity of its glitter almost blinded me. It was gaudy.

"Where is the betrothed, then?"

"Zared? I suppose he's at home."

"You didn't phone him."

"No."

"No." Slowly, with a raised eyebrow and quiet speculation in his eyes. "No. One would hardly dare. This sort of thing wouldn't fit the desired Fraser image at all. Even so, he might have come and held your diamond-bedecked hand."

"I didn't want him. I wanted—" The corner of Danny's mouth tightened and I amended the one-word finish to my second sentence. "I wanted somebody who could keep me out of the clutches of Lon Tirso and his handcuffs. With all his influence, Zared probably couldn't have accomplished that."

Danny didn't smile. "So you're marrying the Fraser Triumvirate."

"I'm engaged to Zared."

"Whether you like it or not, my precious, he comes in triplicate. Hadn't you noticed? He's an integral part of an unbreakable set. How are the twins taking it?"

I shrugged. "Timon treats me like some kind of joke, although I have no idea why. Romney's not amused. Romney is alarmed. He doesn't like the engagement at all."

"Alarmed? Why?"

"Maybe he doesn't want any more little Frasers coming along to take a cut of the family wealth."

"What does the impressive Queen Mother think of her future daughter-in-law?

"Nona?" Nona's reactions puzzled me. Clearly she wouldn't be the mother substitute I always dreamed a mother-in-law should be. "I honestly don't know. She's excited about the idea of a wedding in the family. She's making an effort to welcome me, but I don't feel much personal warmth in it. I don't think she likes me very much for myself."

"It's her loss, then. When's the wedding day?"

"Next week."

Danny's mouth puckered in a silent whistle. "Engagement and wedding in under a month. What about Miss Amanda?"

How dare he bring Gram into it. "What about her? My great-grandmother's dead."

He looked quickly away. "I know now, but I didn't until two days ago. I'm sorry. I was out of touch with Fraserton for several weeks. I didn't hear until I got back, and then, I wasn't sure you would want my condolences, or any other word from me. Amanda Casey was a very special woman."

"I didn't ask you here to talk about Gram's death or my wedding."

"No." His voice sounded sad. "No, why should you?"

Maybe I was being too harsh. He had adored Gram, and she him. I gentled my voice. "Danny, if I didn't imagine the body in my kitchen, what's happening here?"

He looked up at me again and that investigative gleam reignited in his eyes. "You didn't imagine the body. There's no saying you did. Are you given to imaginings otherwise?"

"Maybe."

"Look, even if you're not wanting your coffee, I could use some," he said.

"Sure." I followed him into the kitchen, suddenly more concerned for Danny than for myself and the missing corpse. The man looked like he'd been living exclusively on coffee. "Do you ever eat anymore?"

"I sometimes pick up a pizza or a sandwich. When I remember."

"When was the last time you remembered?"

He shrugged.

"Then I'm going to fix us some scrambled eggs while you make your coffee. Unless you think that'll, what do you call it? Contaminate the crime scene?"

"Is this an invitation to breakfast?" It sounded like a warning.

"No strings attached," I said. "It's only because you look half starved. Like you, I don't want my friends starving. You can call the food medicinal, too, if it makes you feel less threatened."

For the first time since he'd arrived, he smiled a little and, to my surprise, accepted. "Thanks, then. It sounds lovely."

While I got out the skillet and eggs, he rinsed my cup, measured a scant teaspoon of coffee powder into it and stirred in the hot water. "Here."

"Much better, thanks."

He made a cup for himself (four heaping spoons) and perched on a stool by the counter where I was breaking the eggs into a bowl. "Let's have the rest of it," he said.

I shoved bread, a board and a knife at him. "Make yourself useful."

He was quick and efficient with the knife. "Now, what other adventures have you been having?" he asked.

"Shouldn't you report in to headquarters or something?"

"What have I got to report but one clean chair? Tell me the rest. Then we'll see."

"There's nothing much to tell."

I felt another of those official police glares boring into the back of my head as I put the skillet on the burner and took down glasses and plates from the cabinet. Did instructors teach all incipient crime fighters that method of interrogation at the academy? Or did officers pass it down among themselves as a sort of folk remedy? However they learned it, it worked on me every time. I started talking despite myself. "I think somebody searched my apartment while I was at Gram's funeral. That wasn't the first time, but it was the most obvious. Do you want orange juice?"

"I'll pour it. It's in the refrigerator, is it?"

"Yes, and you can get the milk out while you're there."

"Have you not reported any of these incidents?" he asked.

"Nothing was ever taken."

"Then what makes you think the place was searched?"

The eggs sizzled as they hit the hot skillet. I took time to put the bread into the toaster before I answered. The slices were as uniform as if they had been done by machine.

"Sometimes it looked or smelled funny after I'd been out," I said. "Different, but never enough that I could be sure. Things weren't always where I thought I put them, but maybe the wind shuffled the papers on my desk. Maybe the aftershave scent drifted in from outside, too. Why should I bother our dedicated police force with that?" I didn't dare look at the nearest representative of our dedicated police force. "Besides, I thought the police might have had something to do with it."

"Why?"

The intensity of his short question startled me. "Oh, you know. Lon Tirso doesn't give up easily. Since he couldn't get me on a murder charge, he might try to connect me with some other crime."

"The police are supposed to operate within the frame of the law, too, darlin'. Even Lon Tirso."

"Right. Like you were doing a few minutes ago, jiggling locks and poking around Mrs. Jamison's place without a search warrant."

"For your information, a warrant isn't necessary if one is searching for a crime victim or suspects the perpetrator may be still on the scene. Both of those conditions were met." He smiled sweetly.

He was, without doubt, the most irritating man on earth. I piled most of the eggs and toast on his plate, banged it down in front of him and gasped as it clipped the handle of his mug, tilting the scalding coffee toward him.

Chapter 3

Danny caught and righted the cup, losing only a few drops on the counter. He shot me a look of pained resignation, then bowed his head as if in prayer. Maybe he was giving silent thanks for the food. Maybe he was praying I wouldn't accidentally poison him or drop a whole kettle of boiling water in his lap.

He raised his head and picked up his fork. "Sorry," I muttered.

"Don't worry about it. I've learned to stay alert for signs of imminent danger when I'm near you. Now, darlin', let's get back to the subject. Are you telling me you had your windows open while you were away?"

"I lock them now."

"I should think so, and some of them opening onto the landing as they do."

"Locking my apartment didn't do much good last night, did it? You want some of this blackberry jam?"

"Please." He spread it thickly on his toast. "There's no need making it easy for them altogether. This is delicious. Did you make it?"

"No. I made the bread."

"Equally delicious."

Not to me. I took a couple of bites of my own breakfast and pushed my plate away. My stomach was still queasy.

"If you aren't eating, keep talking," Danny said.

"A car almost ran me down yesterday after lunch."

Danny's fork full of eggs froze halfway to his mouth. "The same day you got the ring, was it? Heaven preserve us!"

"Do people really talk that way in Ireland?"

He swallowed the eggs. "It was a serious request for help, if you please. What am I to do with you, woman? You didn't report that, either, I suppose. Are you blaming the police for attempted murder now, as well as unauthorized search?"

"It wasn't attempted murder. It was my own fault."

"Was it now? How do you account for that?"

"It was nearly dark. I guess I just didn't look before I stepped off into the street."

He frowned. "You're not normally that careless, are you? More coffee?"

"No, thanks." I sipped the orange juice. "I must have been thinking about something else. Or maybe I stumbled. I really don't remember."

He made himself another cup of that thick coffee. "I'd have thought you would remember every moment of your engagement day. How close was it?"

"If the man had wanted to kill me, I'd be a grim little statistic in your accident reports today. He was quaking like an aspen leaf when he got out of the car."

"You mean he stopped?"

"Of course he did. He had to or he would have flattened me."

"There's no 'of course' about it, my precious love. People get, em, flattened every day without the driver of the vehicle stopping. I suppose it's too much to hope you took his name and address, or even noticed the make or color of his car."

"Color? It was a funny color. Noisy."

"What? You mean the engine?"

"No, I don't think so." I shrugged. "I honestly can't remember. I didn't get his name or address either. What does it matter?"

Danny and his usually eloquent tongue seemed to be struggling to find the right words. "You are not safe left on your own in this world," he said, finally. "Neither is anyone who has the misfortune to cross your path. It's a keeper you need."

"Are you applying for the job?"

A withering blast from those green eyes. "You've got your Zared Fraser," he said. "What's the man thinking of, leaving you off your leash? He should hire a guard."

"I don't need a guard and I don't need a lecture. I phoned you because I found another body. The body's gone. So's your food and coffee. You'd better go, too."

"Oh, not yet, love. Not yet. Will you be finishing your breakfast?"

"I can't eat. I don't see why you can't leave."

Danny picked up his empty plate and my barely touched one and put them into the sink. "You phoned me with a complaint. Even though I was dragged prematurely from my bed, I'm in this now. Or maybe you'd rather speak to our friend, Lon Tirso?"

"Where's your nasty little notebook?"

He tapped his head. "I'll write it up later if I need to. I don't forget."

He didn't, more's the pity. "I can't stand this kitchen anymore. I'm going to go sit in the rocking chair."

"Fine." Danny followed me to the living room, took off his jacket and settled himself on the couch. "Tell me, now," he said, "what was the man like?"

"The body?"

"The man in the car. Describe him."

"Describe him? I could hardly see him. I told you. It was almost dark."

Danny sighed. "Was he young, old?"

"Older than me, I think, but lots younger than you."

"Don't be spiteful, child. Just exercise your brain and see if you can remember anything at all about him."

"I can't."

"Come on," he said, gently encouraging. "You did fine describing the body."

"I spent an eternity staring at that body, trying to figure out for sure if he was dead. I don't know anything more about the man in the car except he was nice."

"Nice." So much for Danny's gentleness. "NICE! Lovely. I'm sure we'll be able to find him with no trouble now. Nice? What kind of description is that at all?"

"Why do you want to find him?"

Danny rolled his eyes upward, but he didn't repeat aloud his plea for heavenly help. "Are there any other adventures you've not reported?"

Well, if he wanted it all, he could have it. "I think I'm being watched. I've never caught anybody doing it. I can't prove it's happening. It's just a filthy feeling of wanting to look over my shoulder all the time."

"I've felt it." He eyed my ring again. "Perhaps it's the Frasers spying on you."

"You can't think Zared would do such a thing?"

"I don't think about Zared Fraser at all when it's avoidable, nor any of the rest of that lot. Never mind the hurt look. It's a logical deduction I'm giving you. They're business men. They'd want to know what sort of woman they're taking into the family. If your Zared was too besotted to do it, the other two-thirds of the Triumvirate would take up the slack."

"Danny!"

He rubbed the back of his neck. "Constancy, I wasn't meaning to insult you, or the man you'll be marrying. It'd be the simplest answer to your feeling of being watched, that's all. It might even explain the searches of your apartment. Unfortunately, I don't see where the body fits into it, though I have no doubt it's something to do with the Frasers. When a family has that much power, it can accumulate enemies almost as quickly as money. There's always a chance somebody's trying to get at them by using you. Or perhaps they're trying to frighten you away from becoming a Fraser. Whatever their intent, it wasn't at all clear."

"Everybody knows I'm already a Fraser."

An odd expression flitted across Danny's face. "I didn't."

"I thought everybody knew that Zared and I share a great-grandfather. Zared's great-grandmother was Lucian Fraser's second wife. Gram was his third."

"She called herself Amanda Casey. Did she remarry? No. I remember. Her grandfather Michael's name was Casey."

"Right. She took back her maiden name when Lucian died. She never liked to talk about that time of her life, but between her and Miss Irma, I got most of it pieced together. Gram left the mansion and cut her ties with the remaining Frasers the day after Lucian's funeral. She never socialized with them again after that. Not that they asked her to. There were no family reunion picnics and stuff. I was sixteen before I even knew the Frasers in Fraser House were my cousins."

"The Triumvirate at a common picnic. It's beyond thought." He gestured toward my left hand. "Zared obviously decided an intense bit of socializing was in order."

"He came to Gram's funeral. I don't suppose it was to socialize, but that's the first time we'd ever really talked."

"It surprised you that he came?"

"I didn't expect any of them to bother. I was surprised that he came. I was more surprised *how* he came. He wasn't ostentatious about it, and he wasn't acting as an official representative of Lucian's family. He just showed up as a fellow mourner.

"You were touched by that?"

"Yes." I was equally touched by the one perfect red rose, the first of many, that a florist delivered to my apartment the next morning.

I'd been touched enough that yesterday, when Zared asked me to marry him, I agreed without any hesitation. I didn't bother to probe into his reasons for asking, or mine for accepting. Looking at the guarded concern on Danny's face, I began to have an uneasy feeling that I'd done a very stupid thing.

He was slowly tracing the faded flower pattern of the upholstery with one finger. "So you fell in love. Are you happy?" He sent a quick glance in my direction. "No. Forget I asked. You'd say you were just to spite me. I deserve that, don't I?" He fidgeted with a pillow. "I've got an appointment," he said. "Will you be all right?"

"Why wouldn't I?"

"Is there someone who could come stay with you until I'm off work?"

"I don't need a baby sitter now or when you're off work. You don't need to waste any more of your time on me."

"I'm not so sure. This doesn't, at the moment, appear to be a physical threat aimed at you, but should you end up a corpse yourself, think of all the trouble you'll cause. I'll be back later with a bolt for that door."

"Don't bother. I'm not going to stay another night here. With or without bolts."

"Where will you go? To Fraser's?"

"Why should it matter to you where I go?"

"That doesn't answer my question." He ran a hand through his already tousled curls. His hair was much longer now than it had been in May. He looked as if he gave no more thought to haircuts than he did to eating. "I suppose I deserve that, too," he said.

But Danny had answered my distress call. I owed him

cooperation, at least. "Gram left me her house, among other things," I said. "I'll go over there. I should have before now."

"I didn't intend to pry into your personal life, my soul. This may have nothing at all to do with you, but we don't dare assume that. It's a dangerous game somebody's playing. One man's died. Sooner or later he'll turn up. Until he does, and until we learn more about why he was here, I'd like you to be especially careful." He sighed again. "If only you'd keep out of trouble."

"I don't do it on purpose. Do you think I enjoy this kind of thing?"

Danny's grin drooped with exhaustion. "Considerably less than I do." He moved around behind me, rested his hands on my shoulders and began to massage the back of my neck with his thumbs. "Relax," he said. "This is medicinal, too. It'll help your headache."

I hadn't told him I had a headache. I resented the fact that he had seen it for himself, but the warmth and gentle pressure on my tense muscles felt like pure bliss.

"Constancy, should anything else unusual happen, promise you'll phone me immediately."

"Why?"

He gave my neck a little shake. "Promise!"

"Oh, all right."

"If I'm not in, leave a message."

"Last time you didn't have an answering machine."

"I do now, and I check the messages. If you phone me, I'll be with you as soon as possible. Don't talk with anybody else."

"Now you're saying don't phone the police station or 911?"

"I am."

"Why not?"

"Just, please, do as I say." Danny worked a few moments in silence, then added, "I'd be your enemy myself, beloved, if you weren't so like a lost, frightened puppy under all your prickly exterior."

"It's fright that makes puppies prickly, isn't it? Makes them bite, too." I was feeling very prickly and ready to bite.

"When they do bite," he said softly, "often as not, they haven't the faintest idea how to make amends."

I escaped his grip on my neck and glared up at him. "It's not very flattering being compared to a dog. Zared would never say a thing like that."

"Zared would never see a thing like that unless it served some specific purpose, most likely a financial one. It's survival of the most financially fit in the Fraser world. Be sure you know that, head and heart, Constancy, before you get in past recall." Abruptly he collected his jacket and made for the door.

I wandered after him. "Why do you hate Zared?"

"It's not a question of hate." He looked thoughtful. "It could be envy."

"I never saw you as the money-hungry type."

"I'm not. I thought you weren't, either."

"You know I'm not."

He dropped a brotherly kiss on top of my head. "That's for luck," he said, "and the happiness I hope you find."

Nothing in his face, no expression at all. Yet there had been something in the words. Regret? Couldn't be. I was imagining things again. Danny wouldn't feel anything but relief over my engagement. His dissection of my feeling for him had been thorough and brutal and irrevocable. What I felt was mere gratitude, he said. I was no more than thankful to him for his help when I was in trouble. It was like a schoolgirl's crush on a favorite teacher, or a patient's on a successful doctor. It couldn't possibly be love, he said. It was nothing at all. In a few days I would be over it.

On the strength of his certainty, I was able to convince myself I could make a good life with Zared. So why turn to Danny when trouble came again? If he'd been right, how could he, even after five long months, so effortlessly fire up every emotion I was capable of feeling? When I was with him, why did I have to work so hard to remember Zared even existed?

I shivered and opened the door for him.

"Cold?"

"Maybe it's just that feeling of being watched."

Any other human would have swiveled his neck like an owl trying to spot the spy. Not Danny. He gazed into my eyes as if he were reading my mind. I dearly would have loved to be able to read his.

"You'd better tell your Zared about all this, you know, before he hears it from another source."

"What other source?"

He shrugged. "The town's a hot bed of gossip, remember? You've not forgotten that, have you?"

"I haven't had much chance to forget it."

"I'll come round to the house later and do a security check there."

"Why bother?"

"Call it an over-inflated sense of duty." He paused with one hand on the door. "Do you know," he said, "there are maybe things other than money and power that could cause a man to envy Zared Fraser."

"What things?"

"Thanks for the breakfast, love."

The second kiss landed full on my mouth. It was not brotherly.

I slammed the door behind him. Hard. Only then did I realize that the pain had vanished from my head as suddenly and completely as the corpse had vanished from my kitchen.

Chapter 4

Brendan of the melodramatic exits.

I didn't know whether to laugh and be thankful that the headache was gone, or have a major fit and smash something.

Impossible, irritating man! It wasn't the first time he'd done that to me. I could have lived happily, much more happily, without a repeat performance of his kiss-and-run tactics.

Tell Zared. How on earth could I tell Zared?

What would I say? I woke up and found a dead man in my kitchen and then I phoned Danny Egan.

I did not want to talk to Zared about Danny Egan.

Ah. Was that it? If I began talking about Danny, Zared might see more than I wanted anybody to see, including myself.

Not that I was planning to throw my fiancé over for something as unreliable as a blarney-cursed Irishman's capricious kiss. But why had he done that? What had he meant?

If I tried to think about that anymore, my headache would be back for sure. I double-locked the door and headed for the bathroom. Maybe if I spent some time in a hot, hot shower, I could wash away some of the chill and frustrations of the morning.

The shower, of course, did nothing to ease my mind or clarify my thoughts. I threw on jeans and an old sweatshirt and sat down to brush the tangles out of my hair.

A dictatorial knock on the door shook the whole apartment.

Oh, please. Not Danny again. I wasn't ready for another visitation from him. Maybe if I ignored him, he would go away.

"Constancy! Open this door. I know you're in there."

Not Danny. But Heather Hudson was, if anything, less welcome. She'd been a major thorn in my life since she and her family moved next door to us thirteen years before. Aging hadn't improved her. Now that she was nineteen and working as Nona Fraser's private secretary, she didn't bother hiding her opinion that it should be herself and not me wearing the family diamonds.

"Heather, go away and leave me alone."

"No chance. Nona Fraser sent me. Let me in!"

In her younger days, Heather would have punctuated the demand with a vicious, well-aimed kick at anything or anyone within range.

More out of concern for the door than for whatever message she was bringing, I let her in. "Well? What does Nona want that's so important?"

Heather gave me a disgusted glare and began to unwrap some kind of garment she'd carried up. "She sent you this dress." She held out the slinky purple thing as if it were some kind of royal robe. "It's for the party Friday night."

I might have known. That party. They said it was in my honor. If they wanted to honor me, they wouldn't do it with a party. I was looking forward to this one like people look forward to a rerun of their worst nightmare. Designer gowns and caviar. Champagne and an orchestra. A guest list of hundreds. All those high class business associates of Zared's. Billionaires. Celebrities. Politicians. Maybe even royalty, for all I knew. I wouldn't have a clue how to act. I'd spill ginger ale on the lady with the most priceless designer gown. I'd trip up some visiting head of state with one of my clumsy moves and have security officers carting me away. Just thinking about it turned me into a veritable bog of cold shivers.

Heather's perfectly-shaped lips moved into a kind of sneering smile. "Nona's aware that you can't afford to dress up to Fraser standards, so she asked me to bring this over for you to try on. Zared wants you looking good." *For a change.* She didn't say the last three words out loud. She didn't have to.

There wasn't much to the dress, not quite enough even for a decent nightgown, but it probably had cost a whole year's worth of teacher's salary. Heather obviously thought it was perfect. It might have been perfect for her or Nona, but not for conservative, straight-laced Constancy Stafford. I preferred a few more yards of cloth between my body and open air. Both of them would have known that, and that I didn't look good in purple, however much of it there was. I didn't even like purple except as a color for violets and irises and lilacs and hyacinths.

"Thanks, anyway," I said. "But I'll find some old rag. I won't disgrace the family too badly. Now, if you'll excuse me, I need to water my ivy plant."

Heather didn't take the hint to leave. She followed me into the kitchen, antagonism radiating from her like fever heat.

"You've done your duty and shown me the dress, Heather,

and I've told you I don't want it. Why don't you just get out of here and leave me alone?"

"Constancy, do you love Zared or don't you?"

I dumped water on the ivy and turned the glass upside down on the drain board before I answered. "As far as I can see, that's absolutely not your business."

Her mouth curled into a snarl. "Answer my question."

"Not until I hear why you think you've got a right to ask it."

She practically spat at me. "I saw that man coming out of here this morning. Your precious Danny. Only half dressed and looking very smug and pleased with himself."

"Danny nearly always looks smug, and he usually has every right to look pleased with himself. He's a good man. As for what he was wearing, it was a lot more decent than that purple scrap of stuff Nona wants me to wear."

"Just look at this." She gestured toward the dishes Danny had stacked in the sink. "Breakfast!"

"Heather!"

"I saw you kissing him good-bye."

"Heather, that's enough." She backed off a step at my tone, or maybe it was because I had picked up that long, thin knife Danny had used to slice bread for our toast. "You don't have any idea what's going on." I wiped the knife and put it back into its drawer. "What happened this morning has nothing to do with how I feel about Zared."

"I'll just bet."

Screaming at her would be a total waste of time and energy. So would trying to explain, but I had to do something. "All right, I did invite Danny here. He was asleep when I phoned him at his apartment and since it was urgent, he didn't take the time to dust down his best suit. He threw on what was handy and he came. On police business."

"Police business? That's hilarious, Constancy."

"It wasn't. There was a dead body sitting at my table."

"Right. You fixed breakfast for him with a dead body in here." She gave me a sly sideways glance.

"The body was gone when Danny got here. I fed him breakfast because he looked half-starved. For the record, Danny kissed me. I didn't kiss him." Why was I defending myself to Heather?

She laughed. "I think I should tell Zared."

"If that'll make you happy, go to it. Just get out of here, and take that purple thing with you."

"Nona won't like you rejecting something she's chosen for you."

"I prefer to choose my own clothing, thank you. You can quote me."

Heather went, smirking. She said nothing more, but I could almost hear the childish chant running through her head: "I'm gonna tell Zared. I'm gonna tell Zared." She would, too. Zared and Nona, and anybody else who would listen.

If Danny had been available at that moment, I cheerfully would have cracked a few more of his ribs. Or maybe I would have aimed for a more permanent dent in his hard head. Had he known Heather was watching? Had Heather been the spy all along?

If she could find a way to create trouble between Zared and me, she would do it happily and with all her might. Danny had supplied her with abundant ammunition.

So now, if I didn't want my engagement to end almost before it started, I would have to tell Zared about the body, and about Danny. He might hear Heather's version of it directly or filtered through Nona, but he would hear it soon. He would get it fully embellished and liberally laced with Heather's bias.

Well, why not? Why not let her do her worst? If Zared broke off our engagement, I would be spared the trauma of that party, and of many more to come.

Besides, if Zared preferred to believe Heather's fabrication over my true story, he wasn't worth having as a husband. You couldn't have a good marriage without trust, could you?

Maybe Heather was right. Maybe she should have been the one marrying him, anyway. She was beautiful to look at, naturally elegant. She'd never been clumsy a minute in her life. She would fit right in with Zared's distinguished acquaintances, and she loved diamonds as much as any Fraser ever born.

I changed into something a little more presentable and packed a few things to the insistent echo of Heather's accusing voice. Did I love Zared or didn't I?

In all honesty, I had been content enough with my decision to accept Zared's proposal. I had, until I saw Danny Egan this morning.

I slammed my suitcase shut on a couple changes of clothes, Gram's jewelry box, a few books and personal items. Despite Danny's final kiss, any longing I had in that direction was a striving after the wind. He had made that more than clear last spring.

But that was last spring. What about this morning?

I marched the suitcase, along with my ivy plant, down to the car. All right, I would stop by Zared's office on the way home and confess everything. Well, almost everything. Then, with a *nearly* clear conscience, I could begin again the tedious, exhausting task of erasing Danny Egan from my system.

Fraser Enterprises boasted exclusive jewelry and antique shops in San Francisco, St. Louis, Chicago and New York, but Lucian had kept his headquarters in Fraserton. The Fraser office building was, of course, the tallest building in town, twelve whole stories. Not gigantic, but impressive for a town whose population was less than 10,000. Lucian wouldn't have had it any other way.

I had never before had reason to be inside, but I took the

elevator to the eleventh floor and pranced into the Triumvirate's private lair as if I owned it. "Lair" described the place perfectly. Around town, people called that complex and its inhabitants the Den of Lions.

The receptionist, whom I'd never met, frowned. "Do you have an appointment? If you don't, I'm afraid I can't let you in."

"I need to talk with Zared Fraser. I don't have time to wait for an appointment. My name's Constancy Stafford." I leaned on her immaculate desk, my hands where she couldn't miss seeing them clearly.

A gaudy diamond carries certain advantages. She might not recognize me or my name, but she recognized the diamond.

When she did, she couldn't apologize enough. "I'm sorry, Ms. Stafford. I'll tell Mr. Fraser you're here. Wait just a minute." She pushed a couple of buttons and spoke into her phone.

Zared's reply seemed to take a long time.

I spent the interval hoping angels did exist and that a spare one was handy to close the mouths of these particular lions. What if Zared refused to see me? Or wouldn't see me alone? I'd already had enough of Romney's sharp claws.

"You can go in," the receptionist said. "Through there."

I smiled my best smile at her and stepped through the ornately carved double doors.

The Triumvirate was sitting center stage around a large mahogany conference table which was positioned below a life-sized portrait of our great-grandfather.

It looked like a cloning session. I didn't doubt for a minute that they'd planned it that way. Three living men and one gold-framed portrait. All of them had the same ash-brown hair, carefully styled; the same small, neatly set ears and long, thin nose; the same slender, pale hands and arrogant expression.

Romney and Timon were identical twins and entitled to look

alike, but I'd never before realized that Zared, who was two years older, could have passed for either of them. That they should all resemble Lucian to such a degree was startling, to say the least. The scene, as a whole, was every bit as intimidating as they'd obviously calculated it to be.

All four of them seemed to be watching me intently. Living men and portrait. All watching. All disapproving. The twins both wore an exact copy of Lucian's approach-the-throne-if-you-dare expression. Did they practice together with a mirror in front of the portrait?

Zared didn't look quite as daunting as the others, but even he didn't look welcoming. Had Heather got to him already? Or was he one of those people who hated being interrupted at work? Amazing how little I really knew about him.

"We need to talk, Zared."

"I'm listening."

"How about a private audience?"

"We're all family."

Too right. I glanced up at Lucian. He was as much my ancestor as theirs. I also wore a version of that face, though it was modified somewhat by other additions to the gene pool. I had my hair and eye color from the Caseys, along with my general opinion about diamonds. Still, maybe I could tap into a little of the Fraser arrogance. I glanced once more at old Lucian, who suddenly appeared to have more of a twinkle in his eye than I had noticed the first time.

"All right, then, you can all hear it," I said. "When I woke up this morning, there was a dead man in my kitchen. I phoned Danny Egan and went down to the porch to wait. By the time Danny arrived, the corpse had vanished."

Tim looked highly entertained by my recital and Zared merely puzzled. But Rom looked like I'd given him an unpleasant, though not altogether unexpected, shock. Interesting.

"Surely you didn't need to call Egan," Tim said.

I was trying to be patient, I really was. "This is the second body I've found lately, remember? People get suspicious about things like that. I might have been facing a murder charge."

"Because of a nightmare? I don't think so. If you thought it was real, you should have called the police." Rom this time, in that slick, snide voice of his.

"I called Danny, and the body wasn't a nightmare."

Zared sounded even more puzzled than he looked. "You just told us there was no body."

"That is not what I said."

"Now, Constancy, calm down. If there was a body, how could it have vanished? Why would it have been there in the first place? Surely you dreamed it. You've been more than a little stressed lately."

"He wasn't a nightmare," I said again. "I don't know who he was or why he was there, but he was as real as you are." And, I wanted to add, almost as cold.

"Have you seen a doctor lately?" Tim asked.

Rom looked down his long nose. "You could use a tranquilizer."

Zared was still watching me, but I couldn't read anything more than arrogance and maybe a little impatience in his face, despite the twins and their comments. The younger Frasers took as much delight in causing trouble as Heather did. The three of them were enough to drive anybody to tranquilizers. "There's something else you'd better know." I addressed that directly to Zared. "Heather saw Danny coming out of my apartment. She assumed he'd spent the night. I expect she means to tell you that, if she hasn't already."

"You really don't need to be jealous of Heather," Zared said.

"Jealous!" Was he deliberately misunderstanding my every word? "Will you just listen to me? I'm not here because I'm jealous. That thought never crossed my mind. Danny said I should tell you about the body. He thought you might want to offer some kind of moral support or something." I had hoped he would. I wanted Zared to convince me that marrying him was exactly the right thing to do. I wanted him to make me forget Danny Egan.

They all laughed as if I were a world class comedian. "I'm sure Egan was much better at that sort of thing than Zared would be," Tim said. "After all, he's had a lot more practice. Especially with you."

As much as I ached to tell Tim exactly how wrong he was, I clamped my mouth shut and kept my eyes on Zared. He was looking more bored than anything else now, as he shuffled some papers on the desk in front of him.

Funny. He had been quick enough with the moral support and hand-holding after Gram's funeral. He had been very good at it. Why the sudden change? I hated to think that Danny's observation about Zared's seeing things only when it served a specific financial purpose was more on the mark than it ought to be, because if it were true, there wasn't much to see in me.

"Danny was wonderful," I said. It wasn't unqualified truth, but the faintest hint of anxiety touched the arrogance and boredom in Zared's face.

"If that's all, we need to get back to work," Romney announced.

"Of course. Will I see you tonight, Zared?" Maybe all that was wrong with Zared was the close proximity of his brothers.

"Didn't Adams let you know? I can't make it to dinner tonight. A client's flying in from Paris and I'll be busy with him most of the week. I probably won't see you till Friday."

I clutched my fraying nerves tighter. "Zared, that huge party Friday night scares me silly. I'm no good in crowds."

"You have to be introduced properly." He turned his attention to the papers, effectively dismissing me in the same way he would dismiss some business underling.

"Be sure to wear something elegant," he added. He didn't even look up.

I walked out without bothering to reply. Elegant. I'd just found another dead body, had it vanish, been turned inside out again by Danny, and all my fiancé cared about was a party and whether or not I would be suitably dressed.

I took a deep breath of air as the front doors of the building swung shut behind me. Nice, plain, unassuming air.

Elegant! If I lived a hundred years and had all the money in the world I could never be elegant. The only time I'd ever in my life felt anywhere near it was when I was a child playing dress-up with Gram in the old Victorian cast-offs in her attic.

Maybe I would go dig in the attic and wear one of those antique gowns. Why not? Any dress I found up there would be better than that purple thing of Nona's. Let her and the Triumvirate and all their snobbish connections make of it what they liked.

"Constancy, wait. Please." Zared. What did he want now?

"I wanted to apologize for that little episode," he said, panting slightly as he caught up to me at the car.

"Good. It was a vicious little episode, wasn't it?"

"I'm sorry if it struck you that way."

"It did. It struck me as vicious and cold and plain mean. Zared, I know your brothers don't like me the least bit, but did you have to act like you agreed with them?"

"Maybe I'm a little jealous myself." He sounded almost surprised. "Why?"

"Because you called Egan instead of me."

"Would you have come if I'd phoned you?"

He blinked under my direct gaze. "Well, I could have sent somebody."

"Exactly. I didn't want some strange lawyer or one of your hired men. I wanted somebody I knew. Somebody who—" *Somebody who cares?* I was getting things a tad mixed up, wasn't I? Zared was the man who said he wanted to marry me. Danny had told me, more than once, that he never wanted to see me again. "I wanted somebody who knows police procedure."

"I can understand that, but I don't like it. A man doesn't want to think that he can't do everything for his fiancée. Forgive me?" His smile was warm now. Apologetic.

He really was much nicer when he was separated from the twins. "I'll consider it. Do you know that outsiders call that office of yours the Lions' Den?"

He grimaced. "With good reason, I suppose, but the lions shouldn't have stuck their teeth and claws into you. I don't know what's got into Romney and Timon. I can't think why they don't want to accept you."

"Maybe they're afraid we'll produce heirs."

Zared laughed. "Am I truly forgiven?"

"If you're truly sorry."

He kissed me lightly, then opened the car door for me. "Taking your plant for an outing?"

As I got in, I glanced down at the comic-ugly pig planter Gram had been so proud of. Suddenly I felt as if it were the only true friend I had in the world. Why should I tell Zared where Pig and I were going? He would be busy with his client until Friday, wouldn't he? "Pig enjoys a change of scenery now and then." I smiled at Zared. "He's about as close as I've got anymore to family. I like to humor him."

I drove away, leaving my fiancé behind with an expression that almost looked concerned.

Chapter 5

When my mother dumped me on Amanda Casey's rose-framed doorstep, I was six years old and Gram was sixty-two. I still remembered vividly the warm sunshine of that late May morning and the overwhelmingly sweet scent of the roses.

With her only daughter dead and her only grandchild (my mother) seemingly intent on making a total mess of her life, I think Gram was truly glad when I came to stay with her. I know I was glad to be there. Glad of the stability and peace and unconditional acceptance. Glad to belong, even though the knowledge that my own mother hadn't wanted me had never totally stopped hurting. Now although I knew it was ridiculous, I felt like Gram had deserted me, too.

Gram's tall, symmetrical stone house with chimneys on both ends was nowhere near as grand and imposing as Fraser House, the Victorian museum of a place Lucian had built in 1900 for his first wife. Gram wasn't impressed by grand and imposing. She had been born in the stone house and that's where she returned when she left the Frasers.

With Gram at its heart, it had been the coziest, warmest, most welcoming place in the world. Now its heart was torn away.

Coward that I was, I hadn't been inside since the day of the funeral, and I had taken great care not to be alone in there that day. Sooner or later I would have to go in and confront the emptiness and pain. So far, it had been easier to find or manufacture excuses to stay away. Now, given a choice between familiar emptiness and unexpected dead bodies popping up, the house seemed like a better bet. Even with Gram gone, it felt more secure.

With a little sigh and something hard and cold beginning to form in my stomach, I turned the car into the narrow drive that led to the parking area and detached garage in the back yard. There was a pick-up parked in front of the garage. The sign on the side proclaimed: "Eddie's Yards and Gardens".

I distinctly remembered canceling Gram's last order to the town's only gardening firm. What were they doing here?

The leaves had been neatly raked, the yard mowed. An ancient, bent man was still working with his rake, smoothing the surface of one of three new flower beds Gram had wanted. A larger, younger man, powerfully built, weasel-eyed and sullen, was lazily poking bulbs into the bed nearest the house.

I didn't recognize either of them.

The ancient one looked apologetic. "Guess we're in the way, parked there. Pretty near got her finished," he said, gesturing toward the newly dug beds. "It'll be a good show, come March and April. Lots of daffodils and tulips just like Miss Amanda wanted."

"There's been some mistake. Gram won't be needing this."

"I know." He took off his cap. "You don't worry about it. This is just our way of payin' our respects. She was a good woman, Miss Amanda. She wanted these beds and we put them in. You enjoy them now. No charge."

"That's very nice, but you shouldn't have."

"Naw. Don't fuss. We wanted to do it. You just let us know if you need us again."

It was a nice gesture, even if it was possibly motivated by an eye to future business. "Thank you. Gram loved spring flowers."

He smiled and turned to the other man. "Got them bulbs in, Bryce?"

"Yes, sir." Bryce spoke to his co-worker, but his eyes were on me, insolent, a little amused.

"Let's get out then, and give Miss Constancy some decent privacy. She's still mournin'."

"Sure." Bryce smiled slowly before turning to help the old man load some equipment.

That smile instantly gained him a spot high on my *Wouldn't Trust Him Any Further Than* list. My reaction probably wasn't fair. Sure, I normally bristle when men smile at me like that, but this time my poor mind was probably only trying to invent other things to worry about so it wouldn't have to deal with the empty house.

How could I walk in knowing there would be no welcoming smile, no smell of fresh-baked pie? Why is it so hard to grow up?

Well, Gram didn't approve of cowards. "Stand up to your troubles," she always said. "Stand up to them, and like as not, they won't be near as hard on you as worrying about them was."

Oh, Gram, I hope it's true this time.

I opened the back door and stopped dead.

Trouble? Here was trouble, maybe more than I was capable of standing up to.

Whoever had searched Gram's house hadn't bothered to be as subtle as he had in my apartment. The closet and cupboard doors were open, their contents strewn carelessly down the long central hall. That horrible leaden knot in my stomach gained a few more pounds and turned several degrees colder.

Why should I be surprised? My cowardice had given him plenty of time to search, hadn't it? Had he found whatever it was he wanted?

What had he wanted?

I did a quick run-through of the house with Danny in mind, peeking into each of the rooms from its doorway, touching nothing. Then I went back and looked at a few items in particular.

Lon Tirso, the professional, couldn't have made a worse mess while he searched. The family room/kitchen, the library, Gram's bedroom on the first floor; the four upstairs bedrooms, even the baths had been searched. The library was the worst, with books pulled off shelves and papers scattered everywhere. I didn't bother going into the basement or garage or workshop. He would have been there, too, and I couldn't stand to see more just then. It didn't make sense.

The thief hadn't taken any of the usual things. Gram's old silver and her few pieces of jewelry, her television and stereo, even an antique rifle that had belonged to her father were all still in the house. Obviously he had been after the same thing here that he had been looking for in my apartment. Whatever that was.

I sat down on the couch in front of the family room fireplace merely because my knees didn't seem to want to hold me up any longer. What was going on here?

Danny had made me promise to phone him if there was any more trouble, but was this the kind of thing he had meant? Why should I bother him with this? If there had been any danger, surely it was past now. With all the time he'd had, the would-be burglar had either found what he wanted or convinced himself the thing wasn't on the premises.

The back hall door slammed. Hadn't I remembered to close it? A sudden, uncomfortable vision of Bryce's leer shimmered before me. I leapt to my feet, remembering too late that the pepper spray a favorite student of mine had given me was in my bag beside the back door.

Danny popped around the corner. "You certainly keep a messy house."

It took a minute to get my breath back. "You scared me half to death." Or maybe it wasn't fright that had kicked the breath out of me. Maybe it was the sheer joy of the thought that he had appeared, without my summons, just when I needed him. Forget it, Constancy. It wasn't intentional on his part. "Didn't your mother ever teach you about knocking?" I asked.

"Why should I knock? The back door was wide open. Did your mother not teach you about locking?"

"Never mind my mother. What are you doing here, anyway?"

"I told you I would come round to check your locks and install bolts if necessary. I'm a bit late with it, eh?"

I shivered. "What are these people looking for?"

"You really have no idea?" Danny's mouth moved into a grim line.

"Not the slightest glimmer. You don't, either. Do you?"

"As an intelligent guess, I'd say it's diamonds they're wanting."

"Diamonds!"

"You've let it get cold in here with your open-door policy." Danny went into the hall and turned up the furnace thermostat.

It answered with a familiar, comforting thump and whoosh. A gush of air from the floor vent tickled my ankles and filled the room with the smell of toasted dust. I sat down beside the vent and bathed my icy hands in the warming flow. "What about diamonds?"

With a weary groan, Danny stretched himself full length on the couch I had deserted and closed his eyes. "Amanda was a Fraser by marriage, you are by blood. Frasers and diamonds are nearly synonymous in this town. It's at least a place to start." His eyes flicked open. "Did Amanda own any that aren't accounted for?"

"I don't think she owned any at all. She hated them, because of George."

"Who's George?"

"Lucian's first son. It's common knowledge in Fraserton."

"I didn't grow up here, thank goodness. Enlighten me."

My hands were almost warm. I moved to the fireplace and began straightening the ornaments on the mantel. I could still feel Danny's presence, but at least I couldn't see him. It was easier that way.

"I told you Lucian Fraser married three times," I said. "George was the only child of the first marriage. He was the apple of his father's eye and a full partner in the business, until he was twenty-seven and some of the diamonds disappeared. Lucian, egged on by Bartholomew who was the only child of the second marriage, chose to believe the circumstantial evidence instead of George's denials. George couldn't prove his innocence, so he left."

"Was George guilty?"

I moved around to pick up some scattered papers. "Gram was convinced Bart had framed him. Especially when the diamonds showed up a few months later with no explanation as to where they'd been. Bart claimed George had sent them back in a fit of guilt. Lucian didn't buy that, but he was too stubborn to try and bring George back. There was never enough real evidence against Bart, or maybe Lucian was afraid of losing both sons. So Bart got away with it. Gram couldn't stand Bart. I think that's a major reason why she left when Lucian died." Only silence from the couch. "Are you asleep over there?"

"I'm not."

I glanced at him and caught another strange expression. "Danny, are you okay?"

"I'm fine. Why?" He sat up like it was a major effort.

"You looked like you had a bad pain."

He grinned. "You are a pain, love. You said so, yourself. Were all the missing diamonds returned?"

"As far as I know."

"Can't be those, then. Is that not diamonds in the portrait?"

I didn't need to look at the small wedding portrait of Gram that hung above the fireplace. I knew it as well as I knew my own face in the mirror. "They're garnets. I have them with me."

"May I see them?"

"Sure. They're in the car. You can help me bring my suitcase and stuff in."

He smiled at the ivy pot when he saw it. "That reminds me of home," he said.

"Of Ireland?"

"Of the farm." He put the suitcase down with a thud. "What are you carrying in here?"

"Some clothes, some books." And the teddy bear he'd once given me, but I wasn't going to let him know about that if I could help it.

"Ah, books. Of course. Where are those garnets?"

I put the ivy in its old place on the wide sill of the kitchen's south window. "Go sit down. I'll get them."

I unlocked the little case and brought it to him. He examined the jewelry in silence. The deep, brownish red of the garnets glowed softly in the gold settings. Each of the stones was oval cut and encircled by small, fiery opals. The largest garnet was set as a pendant hanging from a filigree gold choker necklace. Dangling earrings, a small brooch and a ring, each set with one garnet and the surrounding opals, completed the wedding ensemble.

"They're beautiful," Danny said. "Are you sure they're garnets?"

"Believe me, I have enough Fraser blood to know the difference between diamonds and garnets. The burglar who visited my apartment knew, too, if it was diamonds he wanted. These were in my dresser, untouched."

"How do you tell the difference, then?"

"Look." I pulled off Zared's ring and held it up to the largest garnet for comparison. "Look at the deep, warm glow in the garnet. The diamond doesn't glow. Cut diamonds never do. They always glitter or sparkle. I've never seen any that weren't hard and icy cold, no matter what their color. I've never seen or heard of red ones, by the way. If that color exists at all in diamonds, it would be very, very rare. No, Gram's jewels are definitely garnets. You don't have to take my word for it, though. Before Gram gave them to me on my twenty-first birthday, she had a jeweler clean and check them. If they'd been rare diamonds, he wouldn't have let us get by with calling them garnets."

"I suppose not. You'd better put Fraser's diamond back on your finger, hadn't you?"

For some reason, it was very hard to put the thing back on my finger. Fortunately Danny was occupied with something else.

He carried the garnets closer to the portrait and looked from the real stones to the painted ones several times. "The ones in the portrait are different," he announced.

"They aren't."

"Use your eyes instead of your heart, my darlin'. The gold settings are identical, but the painted stones are altogether more glitter than glow, unless the painter used his artistic license and portrayed them as diamonds in honor of the Fraser obsession. Isn't it a bit odd that there are only the five garnets? I've seen a bit of Victorian jewelry. All the garnet pieces seemed to be composed of masses of wee garnets. They must have been readily available and not terribly expensive at the time. Why stop with just five? Now if the five red stones were rare diamonds, there'd be an easy answer to that question."

He made a good argument, even if he didn't have all the facts. Maybe I had always seen garnets in the portrait because I'd grown up knowing the garnets first hand. Maybe red diamonds did exist, but Danny obviously didn't know the cardinal Fraser rule concerning their collection. "Danny, if those are diamonds, where are they?"

A smug smile. "There you have it. That'll be the motive for the searching."

"But you don't understand. If it's diamonds Gram's wearing in the portrait, they should have gone back into the collection when Lucian died."

"When Lucian died? Why?"

"Because the Fraser Collection is the black hole of diamond collections. When Frasers acquire a diamond, it's forever. Standard procedure is that the family can lend them for a few hours or a lifetime, but they never ever sell or give them away. Zared's lawyer made me sign a statement promising to return this ring if our engagement is broken. If the wedding goes as planned I have permission to wear it all the days of the marriage. In case of divorce or death of either spouse, it immediately goes back to the collection. I'll never own it. It remains Fraser property."

Danny snorted. "Lovely folk, these Frasers. I suppose it also precludes the bit in Zared's marriage vows about endowing you with all his earthly goods."

"I wouldn't know. I'm not marrying him for all his earthly goods. I wouldn't marry anybody for that reason."

"I'm glad to hear it. Still, it's a right insult, and you already a Fraser."

"I'm not that kind of Fraser. I never asked to wear this particular ring."

He glanced at my hand. "It doesn't suit you, either, thank goodness. Garnets would look much nicer on you."

"Danny, if those are diamonds in the portrait and for some reason Gram wasn't obligated to return them to the Frasers, why weren't they with her other things? Why should people start looking for them after all this time?"

He closed the case and handed it back to me. "I don't know why they've disappeared, but perhaps somebody thought they might be easier to find now that she's dead. Could be somebody thought you might be an easier mark. There's no knowing why until we know who."

"Before we do anything else, shouldn't we find out whether the diamonds existed only in the eyes of the artist?"

"Excellent work, Holmes. Who was he?"

"She. She signed the painting. I've never heard of her, otherwise. Why don't you use your police connections and check records to see if she's still alive?"

"We might." But he didn't seem very eager. "Is there anyone left in town who would know?"

"Irma West, maybe. She was Gram's maid of honor."

"And her best friend since childhood, I've heard."

"That's right. If they could help it at all, Gram and Irma never let a day go by without seeing each other, or at least talking on the phone. They never ran out of conversation."

"Have you talked with Irma lately?"

I know my face turned red.

I had been avoiding Irma with as much dedication as I had the house.

"I haven't seen her since the funeral." The pain of loss stabbed again. I was ashamed of myself for avoiding her, but how could I go to Irma's without Gram and sit there remembering?

Danny was silent for a moment. When he spoke, his voice was gentle. "You'll need to see her again. Even though she has her own family, she's needing you. You'll be more help than hurt to each other, you know."

"How can you come up with answers for my arguments before I've even got the arguments straight in my own mind?"

"I know all the arguments. Today's one of Miss Irma's volunteer days at the library, I believe. I suggest you go see her there as a beginning. It's neutral ground, so to speak, and this question about the portrait will ease the way for you both."

Danny knew Irma West as well as I did. It had been Irma

who'd suggested Danny as prime material for one of hers and Gram's infamous plots, a plot that had failed dismally.

"You'll be safe enough with her at the library," he said. We'll meet back here and compare notes later." He hesitated. "If you're not in by five, I'll come looking."

One glance at his stern face stifled the protest I wanted to make. "Danny, you do think I'm personally in danger."

"Depends on how badly your burglar wants the diamonds, doesn't it? Or how much he thinks you know about them."

"Surely if somebody wanted information from me, they would have tried to get it before now. If they wanted me dead, they could have finished me off last night. What better opportunity with me so out of it that I didn't hear people coming and going through my apartment."

"Will you be staying here tonight?" he asked.

"Where else would I go?"

He gave me a long, level look. "There's my place."

"Oh, sure. Heather would love that."

"Heather, the Queen Mother's personal secretary? Is she the same Heather that Amanda wanted so badly to paddle?"

"The very same."

"But what does Heather have to do with this at all?"

"She saw you leaving my apartment this morning and jumped to some classic soap opera conclusions, which she was promising to deliver immediately to the Fraser clan."

"Ah. The old gossip network again."

"With malice and vengeance thrown in."

"It's protective custody I'm offering for the night, not a soap opera script."

"I know that, but Heather wouldn't believe such a thing was possible."

"It's the farm I'd be taking you to, anyway, not my apartment. There are chaperones in plenty there."

I was greatly tempted. I didn't know much about Danny's

family on the farm. I wanted to know more, but maybe this wasn't the best time. I had a feeling I would like them all very much, which might be awkward, considering the precarious relationship between Danny and me. "That wouldn't matter to Heather," I said.

He grimaced. "I do cause you untold grief, don't I? Are you in trouble with the Frasers?"

"Probably, but at the moment I'm not sure I care."

A flickering smile, quickly masked. "Have you told anyone else you're here?"

"No."

"Not even your fiancé?"

"I said I hadn't told anybody."

"Just as well. All right, go talk with Irma West, a chuisle. It'll do you both good and maybe you'll learn something useful about those diamonds. I'll lock up when I leave, but I'll see you here at five."

"Gram's key is on the kitchen counter. You can take it in case you get back before I do. I have another one on my key ring."

"I wouldn't necessarily need a key."

"No, I don't guess you would. I'm not sure you ought to be so clever at getting into locked doors. It doesn't seem policeman-like, somehow."

"What do you consider policeman-like?"

"On TV, they usually kick the door down."

"You want your door kicked down? I could do it that way, if you'd rather."

"I want you to take the key, like I said in the first place. Do you start these arguments merely for the sake of hearing yourself do it?"

"I'm Irish," he said. "Arguing can be a high art form."

"Whatever happened to your Bible literacy? 'Blessed are the peacemakers', remember?"

He made a droll face. "Point taken. All right. I'll take

the key and use it, if it makes you feel better, and here's a key to the new bolts I'm going to install. In the interest of peace, I'll bring pizza for supper, shall I?"

"That's fine. Danny, do you ever eat vegetables any more? You'll die of malnutrition if all you eat is greasy pizzas."

"There are things people in my line of work are more likely to die of than malnutrition. Never mind. I'll have them put on extra green pepper and onion and tomato, if that'll please you."

"I'll bring fruit and something for a salad," I told him.

"You sound like Rose."

Rose? Well, good. If Danny were in love with somebody else, things would be considerably easier for me. "Just don't let Heather spot you letting yourself in here."

"Oh, my. Heather." He gazed at me, his green eyes much too open and innocent. "What will she say when she learns I'll be spending the night here?"

"Nothing. You won't be spending the night here."

From the determined set of his jaw, I could see he was primed for an argument I couldn't possibly win. Knowing that missing diamonds and desperate thieves might trouble my night, I wasn't entirely sure I wanted to win it. In the interest of peace, I kept my mouth shut.

Chapter 6

Irma West's eyes lit up and she waved from across the library's main reading room as she hurried to meet me. "Oh, Sweetie," she whispered after a generous hug, "you're more like Amanda every day." The tears in her eyes didn't help my composure or my conscience.

She recovered more quickly than I did. "I can't flatter myself by thinking you've come just to see me," she said.

I cleared my throat. "Yes, you can. Miss Irma, I'm so sorry I haven't been to see you since Gram died."

"It's hard. I know." She patted my cheek. "Sometimes even the good memories are too painful at first, but she wouldn't want us to lose touch."

"You're right. I don't want that to happen, either. I was just being a selfish coward."

"Don't call yourself names."

"Gram would be disappointed in me."

She grinned. "Amanda was never disappointed in you a minute in her life."

"I hope not. Miss Irma, I need to talk to you about her."

"Nothing I'd like more. How long do you have?"

"I'm free until a few minutes before five." I intended to be home on time. I didn't want Danny to have to come looking for me.

"Good. Go find yourself a book. I'll be off for lunch in half an hour."

She found me thirty minutes later with my nose in a travel book. "Ireland," she said, with a twinkly little sideways glance. "Amazing people, the Irish. Check out the book and come on."

I left the book behind, trying to pretend to myself that I'd chosen it only for the beautiful landscape photography.

The day had warmed up considerably. Irma and I walked together to the city park. "I always pack enough lunch for two," she assured me. "If I don't find a person to share it with, the ducks and geese are happy to oblige. I tried a new cookie recipe this week. Turned out pretty good, if I do say so."

The park was a pleasant place on the shores of a small lake. Autumn had dressed the maples in fluorescent oranges and reds. The oaks, with the sun shining through their leaves, glowed like over-sized garnets.

Gram had brought me here often to feed the ancestors of today's ducks and geese. Irma and I settled on a park bench overlooking the water. A mother with a baby in a stroller walked slowly past us and smiled. Farther along the path, a kneeling gardener pulled weeds from a bed of blazing chrysanthemums.

"I love this weather." Irma handed me a tuna salad sandwich and started one for herself. No doubt the food was delicious, but I still didn't have much appetite. I nibbled at it to please her and watched a toddler on the lakeshore lunging with arms outstretched at a large, white gander. The bird was not amused. With a squawk of rage and strong wings flapping madly, he turned on the child and chased her, screaming, back to her mother.

Lucky child, having a mother there to run to.

Irma reached over and squeezed my hand.

"You'll be hungry later if you don't eat," she said.

I answered without thinking. "Danny's bringing pizza for supper tonight."

"Well. You mean our Brendan Egan?" She tapped the gaudy ring with one inquiring finger. "That doesn't look like his style."

"You're right. He's part of what I need to talk about, but this isn't his."

Her eyes twinkled. "I didn't think so. I could almost swear you're sorry it's not. I know I'm sorry, but I won't say I told you so."

"Good."

She sighed and shook her head. "I really believed you two were just right for each other. So did Amanda. Brendan's such a sweet boy."

Off and on. "I suppose sweet, like beauty, is in the eye of the beholder."

She ignored that. "He stops by the retirement village once in awhile now with his fiddle."

"His fiddle!"

"Why not? He knows it brightens everybody's day when he shows up to play for us. He wouldn't have to do it. He's very good with it, too. No. He's better than good. He could make his living with his music if he had a mind to. Didn't you know that?"

"Meg Ferguson told me he played, and I may have heard him on a tape once, but all of that kind of got lost in the shuffle. I'd forgotten."

"I can understand that. You've had a rough few months."

Months that I didn't particularly want to rehash just now. "If Danny was the fiddler on that tape I heard, he seems to be able to play almost any kind of tune."

"I don't know about the tape, but I've personally heard him play everything from Ozarks old-time fiddle to Irish trad to concert-hall classical, with a good dollop of some pretty hot bluegrass on the side. He plays best when the piece is something he's composed himself. Ask him to play for you sometime."

"I wouldn't dream of it. We're supposed to be associating on a purely professional basis."

She shot me a questioning look. "Professional?"

"I needed a policeman. Again."

"But he's... Again, Constancy?"

"Not quite the same as last time. It's a long, complex story. I'll get to it, but first I want to ask you a question about Gram. Do you know anything about the jewels she wore for her wedding portrait?"

"A little. Why do you ask?"

"I always believed the jewelry in the wedding portrait was her garnets. Danny says it's diamonds."

Irma sighed. "He's right. Every red stone in that set was a diamond." With great care, Irma shaped a piece of aluminum foil into a perfect sphere. "Amanda never wanted any diamonds. She loathed wearing them, but she did it for the wedding and again for the portrait because Lucian asked her to. The Frasers called them the Soillse Flann set."

"But what happened to them? They aren't in the collection, not even the private section. The garnets she gave me are in settings identical to the jewels in the portrait."

Irma was silent for a long moment. "You think this trouble may have something to do with those diamonds?"

"Danny thinks so."

"I'd say it's possible he could be right. Amanda didn't like anybody even mentioning them, but she sure wouldn't want you having trouble because of them. I'd better tell you the little I know."

"Please."

"It's not much. She told me a little bit one time when I caught her crying and wormed it out of her, but she wouldn't ever talk about it again. She said Lucian gave her the set as a wedding gift, the only diamonds any Fraser ever gave up voluntarily, as far as either one of us knew. He did it over Bart's howls of protest, because that set was by far the most valuable thing in the collection. Lucian told her that those five stones, because they were garnet colored, were probably worth more than double all the rest of it put together. I guess that color doesn't show up very often.

"I don't mean now that Lucian just let her wear them. They were hers, absolutely, with appropriate papers drawn up by lawyers and all the rest of it. Lucian must have wanted her to have something of her own, something incontestable. Maybe he even wanted to get back at Bart a little for what he'd done to George. Amanda didn't say that. That's my own idea. Anyway, Lucian was forty years older than Amanda and he must have known Bart would squabble over anything he left her and her child in his will, which, of course, Bart did."

"Gram never liked Bart."

"Neither did I. He was slick, sneaky. Even as a boy, he had a downright mean streak. Beyond that, Amanda seemed to have some special reason for disliking him. She didn't tell me so in words, but I sure got that impression."

"I don't suppose she told you what she did with the diamonds."

"No, Sweetie. She did tell me she intended to make sure Bartholomew never got his covetous hands on them. She never wore them after Lucian died, but she did wear the garnets soon after that. I don't know if she sold the diamonds out of the settings and replaced them with the garnets or if she sold the whole business and had the garnet set made to wear instead. It could be that she just hid the diamonds away somewhere."

Evidently somebody thought she had hidden them.

"Whatever she did, Bart was furious. He offered to buy them back at something over their appraised value. If Lucian was right about what they were worth, I don't know where he would've gotten that much money. Even if he mortgaged everything the Frasers owned it might not have been enough. It didn't matter, anyway. Amanda refused his offer. Then she wouldn't tell him what she'd done with them. Having those rare red stones in the collection and then losing them about drove him crazy. In fact, I think he was crazy, at least on the subject of diamonds."

The gardener finished the chrysanthemums and turned slightly to bag the wilting weeds. Bryce. I hadn't recognized him from the back. As a gardener, he had every right to be working with the flowers. He couldn't have known Irma and I would have our lunch in the park or be talking about the diamonds. At least from where he was, he shouldn't have been able to hear.

I lowered my voice, anyway. "Miss Irma, that guy with the flowers. Do you know him?"

"If he went to school in Fraserton, he got into the system after I retired. Why?"

"He and some older man from Eddie's Gardens were over at Gram's putting in bulbs. I'd canceled the order, but they did it anyway. For free, they said."

"It must have been Eddie's idea. That youngster doesn't look like the generous type."

"No. In fact he gives me a bad feeling. Gram always told me not to judge people on appearances, but Danny said I should listen hard to my inner feelings. They might be my subconscious way of seeing danger. I'm all for giving Bryce the benefit of the doubt, but I think I'll go with Danny's advice on this one."

Irma nodded. "I would, too."

Bryce set the bag beside the path, picked up his equipment and left the park. Good.

"Was the rest of Bart's family as interested as he was in getting back that set of diamonds?" I asked."

"His son, Oliver, wasn't much account. He wasn't mean like

Bart, but he just wasn't worth road dust on a hot day. Nona was more diamond-crazy than Oliver was. As far as I know, he never pestered Amanda about them. He didn't have much in the way of gumption. For the sake of the business, it's just as well he died the same year as the old man and control went directly to the Triumvirate. I don't know how the younger generation feels about that feud over the red diamonds. Which one of them put that silly ring on your finger?"

"Zared," I said meekly.

Irma West never hesitated to say what was on her mind. "You're not the least bit in love with him, are you? I hope you know that when Amanda and I were plotting to get you married off, we never even looked at Frasers. None of them's your type. Why on earth did you agree to marry Zared?"

"He came to Gram's funeral," I said slowly. "You saw him there. He was sweet and reassuring. I didn't have any backbone left at all. He made me feel wanted and safe when it seemed like everything in my life was falling apart. I convinced myself I loved him, or at least that I could learn to love him."

"You don't look convinced now. What happened?"

I glanced sideways at her. "Your musical policeman came when I called him."

A quick grin. "It's harder and harder not to say I told you so." The grin gave way to a frown. "Why did you need a policeman?"

"I found another dead body. It was in my kitchen, this time."

"Another dead body! I never heard a word about that."

So I told her, too, about the vanishing corpse. "Seeing that body, I didn't know what else to do except call Danny. I wasn't sure he would come after last time, but he did. When I saw Danny again, Zared, uh, kind of faded into the background."

"As well he should. But what about the body? Who's handling the investigation?"

"Danny says since it disappeared and he never saw it, he has nothing he can report, so I don't suppose he did. He seems to be taking it seriously unofficially, bless him."

She raised both eyebrows. "I hope that boy knows what he's doing."

"I trust him."

"You're in love with him."

"I can't be in love with him." I waved the diamond at her. "I'm engaged to another man. It's funny. Danny wasn't as thrilled by that as I thought he would be."

"Of course he wasn't. If you had any good sense, you'd know why."

"Miss Irma, he feels nothing for me, unless it's annoyance. I was surprised he even answered my SOS."

"Really?"

"Well, maybe not. Underneath all that blarney and bluster, and despite our…differences of opinion, he's truly a good man. He cares about things like justice. But at the end of that last episode, Danny informed me with great enthusiasm that he never wanted to see me again."

She smiled. "Did he tell you that from his hospital bed?"

"The second time. The first time was just after I tripped him, but that shouldn't make any difference."

"It might. The man was in pain and I expect he was frightened out of his mind along with it."

"Danny Egan doesn't know the meaning of the word."

But even I had seen fear in his eyes. Once.

"He wants the world to believe that nothing gets to him, but it's not true. When he was just a boy, he witnessed a murder. The man who died was a policeman who was very close to the family. Brendan experienced firsthand the trauma that man's wife and child faced. Because of that, he swore he wouldn't ever put a woman in that position. With him it would be police work or a wife. Not both. You scared him, Constancy, that's all there is to it. When he found you, he had to put that resolve to its first real test."

If that were true, even if he had chosen the police work, why didn't he just tell me? It would have been a lot easier to take than what he did say. "Did he tell you that?"

"Let's say his mother worries about him. It'd serve him right if you did marry Zared." She gazed at me a long moment. "Wouldn't do you or Zared much good, though. You want some of these cookies?"

"I'm sorry. I'm not very hungry."

She handed me the whole bag. "Here. Take them home and share them with Brendan later."

"Okay. He needs to eat more. He's gotten awfully thin." I stared down at the honey-gold brilliance of Zared's ring and went back to a previous subject. "Miss Irma, somebody's been searching for something in Gram's house, and in my apartment. Danny thinks it's those red diamonds they want, but I don't know who 'they' could be."

She frowned. "If I remember correctly, Bart tried to hush up the fact that they no longer owned that set of diamonds. It was a bad blow to the Fraser corporate pride, as well as to their net worth. Not that it turned them into paupers, but they certainly would have felt it financially. Mostly they hated it because a set of diamonds had escaped their clutches. If they thought there was a chance they might get them back, I believe they'd take it in a minute. That makes them the obvious suspects, if you want to use that word.

"If you'd rather look outside the family, there are bound to be people besides me who remember, or whose relatives passed on the story. People would have seen them at the wedding, or in the museum display or the portrait. Or there might be people who just heard rumors about them. There may even be a record in the library." She stretched and checked her watch. "My lunch hour's nearly over. Now I have a question for you. Constancy, I want you to think hard before you get angry with me."

"I won't get angry."

"Have you considered the possibility that Zared might be marrying you for the Soillse Flann diamonds?"

"You're kidding!"

"Why did he wait until you inherited Amanda's estate before he took any interest?"

The more I thought about it, the funnier it became. "Miss Irma, I have never, in my wildest dreams, imagined anybody would want to marry me for my money."

She gave a lady-like version of Danny's derisive snort. "I didn't say money, did I? It's not the money. In the long run, Frasers don't care beans about the money the diamonds represent. It's the diamonds themselves they covet. If it came to a choice between selling off part of their collection or starving, I expect they would choose to starve. It's a family disease. All of them have it except for you and George, and maybe your mother. I don't know about her. Anyway, you and George escaped somehow. Count your blessings." She carefully picked up the remains of our lunch. "If you find out that's why Zared wants you, will you give back this monstrosity of a ring?"

I blushed, probably to the tips of my toes. "I don't know. I've got to consider Danny."

"Danny! What? Are you trying to make him jealous?"

"If it were, it wouldn't work. But if I scared him the first time, I can't afford to do it again. Not until this mess is cleared up. If you're right and I broke this engagement, he would probably be heading all the way back to Ireland on the next plane. I'd be left with Lon Tirso or somebody worse who would just as soon arrest me as not."

"Lonnie Tirso was the worst bully I ever had in kindergarten."

"He still is."

"I wish I'd known young Brendan when he was five. He must have been an adorable child."

I couldn't argue with that.

Chapter 7

Danny wasn't at the house yet, but it was only three o'clock. I went in through the back as usual, set the groceries I'd brought on the counter in the kitchen and carefully secured the door, including Danny's new bolt.

Besides doing the bolts, Danny had straightened up some of the mess in the hall and the kitchen. I couldn't imagine Zared, or any of his family, cleaning my house. They might hire it done for me, but they would never get their own hands in it. Irma was right. Despite everything, Danny was a sweet man.

And I was about to be formally engaged to somebody else. What was I going to do about Friday night? My interview with Zared had in no way reassured me. Not about anything. The more I considered life as Mrs. Zared Fraser, the less I felt able to cope. I wasn't cut out to live that way and I wasn't sure I could learn how to do it. Or that I wanted to.

Gram and I had lived comfortably, but not extravagantly. What was that verse in Proverbs? "Give me neither poverty nor riches." Moderation had been Gram's hallmark, but the Frasers didn't even know that word. All those parties. All that diamond-trimmed elegance. I may as well face it, I didn't have enough of the right kind of feeling for Zared to make it bearable.

Did we have anything at all in common except our Fraser ancestors? Possibly not. If Zared kept insisting that I look elegant all the time, I would be a constant disappointment to him. That wouldn't make for much of a marriage, either.

With a deep sigh, I began to put away the groceries. When I was a child, fancy dress had been such fun, elegance as easy as pretend. Gram and I spent hours at it the first summer I was with her. She had a huge, old domed trunk full of beautiful gowns with all the accessories. They had belonged to her mother or grandmothers. Victorian laces and velvets, silks and satins.

A flutter of pure excitement, left over from a very young Constancy Stafford, tickled my stomach. The first time I'd thought about it, it had been no more than a self-defense tactic, a reaction to Zared's use of the word *elegant*.

What if I could find something that would work?

The clothes wouldn't be quite what I remembered, of course. I knew that. Cloth gets fragile with age, or moth-eaten, or rotted by mildew. Even if the garments had survived the hazards of aging and were in perfect condition, they'd surely be too small for me now. Wasn't it the Victorian ladies who dreamed of sixteen-inch waists and compressed themselves mercilessly to make it so?

Besides, the dresses probably weren't velvet and satin and lace. A child's make-believe has as grand an effect on rags as a fairy god-mother's magic wand, but like the clock striking midnight, the eyes of adulthood would reduce them to their state of sad reality.

That trunk was still in our attic, though I hadn't looked into it since I was ten years old. That was the year I decided I would much rather be climbing trees and playing ball with the neighborhood boys than dressing up in ancient clothing. That phase didn't last long, but somehow I never got back to playing with the things in the trunk. Maybe I *could* find something in it that would do. It wouldn't hurt to look.

If, by some miracle, I did go through with the official engagement, maybe one of Gram's dresses could help me pretend elegance and poise the way I had as a child. The very fact that it was associated in my heart with her would get me through Zared's party better than any modern gown.

I shoved the milk and fruit into the refrigerator and ran up to the attic.

The burglar visited there, as well, but not with much enthusiasm. He had pulled out and scattered a few things, but most of it looked just like I remembered. It was a far cry from Mrs. Jamison's sterile and empty place.

Gram somehow managed to keep things in fairly neat stacks, although until she was too feeble to climb the stairs, she was always piling more in, adding to what had already been deposited by several generations. The attic would have been a junk dealer's fantasy, a selective burglar's nightmare. If Gram had hidden any diamonds in the attic, any burglar would need months to find them.

Even digging out the trunk took time. As I moved all the more recent stacks of stuff to get to it, I took a good wallow in nostalgia. Among other things, Gram had kept boxes of my school papers, furniture that had been moved when she let me remodel my room on my thirteenth birthday, and suitcases of more modern clothing that she couldn't bear to part with. I had to look through all of it, of course.

Finally, after I made nearly as much mess in the attic as the burglar made downstairs, I pulled the magic box out of a cobwebby corner and shooed away a couple of strolling spiders. The black trunk was ancient and dusty, its leather straps cracked from disuse, its brass hinges dull and tarnished. Probably locked. No. The stiff clasps needed a few seconds of coaxing but they finally came free. The lid creaked when I lifted it.

Instead of the mildew I expected, the contents smelled exactly as I remembered them. They smelled faintly of roses and violets and fine, old face powder. They smelled as if I were still six and Gram and I were about to begin one of our games.

The first garment was heavy, black, well-worn. A widow's mourning gown? I held it up to me. Too small in the middle and absolutely no good for looking elegant. I found a lace-edged baby's dress, once white, now ivory with age. Had Gram worn it? Had she dressed her baby daughter in it? I refolded it gently. Maybe someday I could use it for a child of my own.

What was that? It was only a tiny noise, so soft and nondescript that I couldn't quite place it. Was it even in the attic?

I listened hard for a couple of minutes. Nothing else. No noises that shouldn't be there. Probably some old treasure I had disturbed was just getting settled again. I turned my attention back to the trunk.

Here were some dresses that I remembered. I sighed. The velvets, satins and laces of childhood were actually much more prosaic stuff. Just everyday clothing. They, too, were worn, fraying. A few of them had been carefully mended and pressed. Gram must have done that after I lost interest. She always enjoyed our games as much as I did and would have missed them more when they ended.

I kept on, digging through yards of petticoats, some odd handbags, an uncomfortable-looking corset, a clutter of glass beads and a fan or two.

Only dim light penetrated into this part of the attic and as I neared the bottom of the trunk, I was going as much by feel as by sight. Beneath the loose garments I touched something different, a hard box of some kind.

Somebody's watching me! Horrible, creepy feeling! I scrambled to my feet. If I wasn't the only person in my attic, I wanted out. Quick.

I took one step toward the stairs and saw the intruder. Tiny beads of light reflected from a pair of little eyes near the floor in the corner. Another step and their owner gave a shrill squeak and skittered away to darker shadows.

Mice! They were probably the cause of the first noise, too. I sat down by the trunk, laughing.

They had no doubt decided an empty human house was the perfect winter hideaway for them. I didn't mind mice, but I couldn't let them stay here. Rodents liked chewing too much and they could carry disease.

Somewhere I had some traps. It wouldn't be the first time I had captured mice, driven out of town with them and released them in the woods. First things first, though. I had to see what was in the box at the bottom of the trunk.

I pulled it out and opened it, hardly daring to hope. My fingers encountered cool, smooth silk and a touch of warm velvet. This wasn't for normal, everyday wear. I carried the box to a window.

We had never played with this dress, but I recognized it from an old photograph of Gram's mother. The deep garnet-red silk, with its aged-ivory lace and darker maroon velvet accenting the neckline and sleeves almost glowed in the dusky attic.

If it weren't damaged in some way, and if it fit me, it should be elegant enough to suit even Zared.

I lifted the bulky, heavy garnet out of its box and carried it down to my room and examined it in really good light. No defects. It had been folded so carefully that the material was uncrushed, undamaged. It looked as if Gram, or her mother, packed it away only yesterday.

Half holding my breath, I took off my skirt and sweater, undid the many tiny hooks down the gown's back and slipped it over my head. No way was I going to do up all those hooks until it was absolutely necessary, but by fastening the waist and top and one somewhere between, I could tell it would do.

Gram's mother had been a bit taller than I, but thank goodness she hadn't squeezed her middle into a scant sixteen inches. A few minutes of hemming the dress would be all the work necessary, and I might get by without that, if I could find the proper petticoats.

That scent of old-fashioned roses floated around me as I stood there in front of the mirror. The color of the silk would be perfect with the garnets. A deep fall of lace overlaid with a cut-out yoke in the darker velvet created a stunning collar. The dress had a rounded neckline that fell a couple of inches below the hollow of my throat, exactly right for the choker necklace with its large pendant stone. The sleeves were short, gathered just above the elbow with a band of the velvet and the graceful drape of more lace. The skirt hung straight in front, but was gathered and longer in back, making a kind of train.

The silk material shimmered in the glass. Even Constancy Stafford could look elegant in this dress, and could almost feel the part. If I could coax my hair into something approximating those old photos, it just might work. Hadn't I seen ancient hairpins among the glass beads?

Skirts gathered high in one hand, I made another swift trip up the attic stairs and brought down an armful of stuff, assorted petticoats, pins for my hair, a tiny black-beaded handbag, a delicate lace shawl. Ten minutes of work and the hair was approximately what I wanted. It gave the illusion of fitting the dress, anyway. To do it right, I'd need the curling iron and a bit more time, but it was going to work.

I stood back and looked at myself. Amazing. The old magic of make-believe still held. At least in my eyes. How the Frasers would react to this antiquity, I had no idea. Truthfully, I didn't much care. The probability that I wouldn't be going to that party at all was increasing by the minute.

In the mirror, I suddenly caught a glimpse of motion outside the door, in the dim hall.

"Danny, come see what I found."

But this time, it wasn't Danny.

What was it with strangers invading my space?

The man and I stared at each other. At least this one wasn't already dead. Quite. He looked so sick and wobbly that I was more afraid for him than of him.

His face was a mess, pearl-pale in the few places where it wasn't scraped and bruised. Blood had soaked into a badly tattered shirt from a small jagged cut on his chin. He kept one arm held tightly across his body. Through a rip in the long sleeve, I could see more dried blood crusting the forearm. In his other hand, he held a gun. He had it pointed in my general direction, but not convincingly enough to make me feel the least bit threatened.

It nagged in the back of my mind that I had seen the man somewhere recently, had even spoken with him and had liked him. But I couldn't put a place or time or name to the memory.

"You're hurt," I said. "Let me help you."

When I spoke, he shook his head, his eyes wide, incredulous. "I must be dreaming. You can't be—"

In bizarre slow motion, he crumpled into a pathetic little heap just outside the doorway of my room.

Oh, please don't let him die, whoever he is!

This one had a pulse. Barely. I grabbed the gun from his unresisting hand, then ran for the stairs. I must have had some vague idea of phoning an ambulance or getting water to revive him, both of which could have been done from the second floor if I'd been in my right mind.

I made it three-quarters of the way down the staircase before that beautiful, over-long silk skirt and my in-born clumsiness clashed. I felt my foot catch and tangle, my ankle turn, myself falling. I grabbed wildly for the banister with both hands. The gun, which hadn't discharged when the man fell with it, did so resoundingly when I banged it against the wooden railing. Surely it shouldn't have. Had I had my finger on the trigger? Ears ringing, I sat down with an ungraceful, brain-shaking thump on the bottom step, lifted my eyes and met the horrified gaze of Danny Egan.

Chapter 8

"Give me that!" Danny snatched the gun from me, his voice harsh, totally Irish, and thick with anger. Or was it shock?

He jerked out the ammunition clip, ejected the chambered round and dropped the whole mess onto the chair by the door. He was breathing like he'd tried to run a two-minute mile. "Is it not enough that you break my ribs? Will you be blowing my brains out now? Look you where the bullet hit. I felt the hot wind of its passing and itself not an inch from my ear. I should be locking you away in the deepest pit this world boasts and never releasing you lest you destroy the whole of humanity and yourself with it. What were you thinking?"

He choked back whatever else he intended to say, dropped onto the step beside me and, to my total amazement, pulled me close with fierce, trembling arms.

I only just managed not to throw my own arms around him and hang on for dear life. It was the one thing I wanted most to do, the one thing I dared not do. With my face jammed into the curve of his throat, I could barely breathe. I didn't care. How very wonderful his ragged, racing pulse felt against my body. Thank God, he was still alive. My stupid panic, aided and abetted by my clumsiness had come within inches of stopping his heatbeat forever.

What if the bullet had hit him? What if I killed this man I loved? *Yes. All right, all right.* I did love him. No matter how much I tried to convince myself, and everybody else, otherwise, that fact remained. How could I have been so stupid as to think I could marry Zared Fraser?

I swallowed a sob, which, fortunately, he mistook for something else.

"Am I crushing you? Are you breathing?"

"Not much." Which answered both questions.

Danny loosened his grip a little, but he held on almost as if he were afraid to release me. "Sorry," he muttered. "I wasn't meaning to smother you." Once again there was fear in his eyes. "Ah, Constancy, I saw you falling and I couldn't reach you in time."

He seemed to catch himself at that point. He let me go and stood up quickly, his voice almost returned to his normal, lightly sarcastic tone. Almost, but not quite. "Are you hurt?"

"I'm okay. Danny, I'm so sorry. Are you hurt?"

He took a deep breath and released it slowly. "By the grace of God, I'm not. At least not physically. I've maybe lost ten years off my life from sheer fright." He remembered he was supposed to be angry with me. "What were you doing with a loaded pistol? You told me yourself you didn't have one in the house, that you'd had no firearms training. You've proved the last part of it well enough."

"It's not mine. It belongs to the man upstairs. He's hurt, unconscious. He looks like somebody tried to put him through a wood chipper. I only picked up the gun because I thought if he woke up, he ought not have it. Danny, we have to help him. That's why I was running."

"The man upstairs. WHAT man upstairs?" He was roaring again, and I found it most heartening.

"I reckon she means me," said a breathless voice from above us. The battered man watched Danny's hand slide swiftly toward the holster under his jacket. "Don't worry," he said. "I've been mostly disarmed. But I'll keep my hands where you can see them."

"Who are you?"

"Name's Stuart. I have identification in my left front pocket."

"Okay. Let's have it. Go carefully."

The man reached into his pocket and slowly brought out a small leather folder. I thought he was coming down. Instead, he wobbled, grabbed the banister, then sank down onto the top step. "Sorry. I don't seem to be steady enough to tackle stairs yet."

"Just drop the identification down to us."

He did.

Danny didn't seem to be taking this episode very well. He looked every bit of ten years older. He probably hadn't slept since I phoned him about the body. By his own admission, he'd had precious little sleep before that. To top it off, clumsy Constancy had nearly shot him. No wonder he was looking shell-shocked. He glanced at the stranger's identification. A smile flashed across his mouth, but vanished as he turned to me.

"Get out of the fancy dress," he growled. "Put on something less dangerous."

More happy than I had any earthly right to be, I grinned at our visitor. "I'm Constancy. This is Danny," I said. "He sounds uncommonly grumpy tonight, but if you need help, you couldn't find a better policeman."

"Constancy!"

"Oh, be quiet for once, Danny." I climbed the stairs with Danny right behind me. "There are towels and soap and first aid stuff in the bathroom," I said. "Take him in there and practice your first aid skills."

As Danny helped the man to his feet, I went to change out of the dress. Thank goodness I hadn't damaged it when I tripped. I hung it in the closet with great care and a pang of regret, combed out my hair, and put on the plain, safe skirt, blouse and sweater that I'd been wearing before. Every Cinderella has her midnight. I could handle that. If only Prince Charming didn't change back into a rodent.

Fifteen minutes later, when I went to check on the repair work, the stranger was looking considerably better. His face was less injured than it had first appeared. There were bruises and a scrape or two under a couple of days' growth of beard, but the cut on his chin had required only a small bandage. Danny was working on the arm wound. They were deep in some serious discussion, as if they'd known each other for years.

Though their features were very different, they wore identical expressions of weariness and watchful tension. Since knowing Danny, I had associated that look exclusively with policemen under unusual stress. Who was this guy?

"Here." I hung a sweatshirt on the doorknob. "I thought you might want this to put on after Danny's done with you. It should fit. Gram got an extra-large by mistake once and never took it back. Would you like me to wash your shirt?"

"Thanks, but I don't think it's salvageable. I appreciate this."

"How are things?"

"I'm no doctor," Danny said, "but I'm convinced he'll live, if he stays out of trouble. It must be a dominant gene."

"What's a dominant gene?"

Danny's mouth twisted up at one corner. "That ability to find trouble without the least bit of effort. Look at him, heart's blood. Look at him and tell me what you see."

I looked. Found ash-brown hair, semi-disguised by sun-bleached blond streaks and a very familiar chin only slightly disguised by the bandage. When the swelling left his nose, it would be thin. A little like mine. A lot like Lucian Fraser's. Why hadn't I seen it before? "You're a Fraser."

"Yep." He watched me warily. "I don't know if that makes you friend or foe, but I'm Stuart Fraser."

"George! Are you from George's family?"

"George Fraser is my Grandad."

"Oh. Oh, Stuart!" Only the fresh bandage on his arm and his wary look kept me from hugging him like a long-lost brother. "Is George still alive?"

"Yes."

"Where is he? How's he doing? Where did he go when he left here?"

"When his family ran him off from here, you mean. After the depression, he settled in South Dakota. He built up a fine ranch that's being run today by his kids and his grand kids. He didn't steal any diamonds to get the money to put into it, either."

"I never believed he stole any diamonds, Stuart. In the end, even Lucian believed George was innocent, though he could never quite convince himself that Bart had framed his own brother. That's what my great-grandmother told me."

"It's too bad Grandad didn't hear that straight from his old man. It would have saved us all kinds of trouble."

"That's hardly Constancy's fault," Danny said gently. "She's no typical Fraser, despite that showy thing on her finger. That much is fact."

Stuart smiled. "No," he said. "I'm sorry. Amanda's great-granddaughter couldn't be a typical Fraser."

Had he known Gram? George would have, of course. George had been much closer to her in age than Lucian had.

"George and Amanda kept in touch until she died," Stuart said, as if he were reading my thoughts.

"In touch! How? They never found George."

"Amanda did."

"It's a shame to be interrupting this grand family reunion," Danny said, "but there's pizza growing cold downstairs. I don't know about the two of you but I'm famished. We can talk just as well or better while we eat and we'll be more comfortable."

"You would remember to eat at a time like this."

"Well, then, I doubt Stuart's had anything at all today. It's him I'm thinking of."

Stuart grinned, then gazed at me hopefully.

"All right. I bow to the majority vote. Can you make it downstairs now, Stuart, or shall we bring the food up?"

He blushed. "I can get down with Danny's help, but I need a few more minutes up here first."

"I'll go put the food on the table."

I had time to set the table, make a salad and reheat the pizza before they came down. I suspected that the delay was no more than a cover for some kind of conference they didn't want me in on. I didn't mind if they had their little secrets, although I didn't like the fact that they both came down looking more grim than they had before.

After Danny gave thanks for the food (aloud, this time), Stuart began to eat as if he hadn't done it in weeks. Danny matched him bite for bite. Food was beginning to appeal to me again, too.

"It honestly doesn't upset you that I've come?" Stuart asked when the worst of the hunger pangs and the better part of two large pizzas and the salad had been conquered.

"Stuart, I've spent months of idle hours thinking about George and dreaming up a family for him and for me. How do you feel about picnics?"

"Cheyenne Crossing," he answered with a grin. "That's where we go for picnics. There or Roughlock Falls. Unless, of course, you'd rather stay on the ranch. If we do that, we can go by horseback and save fuel. There's a perfect spot about a mile from the house. You come up and we'll throw you the best picnic you've ever seen."

I set out Irma's cookies. "Then I don't see any reason why your being here should upset me."

Danny brought the gloom rushing back. "It's upset somebody. You're forgetting Stuart's recently been used for target practice."

"Not exactly forgetting. I'd just rather think about family picnics." I shivered. "Somebody really did shoot at you?"

"Among other things."

"On purpose?"

"No question about that."

"I'm glad he wasn't a very good shot."

"Oh, but he was. Dead on target. Got me right in the heart. You can look at the hole in my shirt if you don't believe me."

He'd been shot in the heart and he was sitting there calmly stuffing down pizza and cookies. Sure.

Callous creatures that they were, they burst out laughing. Or Danny did. Stuart's attempt was quickly stifled, as if it hurt.

"Body armor, delight of my soul," Danny said. "You've tried it. Remember? Marvelous stuff, when it works."

Stuart grinned. "It did this time. God bless the inventor and manufacturer of it and the tax dollars that provided it and my girl and my mother for making me promise to wear it. I reckon, while I'm at it, I ought to throw in a word of thanks for the gunman, too, that his weapon wasn't high enough caliber to penetrate the vest. I'm bruised, that's all."

I shook my head, a thousand questions fighting for voice, but one had been plaguing my subconscious since the first moment I saw him. One thing I wanted to know above all others. "Where have I met you before now? I know I've seen you. It's not just because you have a Fraser face."

"We've met. In a way. I didn't recognize you until you came back to this century clothing-wise, but I didn't think you were capable of remembering anything about our first meeting."

"The car! You were driving the car that almost hit me."

"I get pretty close to a terminal chill every time I think about it. I know you saw me. You looked straight at me, then waltzed right out into the street. I didn't know who you were then. I thought you were suicidal, or out-of-your-mind drunk."

"Constancy, love, I'm shocked. If you were drunk, it's no wonder you weren't remembering details."

"I couldn't have been drunk. I've never touched alcohol, except maybe in cooking. Gram would've skinned me if I'd tried it before I left home and I never did develop any inclination to take it up."

"It wasn't alcohol," Stuart confirmed. "I realized that when we got face to face. It was more likely something from the cannabis family."

"Cannabis! You mean marijuana?"

Danny raised an eyebrow. "At least the liquor's legal."

"I've never smoked anything, either, let alone that."

But something had been wrong with me. I couldn't remember getting from the restaurant on the top floor of the Fraser building to the street in front of it, but suddenly I was there, floating a bit, feeling as if everything were moving in slow motion. As if I had all the time in the world to cross in front of an on-coming car. It certainly wasn't normal.

Danny had been watching me think it through. "Well?"

"I may have been drugged someway, but I sure didn't take anything on purpose. Could I have got it accidentally?"

The two men looked at one another again. "It might have been given you in food," Danny said. "I very much doubt it was accidental."

"Then who gave it to me? Why?"

"Who did you see that day?" he shot back. "Who fed you?"

"Danny, no!"

"Tell me where else you could have got it." With an effort, he softened his voice. "I'm sorry. Constancy, I'm sorry, but we're needing to face facts." He turned to Stuart. "Did you see your attacker?"

"Oh, yeah. I got a real good look at him. The idiot jumped me under a street light, if you can believe it." Without further prompting, Stuart Fraser gave a better description than I had of the man whom I knew only as the corpse in my kitchen.

Chapter 9

"You know him," Stuart said, looking from one to the other of us.

Danny shook his head. "I've recently heard much the same description from Constancy. We've no name for the man yet. When did he attack you?"

"Yesterday evening. About nine, I guess."

"How badly did you hurt him?"

"I didn't," Stuart said, ruefully. "I hate like everything to admit it, but I never got a finger on him. Why?"

"Somebody did. This morning he was dead and stored temporarily in the kitchen of Constancy's apartment, after which he mysteriously and conveniently vanished."

"Good trick."

"Wasn't it. Well, if he wasn't suffering from an overdose of your self-defense, perhaps there's another reason for his death."

Stuart nodded. "Sloppy work on his part? Could be."

Their minds seemed to be running in the same groove. It took me a few minutes longer to get it. "You mean somebody hired that criminal to kill Stuart and he's dead because he didn't do it right?"

"I'd say there's a good possibility of it."

"But why put him in my kitchen? Why take him out again? Who would do that? Why does anybody want Stuart dead?"

"I don't know why they stashed this guy in your kitchen," Stuart said, "but I'm pretty certain why somebody wants me out of the way. I came here to investigate my dad's disappearance. I get a real strong impression somebody didn't like him being here. The same people didn't appreciate me coming to see about him, either."

"Your dad disappeared here? In Fraserton? Why was he here?"

A faint smile. "Stubbornness runs in the family. First there's Grandad. Amanda wanted him to come home a long time ago, but he wouldn't. Didn't want people to think he was after those bad luck diamonds. Last month he had a heart attack. He survived, but the doctor says another one, a fatal one, could be just around the corner. Grandad would like to make some kind of reconciliation between the two branches of the family before he dies.

"Then there's Dad. Grandad said to wait a few weeks longer before we contacted Bart's family, but after the heart attack, Dad wouldn't. He wrote Zared Fraser asking him to meet with us as soon as possible. He was very careful to specify that we aren't a threat to the Fraser empire. We don't want the diamonds or any of the rest of it. We like where we are and who we are. Dad and Zared arranged a time to meet and Dad flew down."

"Zared didn't mention meeting your dad. I wish he had told me."

Stuart gave me an odd look. "They're not likely to tell anybody they met with him," he said. "They denied it to me."

Danny shifted in his chair. "You do know your father actually got here?"

"He phoned Mom from the Fraserton airport.

Everything was fine then. The Frasers had sent a car for him and he promised to call again after the meeting."

"But he didn't?"

"He did. Dad's a cop, too, did I tell you? Over the years, he and Mom have developed a kind of code between them. He can tell her a lot without actually giving away anything to anybody else who might be listening. There's a special signal if he wants back-up or thinks he might be in trouble."

I glanced at Danny, and didn't like what I saw there. "Did your father give that signal?"

"No. He phoned several hours after Mom was expecting him, but he didn't push any alarm buttons. He told her he was going to stay in Fraserton awhile longer, get better acquainted with the relatives, work out some details for them to have a visit with Grandad George. He promised to be home in about a week. She didn't buy a word of it."

"What alerted her?" Danny asked.

"The way he talked. A slurred consonant here and there, the tone a little too laid-back. Dad's an easy-going guy, but that trait's inborn, not chemically induced. Slurring consonants isn't inborn. Neither is slow, drawling speech, not for any South Dakota native. Mom was convinced he was on something when he made the second call. Like you, Constancy, he wouldn't choose to be high on anything, legal or illegal. What it added up to, in her judgment, was that he was in bad trouble, and he deliberately wasn't asking for help. He didn't want any of the rest of us involved."

"So naturally you came."

"Wouldn't you?"

"In a minute."

Stuart grinned. "Mom's careful, but she's not paranoid. She doesn't jump to unwarranted conclusions. As soon as I could get down here, I went straight to Fraser House. They calmly and reasonably told me they had no idea what I was talking about. They'd never even heard of Caleb Fraser. I got exactly the same story at the office from cousin Zared."

"Then what?"

"I drove around for a long time after that, thinking about what to do next, looking at the ancestral home town, trying to decide if I wanted to contact Amanda's great-granddaughter." He glanced at me with a wry smile. "About dark, I almost ran down some girl who was under the influence. All that time, I was also keeping my eye on the man who was following me."

"When did you spot him?"

"Right after I left Fraser House. Looked like they were expecting me and had him handy to pick up the trail. I thought they'd try kidnapping me, too. I went walking after supper, hoping I could get my hands on somebody who could take me to Dad. I'll admit that was stupid, but I wasn't expecting attempted murder. Not right off the bat like that, anyway. I thought they'd have better sense. At least I was wearing the vest."

"He just opened fire?"

"Nothing so simple. He cut around in front of me and was standing at the corner. I decided I might as well go up and talk to him. He wasn't much on conversation. He hit me." Stuart touched his chin with great care. His face was red. "I didn't see what with, but I've been knocked down more gently by a quarter horse in a bad temper. You think I would've seen it coming, but I didn't. If that ever gets back to the guys at home, I'll never live it down."

Danny grinned. "They'll not hear it from me. What happened then?"

"The guy got in a few kicks before I finally began to get my brain working again. I thought he'd broken my arm. I couldn't move it to reach my gun. He didn't have any problem with his. Arrogant gentleman. He didn't even check to see if I was dead. Not that I'm complaining about that. When I got enough breath back to move, I realized I wasn't far from Amanda Casey's house. My one thought was to get here."

"Why didn't you call the police or go to the emergency room?" I asked.

Stuart's glance flicked to Danny and away. "In a town like this, you never know exactly what's safe."

"You did exactly the right thing," Danny said. "For a town like this." Their eyes locked for a moment.

Stuart nodded and went on before I could question the unusual bitterness of Danny's statement. "I had no trouble finding the house, but nobody was home. I'd heard Amanda was gone and had left the house to her great-granddaughter. I wasn't, uh, feeling very well. I thought maybe Amanda wouldn't have minded if I came in anyway, and I hoped her heir wouldn't. When I did get in and saw this mess, I got a little worried about the heir."

"I wasn't here when the last uninvited guest came in, either. I don't know who made the mess."

"Thanks for not assuming it was me," Stuart said.

"I never even thought of that." I looked at Danny. "Your bolts were supposed to keep people out of here."

"Timing, love. Stuart was already in the house when I installed the bolts, remember?"

"Stuart, I walked through the house and didn't see you. Then when Danny came, we were talking."

"I wasn't being all that quiet with the tools when I was working on the doors, either."

"Didn't you hear any of that, Stuart? Where were you?"

"I was in the back bedroom upstairs, on the floor on the far side of the bed. When I came in, I was going to lie down out of sight just for a few minutes, but I went to sleep or passed out or something and I didn't wake up until I heard somebody in the attic. I must have been in worse shape than I thought. That was bad enough." He smiled a little sadly. "Grandad has a picture of

Amanda wearing that dress you had on. I thought you were a ghost, or that I was more than halfway over the line myself. You were pretty much identical to that picture—scared what was left of my thinker right out of me." He grimaced. "That's another thing that better never get out."

"Don't worry. It won't," Danny said. "Let's get back to the gunman. I suppose somebody in the Fraser family wanted to make sure your father presented no claims against the estate. Then you arrived to complicate things."

"That would have been their take on it."

"Wait a minute. How can you think anybody in the Fraser family would do such a thing?"

"How can we not?" Danny asked with weary patience.

"Logically, there's nobody else it could be," Stuart said. "I don't know if it's just one of them or all. Don't worry. I'm not going to make the same mistake old Lucian made. Until there's more than circumstantial evidence, I won't make any accusations. I'm sure not going to give up looking for that evidence though."

"But Zared wouldn't—"

Danny's words cut across mine. "Constancy's engaged to Zared."

Stuart glanced at my ring and then at Danny's face. "Oh. I thought it was you."

Danny shrugged, green eyes laughing. "In the unlikely event I should ever marry, my woman won't be getting a gaudy bobble like that one to wear. She'll take something I can afford on my policeman's salary or give me up as a bad job altogether."

Stuart was embarrassed. "Sorry."

"Quite all right." A sideways glance at me. "We all make mistakes."

"Tell us about George and Amanda, Stuart," I said quickly.

He grinned. "It's going to rearrange your family tree, if you haven't heard the whole story. Amanda said she wasn't planning to tell you."

"How is it going to rearrange my family tree?"

"It'll shuffle your ancestors, kick Lucian up a notch. George Fraser and Amanda Casey were secretly married in 1930 and they had a child."

"You're right," I said. "Gram never told me that. Then George is my great-grandfather, not Lucian."

"Exactly. Amanda was only seventeen. Her parents weren't social climbers. They didn't care that their daughter was in love with the heir to the Fraser fortune. Even in the middle of the depression, they didn't care. George was ten years older and they thought Amanda shouldn't marry until she reached twenty-one. So Mr. and Mrs. Casey made the age-old mistake of forbidding the wedding. That's why Amanda and George ran off together."

"You could change Gram's mind, but not by issuing ultimatums."

"Same with Grandad. George and Amanda married and spent a week together before the Caseys found them. Her parents had the marriage annulled because Amanda was underage. They pretty well hushed up the fact that it had happened and Lucian was happy enough to help them do it. But George and Amanda, being young and smitten, swore that as soon as Amanda hit eighteen, they would be legally married and never part again."

"So what happened?" Danny asked.

"Enter the wicked half-brother," I said.

"Right. Bart was one bad character. He was looking for a way to get rid of George. He used the marriage to convince Lucian that George wasn't the normal hard-headed Fraser. He claimed George stole the diamonds to get back at Lucian for not helping him with Amanda's parents. But he didn't stop at that. He wanted to ruin George's life so it couldn't be fixed. George was determined to stay and fight the theft charges. Then he got a letter from Amanda saying she could never marry a thief."

"But Gram knew he was innocent. She never would have sent a letter like that."

"Forgery was another one of Bart's little accomplishments. George should have known, but he was already so battered by everything else that he accepted the letter at face value. There was no way he could get to Amanda to have it out with her. The Caseys weren't taking any chances. They'd shipped her off to some anonymous relatives on the east coast just to make sure no communication got through.

"It was the knock-out punch for George. Why fight to clear his name when the woman he loved didn't want to share it. He packed up and got out, leaving Bart a very happy man, and Amanda, well, Amanda was pregnant."

"My grandmother was George's daughter." I still hadn't quite taken it in. "Are you sure?"

"No doubt about it. When Amanda was certain she was carrying George's child, she ran away from the relatives and came back to Fraserton. George was gone, so she marched right up to Lucian and told him about the baby, even before she told her parents. As I understand it, she threatened to bring the House of Fraser down around the old man's ears if he didn't find a way to provide for his first grandchild."

"She probably would have, too," Danny said.

"You bet. She wanted Lucian to find George and bring him home. He tried, or told her he did. I don't know how hard he worked at it. I do know George never heard from him. Lucian's final solution was to take Amanda into Fraser House, but the only way the Caseys would allow that was if he married her himself, at least in name. The way she felt about George and the other Frasers, I seriously doubt that there was any more to it than that. Maybe she thought that was the only safe way to protect her child. I do know they never told anybody outright that your grandmother was George's. People accepted her as Lucian's, even if she did arrive a couple of months before she should have. If Bart had suspicions, he didn't act on them."

"Maybe he didn't dare while the old man was alive. Maybe he thought he'd pushed his luck as far as it would go with Lucian. That certainly explains why Gram left Fraser House when Lucian died. When did she find George again?"

"I think she knew where he was for quite a long time, but she never tried to see him until after Bart was gone. My grandmother had passed on by then, too. Amanda waited until she was sure nobody would be hurt. You were eleven. Do you remember a vacation to a South Dakota dude ranch?"

"Don't tell me that was Great-Grandad George's ranch."

"No, it wasn't. But while you were being taught to ride and whatever else with the children's group where you were staying, Amanda made a visit to Grandad. We all loved her. She wanted him to come back to Fraserton then, but he wouldn't."

"Oh, I wish I had met you all then. Especially George. Gram never told me any of that."

"She thought you would be safer not knowing."

"But why? It's all so sad and useless. Why did Bart hate George so much?"

"Hate? I don't know. Seemed like greed was more of a motive than hate. Nothing on earth was as important to Bart as having those diamonds all to himself."

We finished eating in relative silence, then Danny and I cleaned up enough of the burglar's mess for Stuart to go to bed in one of the upstairs rooms. Danny stayed to help him get settled.

When he came down a little later, he was almost stumbling with exhaustion. He dropped onto the couch beside me. "That was quite a story about Amanda and George. Does it sound believable?"

"Every word. It explains several things that didn't quite make sense to me, including why Lucian flat-out gave Gram the diamonds. You were right about that. The ones in the picture are diamonds."

He merely nodded.

"How's Stuart?"

"He'll be fine." Danny gave up fighting the yawn that was trying to get through.

"Will you?"

"Ah, sure. The Irish are great survivors."

"Well, if you're going to survive this, Irishman, you'd better go home and get some sleep."

His eyelids were already drooping. "I told you. I'm spending the night here. Never mind making objections. I wouldn't do it if I didn't think it was necessary for your safety, and Stuart's. Stuart could have complications from his injuries. Or someone could come looking for him. In fact, I'm surprised that's taking so long. They're a bungling set of criminals."

"Danny you're exhausted. You won't hear it if somebody screams for help right next to your ear. If you're going to stay, why don't you go to Gram's bedroom where you can rest?"

"I'll be fine where I am, and I'll hear anything that needs hearing."

"Okay. All right. Have it your own way. I'll get you a pillow and some blankets."

"It's only six-thirty. I'm not sleepy yet."

I was back with the bedding in five minutes. He was already asleep, curled up as if he were cold. His face was pale with fatigue and there were dark shadows under his ridiculously long-lashed eyes, but his breathing was slow and rhythmic. When I tucked the blankets around him, he snuggled into them with a contented little sigh and didn't move again.

I stood a long, long time looking down at him, the dull ache in my heart reinforcing the knowledge that I never could marry Zared Fraser; that I must have been delusional ever to think it was possible. Danny, however, didn't need to know that.

When this was over, he deserved to be able to go back to his own life with no encumbrances. If I could be careful enough, he never would know.

I watched a moment longer, then gave in to bitter-sweet temptation and very carefully, very gently kissed him. Just one swift, light kiss at the corner of that weary, vulnerable mouth. I'd never done it before. Not voluntarily. I probably would never have opportunity to do it again. Fortunately, he was sleeping soundly. He didn't need to know about this, either. Zared and Heather and Nona had no way to find out. The only person it could possibly hurt was me. At this point in my life, what was a little more pain?

Chapter 10

Idle hands are the devil's workshop, Gram used to tell me. Belief
in the devil wasn't fashionable, but it was true enough that idle
hands didn't help ease a troubled mind. Both men were asleep,
but they were exhausted. I didn't know what I was, except that
I'd never felt less like sleeping.

All right. I didn't need to stay idle. Gram firmly believed that
hard physical labor was an antidote for most cases of the jitters.
Tackling that awful mess in the library should keep me busy for a
long time. Eventually, maybe I would be calm enough or just plain
bored enough to sleep.

Gram had remodeled the house when she moved back to it.
She turned the large formal parlor into a library; the small study
behind it became her bedroom. After those years in Fraser House,
she no longer wanted formal living areas. The combination family
room and kitchen where she welcomed her guests had been, in
her parents day, a drafty, inefficient kitchen and a dark, cold dining
room. She had made it into a warm living space.

The furniture there was well-used, slightly shabby and
supremely comfortable. Danny had fallen asleep on the worn couch

in front of the fireplace. I could close myself into the library across the hall and not disturb him in the least. He looked so sweet and harmless in his sleep and so overwhelmingly lovable.

The soft chimes of the doorbell grated across my nerves like the screech of Danny's fabled banshee.

Another hit man looking for Stuart? Surely somebody intent on murder wouldn't arrive so early in the evening, or be ringing the doorbell.

The noise hadn't budged Danny. Then neither would I, unless it turned out to be life or death. I peeped through the curtain of one of the slim windows that flanked the front door. Nona Fraser! Of all people. What was *she* doing here?

Facing the next hit man might have been easier. Try as I might, I couldn't think of any pleasant reason for Zared's mother to be at my door. Surely she wasn't looking for Stuart?

The theory about the Frasers trying to kill him had to be nonsense, anyway. Even if there was some truth in it somewhere, how could Nona be involved? Nona's head was full of diamonds and fashion and opera galas and all the other trappings of her elaborate lifestyle. She wouldn't have time for murder plots.

Still, I was glad Stuart was safely upstairs.

But Danny wasn't upstairs. By now Heather would have delivered her load of filth. So Danny was most likely the reason Nona had come. If she wanted to talk about him, she would have to bring up the topic. I opened the door.

"Hello, Nona. I wasn't expecting to see you tonight."

"That's fairly obvious." She sounded angry.

"Do you want to come in?"

"I wouldn't be here if I didn't."

"Let's sit in the library," I said.

She gave the room a long, critical check and smiled that cold, insincere smile of hers. Probably nothing was ever out of place in Nona's world.

I didn't bother making excuses. "Sit down."

Nona picked her way through the mess, chose the chair that was most becoming to her coloring and, before sitting, delicately brushed away dust I couldn't even see. "Amanda spent entirely too much money and energy on books," she said. "I was delighted when she moved all this junk out of Fraser House. It was such a distraction to the boys."

I had expected accusations about Danny, or maybe comments on my lack of housekeeping abilities, not small talk about Gram's books. "Was that what you came to talk about?"

"Of course not, Constancy. I need to know what you'll be wearing to the party Friday. Heather said you refused even to try on the Hugo royal purple gown I sent over."

Heather hadn't exactly asked me to try it on, but if she had, I probably would have refused.

"It'll take some time to decide on just the right diamonds for your dress and to get them from the vault or the collection."

As dedicated as Nona was to fashion and diamonds, the question of my dress shouldn't have demanded a special, personal trip to what she no doubt considered the outer limits of polite society. She could have used the telephone with a lot less effort. Or sent Heather again.

"It's terribly short notice, but if you haven't planned your gown yet, Hugo would be more than happy to run you up a little something else. You'd be ravishing in black and we could use the Fleur Anna set with that."

The Fleur Anna diamonds might be ravishing in black, but I never had been and never would be and Hugo charged about a hundred dollars a stitch for his services.

As much as I would have enjoyed telling Nona that I wasn't about to go to her party, I couldn't do it yet. It wouldn't be fair to tell her before I told Zared. For now I would have to play along.

Even if Nona never would see it, I was grateful to Gram for the garnet silk in my closet. "I have my dress. I'm not wearing diamonds with it."

She frowned. "You must wear something from the collection besides the engagement ring. People expect to see all the Fraser women dripping with diamonds. It's part of the reason they come."

If I were giving a party, it wouldn't be for people who came only to gawk at what I was wearing, but Nona seemed to think it was the most natural thing in the world. Nona always dripped with diamonds, though. Even for this visit to me she was wearing three multi-carat rings and a sparkling, repellent lizard-shaped brooch. "The engagement ring is more than enough diamond," I said. "If I wear any other decoration, I'll wear Gram's garnets."

"Garnets! They'll clash with your ring. Why wear garnets when you could have diamonds?"

"There's not a diamond in the collection that would do this dress justice, unless you can lay your hands on some garnet-colored ones."

That got her attention. "No, I can't," she said, gazing hard at me. "Can you?"

"Nope. Even if I could, I wouldn't wear them. I like my garnets. They have sentimental value."

She watched me as if I were some unsavory specimen from a stagnant pond. "Zared will be so disappointed."

Because I didn't want to wear diamonds or because I couldn't deliver up the Soillse Flann set? "Zared will have to get used to my not wanting to wear diamonds, because I don't intend to do it."

Nona left the chair, strode to the window and back. It wasn't exactly a dignified performance, considering she had to dodge the clumps of clutter on the floor. She stopped in front of my chair and stood glaring down at me. "Will Zared also have to get used to your ongoing affair with that Egan man? Egan's a little beneath you, don't you think? A policeman, of all things."

Now we were getting to the real reason for Nona's visit. After hearing Heather's fractured fairy tale on top of last May's spate of gossip, she felt the need to warn me away from anything not in the aristocratic Fraser tradition. Like fraternizing with mere policemen.

"Zared doesn't approve of him in the least," she added.

What kind of a family was this? It wasn't even the idea of an affair that they objected to. It was Danny. "Why should Zared approve of anybody he thought I might be having an affair with?"

"He wouldn't, of course." Diamonds flashed on her hand as she made a little gesture of distaste. "Really, Constancy! Right before the wedding, too."

I was insulted for Danny, as well as for myself, and angry, probably beyond what was reasonable. At least she hadn't mentioned Stuart. A certain amount of relief over that, spiked by suffocating indignation, made me flippant. "Danny's much like my great-grandmother's garnets," I said. "He has exceptional sentimental value."

"I don't see any value in Egan, or in sentiment. You know those garnets of yours are next to worthless."

"I think garnets are much better for people than diamonds. There's a gentle warmth along with the beauty in garnets. I believe those cold, cold diamonds could freeze the soul right out of you after awhile."

She looked at me like she had no earthly idea what I was talking about. (She probably didn't.) Then she sighed dramatically. "I should apologize." She certainly didn't. "I suppose you were frightened, even if the corpse you thought you saw was only a nightmare. It's still annoying. You'd really better try to keep clear of such things when you're a part of our family. You'd better stay away from that common Egan man."

I was beginning to pity any woman who did eventually get Nona as a mother-in-law. Only the comforting knowledge that she wouldn't be mine kept me halfway civil. "When I'm part of your family? Go take another look at the family tree, Nona. I'm already as much a Fraser as Zared is. I'm beginning to think that's nothing to be proud of, and for your information, I don't go looking for bodies. When I do find one, I want Danny. He knows the procedures and he cares about the outcome.

"I can guess what Heather's told you, but if you're interested in the truth, or even if you're not, here it is: My upbringing was old-fashioned. Gram taught me to practice chastity before marriage and faithfulness after. There are still people who choose to live by that teaching, you know. Believe it or not, I'm one of them. Danny's not my lover. I've never had one. The only one I ever intend to have will be my husband first."

Her smug silence only egged me on.

"As for Danny, Danny is the most uncommon man I've ever met. He's my treasured friend. Nothing more, but certainly nothing less. I will not be told whom I may call friend."

"I know he's here."

"If he is, it's because he's concerned about my safety, which is more than I can say for Zared. Zared's too busy with his client from Paris even to talk to me."

"Poor child. If you're frightened to stay alone, why don't you come to Fraser House? You can begin moving into your suite now. You needn't wait until the wedding."

My suite? The quick change of topic made my head spin. So did the topic she switched to.

"It's truly beautiful," she said, "and very well decorated, though I know you'll want a few of your own things brought in."

Emphasis on the word "few", but that hardly registered then. Zared and I, I suddenly realized, had never discussed where we would live. Now that I thought about it, actual discussion hadn't got beyond the wedding at all, on any topic. No doubt about it. I had been stupid.

Nona kept on. "Poor Zared does stay busy. You'll be able to see more of him if you come home with me tonight."

"I'll stay here."

She allowed herself to look a bit crumpled. "Is it because I've insulted your...friend?"

"No."

"Constancy, we are concerned with your safety. It's not safe to stay here with that Egan man."

Why was she so insistent? I couldn't quite believe it was all because of Danny, but I couldn't see any other reason. "I'm perfectly safe with Danny."

"Maybe not as safe as you think. Don't you see? You'll upset Zared again. Don't push him too far, Constancy. Zared can be unpleasant when he's pushed. It's not something you would enjoy being a part of."

What did that mean? I'd never seen Zared angry about anything. *Just how many hours total have you spent with him? You don't know how he reacts to minor irritations, let alone major problems.* Okay, okay. I already admitted I'd been stupid.

"Really, Constancy, we have your best interests at heart."

"I'll stay here," I repeated.

Nona's eyes could flash the same cold fire as her diamonds. "If you change your mind about the jewels or about staying with us, let me know."

"I won't change my mind about either of those things." The only thing I had changed my mind about was marrying her oldest son. Danny was only part of the reason.

"Then be careful, Constancy." She swept out of the house leaving a faint scent of expensive perfume behind. I hated that smell. Heather wore it, too. It made my head ache again.

Why had Nona kept warning me about upsetting Zared. It was almost as if she were afraid of him. Was she? Should I be? If I broke off this engagement as soon as possible, it wouldn't matter. I would be free of both of them, and the twins, and Heather.

I locked the door behind her, fled back to the library and

feverishly began on my self-appointed job. Sort and dust and re-shelve. Don't think beyond the physical work.

Sort and dust, re-shelve. Heavy books on the lower shelves, the matched set of Harvard Classics all together on the second and third shelves by the window.

Sort. Dust. Re-shelve. Slowly, slowly I became more calm. The books that both Gram and I had loved were like old friends. I found a growing peace in touching them, in muttering their beguiling titles aloud like an incantation against evil, and against all the Frasers stood for. Doing the work and restoring the order brought a gradual, soothing comfort, as if I were rebuilding some lost connection between Gram and me.

I worked hard at it for nearly two hours, hands busy, mind blessedly distanced from anything but the job I was doing.

Then I stumbled onto more corpses. Not human ones this time, though the sight slammed into my consciousness with all the same nasty effects.

From the first night I spent in her house, Gram had made a habit of reading aloud to me before bedtime. That reading opened universes I'd never dreamed of. The Hundred-Acre-Wood and Toad Hall. Greek Olympus and the Celts' Tir na n'Og, Middle-earth and Narnia, and, of course, the Bible stories that Gram didn't count as fiction. She loved those best of all, and since she did, I did, too.

I won't pretend that I understood everything she read. Hearing the stories was wonder enough. My mother had never read to me.

It was some of those precious story books, including a Bible, that I found all in a heap behind Gram's favorite rose-colored chair. Their poor backs were bent at impossible angles, their pages maliciously torn and torn again until they resembled fine confetti. Totally, absolutely destroyed. Why these harmless, beautiful books?

I couldn't make myself touch them. I couldn't weep. I couldn't seem to do anything but sit there, trapped in a choking, black cloud of misery.

"Not getting along with the cleaning very fast, are you?"

Danny peered down at me over the chair. There were too many complications in my life and he was chief among them. "Go away. Leave me alone."

"Not likely. Come out from there."

"No. Go away."

He didn't bother to argue. He simply reached over the back of the chair, took a no-nonsense hold on my collar as if I were a naughty child and gently, but firmly, hauled me out. It was move or be strangled. I moved.

"Let go of me. What do you think you're doing?"

He let go. "I know quite well what I'm doing. What are you doing cowering behind a chair like a beaten puppy?"

"I wish you'd stop comparing me to a dog." Another wave of blackness washed over me. "Oh, Danny, look at Gram's books. Destroyed. For no reason. It's so senseless, so horrible. What am I going to do?"

"You're going to fight, Constancy. You'll not give in to the darkness."

He sounded far away, although I could see him well within arm's reach. "What do you know about what I'm feeling?"

"What do you know about what I feel? I watched my father die, did you know that?" His voice was hard, coming closer. "He didn't die quietly in bed like Amanda. I saw a man who was the devil's own intentionally blast a great, bloody hole in my father's chest. Oceans of blood, Constancy, and I with no power at all to save him. Then I watched it happen again in my mother's eyes when she was told, and over and over and over again in nightmares that still sometimes plague me."

I closed my eyes against that shattering picture and Danny

put a cautious hand on my elbow. The mental shock tactic worked as well as a slap across the face.

So that was the horror that haunted him, the reason he was afraid to have a family of his own.

"Your father. I'm sorry."

"A lot of people were, but the sorrow doesn't bring him back, does it? All the tears in the world couldn't wash away the evil that had been done or the grief it caused. So the darkness uses those feelings. Grief. Depression. Hatred. They're sometimes his best weapons."

I shook my head, bewildered. "You're going on about this darkness like it's a person. It's just a feeling. How can I stop what I feel? How did you?"

"Come with me."

"Where?"

"Outside for a moment. There's something you need to see."

I followed him out only because I didn't want to be left alone again. The cold, damp wind came at us in fitful gusts. Neither of us had put on a jacket.

"What's so important out here?" I huddled close beside him, hiding from that uneasy wind.

"Look up."

"At what?"

"At the sky, you young idiot. Look at it. What's the first thing you see?"

"Stars?"

"Exactly. There is a vast, empty darkness surrounding us, but it's the stars we're drawn to. The light that shines in the darkness."

"Danny, what's the point?"

"It works the same way in the spiritual realm, you know. You asked how I stopped the darkness. I stopped the darkness by concentrating on the light. My father was a Christian. My mother still is. She never gave up believing that the Light they both served was stronger than the darkness that murdered him. She intends to see him again after she leaves this earth, and so do I. Light can be obscured by darkness, but it can never be destroyed."

"Do you really believe that?"

"I do."

"The powers of darkness. All that?"

"The powers of darkness. The Father of Lights. I believe in both."

While I'd always gone to church with Gram and embraced the moral and ethical teachings of Christianity. I didn't have much in the way of personal faith in God or Satan. If they existed, they didn't seem to take any great interest in my life.

Now here was Danny, dead serious with belief and more convincing than any sermon I'd ever heard. To him they were absolutely real.

"You should have been a poet," I said. "Or a preacher."

"I have a job. Let's go in. It's freezing out here."

The house felt warm after being outside. "Danny, I didn't mean to sound like I was laughing at what you said. Or at your beliefs."

"I know."

"How old were you when your dad died?"

"Ten, and I'd rather not discuss it any further."

"Okay, but thanks for telling me. Thanks for being here."

"Always pleased to lend a helping hand." He held out his right hand, palm up. "If you need it again, just say."

It was a good hand. Not thin and pale like the Fraser hands, but long-fingered and wide with it. Calloused and brown and scarred. A working hand. I remembered watching his hands the first time I saw him. Strong, sure, healing hands. Hands capable of banishing pain and darkness and despair with the goodness they wielded so skillfully. If I touched one of those hands now, I would never want to let it go again. Not physically. Not emotionally. That wasn't what he was offering.

"I'll remember," I said. I turned my back on him and walked

a few paces away. "You were supposed to be sleeping. Was I making too much noise?"

"You were making no noise at all. That's when I began to worry. It's wisdom born of having three much younger sisters." A brief smile in his voice, he added, "You and Rose are forever worried about my lack of sleep, but I require very little. We need to talk."

Rose again. "What about?" I turned around in time to see his most wicked grin.

"Things of exceptional sentimental value, maybe."

Oh, mercy. He wasn't supposed to have heard that. "You heard Nona?"

"Every word."

"Every word?" I sat down on the couch, frantically trying to remember everything I'd said. "I thought you were asleep."

"Didn't I tell you I'd hear?"

"I'm sorry we woke you. I'm really sorry you heard all that."

"I'm not."

"Danny, she makes me feel so inferior. I don't know what to say when she's talking about the latest fashion and which piece of the diamond collection will be best enhanced by it."

"Is that all she talks about?"

"I haven't been around her much. I've heard her mention the opera and some grand party she'd been to and her hairdresser." I glanced at him. "Tonight it was that snide comment about my choice of friends. That was a new topic."

"You did very well defending your right to friendship. I was honored, and there's no need your blushing."

It wouldn't take much more time to drown completely in those laughing green eyes. I was already in far too deep. I looked away and kept talking about stupid, safe things. "She also simply can't understand why I don't buy all my clothes from her tame designer. His creations are divine. That's Nona's phrase."

"Why don't you, if it would aid the cause of peace?"

"It wouldn't aid anything except Hugo's bank account. I happen to know his so-called creations run to at least four digits on the wrong side of the decimal point. I'd feel worse paying that much for any dress."

Danny grinned. "You're sounding like Rose again."

He was determined to insert this Rose into the conversation. Fine. If he wanted to talk about his latest love, why not? Whoever she was, talking about her couldn't be as bad as talking about Nona. "Okay. You keep bringing her up. You obviously want me to ask. Who on earth is Rose?"

Chapter 11

His face lit up with the smile. "My Mum. What were you thinking?"

Ridiculous that I should feel so relieved. "If she's your mother, why do you call her by her first name?"

I got into the habit of it because Cameron does. You've met Cam, I hear, but I'm sure you don't want to know all my family history."

"I did meet Cam. Cam was very kind, and I'd love to hear every word of your family history. It seems only fair. You know most of mine by now."

"Then another day I'll tell it to you, or better yet introduce you to all the rest of them."

"Including your sisters?

"Including the three weird sisters."

"Promise?"

"I do. After this is over and if you still want it then, I'll take you out to the farm."

"I'll hold you to that."

"Look, Constancy, there are less pleasant things we're needing to discuss just now."

"I'm cold. Do you mind if we have a fire?"

"Not at all. I'll even start it for you. Where's the wood?"

"Out behind the workshop. I'll help you bring in wood, but you can light it. I always get more smoke coming into the room than going up the chimney."

Between us, we carried enough wood to the back porch to last through a blizzard. Danny brought a few logs and some kindling into the house and I sat and watched as he took great care positioning them in the fireplace.

"Where is this farm you mentioned?"

"It's up in Morris county. Gavin and Rose make a fair living at the work, but even if they didn't, it's where they most want to be. They make it a grand refuge when life turns sour for any of us." He lit a match and stuck it into the dry shavings. The flame caught eagerly. All the smoke went up the chimney. "A few days cutting hay or planting corn soon puts everything in perspective," he said. "It's a good life. They're lovely people, if I do say it. I think you'd like them."

"If the rest of them are like Cameron and you, I'm sure I would."

The fire began to crackle with light and warmth, like his description of that farm. Just talking about it erased some of the weariness from his face. "Your farm sounds like heaven, Danny."

"It's not." I loved the childlike hint of mischief that could come so quickly to his eyes. "You realize that instantly when a cow steps on your foot, or more slowly when you come in hot, dirty and dead tired from a dawn-to-dusk day in the fields. No. It's not heaven, but it's maybe the closest thing we'll ever get on this earth. I wish I could show you the new-born piglets and the field of daisies in the spring." The words ground to a halt and the glow died out of his eyes. He turned back to put one more log on the fire.

"That's why you liked Gram's planter."

"The pig. Yes. I know a sow who puts that exact silly

expression on her face when she's up to something, which is most of the time. Those young, idiot sisters of mine made a pet of her when she was the runt of the litter. She was cute at that stage. Now she's 400 pounds of arrogance and believes she rules the whole farm, humans included. Pest though she is, Gavin can't bear to part with her because his daughters still think she's marvelous. Of course that's one point on which the sow and the humans agree."

I was already laughing at Danny's tale when I had a sudden, ridiculous vision of Mrs. Nona Fraser feeding a whole line of silly-looking pigs, a bucket of swill clutched in her diamond-clad hands. The thing was so vivid I nearly choked over it.

"Darlin', what on earth is so funny?"

"I was imagining Nona feeding pigs and all of them looking at her like that." Danny's expression set me off again.

He was across the space between us in an instant. "Stop that." He grabbed my shoulders and gave me a little shake. "Stop it. You're hysterical."

Was I? The noise I was making wasn't exactly laughter anymore. Well, if I was crying, so what? I deserved to have a good cry over this whole situation. Danny didn't have to listen. He wasn't tied down. He could leave any time he liked.

But he wasn't leaving. He had gathered me close and seemed prepared to let the tears flow for as long as it took. He was crooning soft, healing words that I wished I could go on hearing forever.

Sadly, they probably wouldn't stay soft and healing. In no time at all, I had learned, they could begin to stab and tear and create deep, deadly wounds. No. I couldn't risk that again. I wouldn't. I sniffed and pulled away, though he seemed reluctant to let me. "You're right," I said. "I am hysterical. Sorry about your shirt."

"I'm considerably more concerned about you than about my shirt, darlin'. You're still in deep grief. Why shouldn't you cry?" He fetched a box of tissues and waited patiently while I mopped at my eyes and blew my nose.

Oh, Danny, stop being so sweet. "You'd better forget talking to me tonight and let me go upstairs before I drown you."

"Not yet," he said. "We have to talk this out."

"What won't wait until you've had a good night's sleep?"

"Zared Fraser, for one thing. Stuart, for another. Stuart and his missing father. You're still shivering. Wrap up in that blanket. I'll make us a hot drink if you'll tell me where to find what I need."

"Is that your prescription for everything?"

"Not quite everything, but I find it soothing and I'm rather in need of soothing, myself, just now."

"You?"

"It happens."

"There are tea bags and coffee and hot chocolate mix in the pantry. The kettle's on the burner and the mugs are in the wall cabinet to the left of the sink."

"Got it." He filled the kettle and set it on the burner. "What will you have?"

"It's your party," I said. "Just don't give me anything super strong this time."

"I won't."

I burrowed into the end of the couch, cocooning myself in one of Danny's blankets. "You may as well start talking now," I said. "We'll get it over that much sooner."

"Sorry. I need to watch your face while we talk. I'm going to play policeman and ask you any number of questions that will undoubtedly make you loathe me as much as you do Tirso."

"You'd enjoy that, wouldn't you? If I hated you, you wouldn't have to worry about any misplaced gratitude."

He didn't answer until he had poured the boiling water. "It

might make life easier in the long run," he said finally, "but no, I wouldn't enjoy it at all. I'm only surprised you don't already hate me. Is there milk?"

"In the fridge. I tried to hate you, Danny, I really did. I wanted to. I thought you deserved to be hated, but I just couldn't do it."

Danny laughed, but he was avoiding my eyes. "I did ask for it. I asked for it specifically. I'm glad you found it impossible. The friendship's maybe not such a bad thing for either of us."

Not so long ago, he had thought the idea of friendship with me a major disaster. Or he'd acted as if he did. It might yet be a disaster for my peace of mind. Danny, in this mood, was a little too far beyond being irresistible. Probably it would be easy enough to provoke him back into his irritating, sarcastic self. That side of him would be much safer for me to deal with. Only I couldn't bring myself to do it.

He turned out the kitchen lights, leaving the fire as our only illumination. Then he brought the two mugs and sat down beside me. Not close, but not far enough away.

Had I claimed I would be safe with Danny? This was not safe. "No," I said.

"It's only one tea bag."

"I didn't mean that." I threw off the blanket, carried my cup to the kitchen table and turned the lights back on. "If you're going to ask policeman questions, let's pretend this is that claustrophobic little interrogation room in the police station. You can see my face better in bright light with the table between us."

"We'll do it that way, if you like." He said it so gently that it made me want to cry again. I took a quick swallow of the hot tea instead as he moved into position across from me. "Better now?" he asked.

"Do we have to do this at all tonight?"

"We do. The time element worries me, all of it coming so soon after Amanda's death and George's heart attack. Why now?"

"He's old. So was Gram. She lived considerably longer than

the doctors said she would." It took a moment for what he was saying to sink in. "Do you think there's something suspicious about George's heart attack and Gram's death?"

"There's certainly no proof at this point, but it's possible. Surely there's more at stake than one set of diamonds. Must be. There was something Stuart said. Ah, I wish I could just send you off to Rose and do it all myself."

"I'm sure your mother would love having a strange girl dumped in her lap."

"You wouldn't be the first. She has quite a soft spot in her heart for strange girls."

I didn't want to hear about his girls.

"Of course, they were all Cam's girls," he said, as if he were reading my mind.

"Ask your questions, Officer."

A quick grin, then he sobered. "Right. If we can establish when it was you began feeling ill, we might have a better idea of when you got the drug and how. Tell me everything you did yesterday. That'll be a start."

"Everything I did. Was it only yesterday?"

"So you said. Give me people, places, conversations. What you ate and when. All that sort of thing."

I pushed aside my half-empty cup. "I've told you I don't remember much."

"I'm asking you to try again. There are pieces missing. Discrepancies, things that don't add up. Tell me everything you think of, even if it doesn't seem important. At this point any of it could be."

"I'll try." I told him about Zared's invitation to breakfast at Fraser House, about the fancy food, about Zared's proposal which had sounded more like he was suggesting a business merger than a matrimonial one.

"Not a very romantic thing, was it?" Danny said.

"How would you do it?"

He glared at me. "I'm asking the questions. He wanted you to marry him. You said yes. Why?"

Because I couldn't have you. The truth shot into my head before I could stop it. For half a second I was afraid I'd blurted the words right out of my mouth, but since Danny wasn't headed for the nearest exit at a dead run, obviously I hadn't. I took a long swallow of my tea and thought furiously.

"Constancy, you'll need to come up for air sooner or later. Is that such a difficult question?"

I shrugged. "Why does anybody say yes to a marriage proposal?"

"There's love in all its various definitions. Then there's greed, escape, fear, revenge. That's a start. I don't doubt there are plenty others."

"Choose whichever one strikes your fancy, then."

"I'm not wanting to guess. I want to hear from your own mouth why you agreed to it. Let me put it another way. I asked this once before, then wouldn't let you answer. Now I think I need to know. Are you in love with Zared Fraser?"

"You didn't ask me that. You asked me if I was happy."

"Well, I can see for myself that you're not, but there might be other reasons for that than your relationship with Fraser. So I'm asking you again. "Are you in love with the man?"

What could I say? I couldn't tell Danny the truth, but I couldn't lie about it, either. "Why do you need to know? What does it have to do with all this?"

"Constancy, if this investigation finishes the way I fear it will, I want to know how badly you'll be hurt."

If I answered his horrible question, I could be hurt much worse. "Danny, what I feel doesn't matter right now. You have to dig out the truth. If Zared or any of the rest of the Fraser family is involved in this, it needs to be exposed. Any person who would hire a gunman to murder somebody has to be stopped. Any person."

"You mean that?"

"I mean it with all my heart. Wrong is wrong, no matter who does it."

"Bless you, love. That seems to be a rare attitude these days. Constancy, I will be fair."

"I never doubted that."

He stared at me a moment, then gave himself an almost visible mental shake and went back to being an efficient policeman. "Thank you. Now, where were we? Right. The proposal at breakfast. What happened next?"

"After breakfast, Zared took me to his lawyer to do some legal stuff."

"Legal stuff. Elaborate."

"I already told you about the papers for the engagement ring. I made a will, too."

Danny's face darkened. "So am I to assume you made Fraser your beneficiary?"

"Why not? He's worth millions and all I have is what Gram left me."

"Exactly my point, darlin'. You inherit Amanda's estate and suddenly..."

I had got over being tickled by the idea. "Suddenly Zared takes great interest in poor cousin Constancy." I looked away from that intense gaze. "I'd like to think the attraction wasn't completely mercenary, but I don't know now."

Danny was silent until I looked at him again. I saw a kind of wary respect in his expression as he asked his next question. "Just what did Irma tell you?"

"I told you she said the jewels in the portrait are diamonds." He nodded. "What else?"

I reported the rest of Irma's information about the Soillse Flann diamonds.

"So that could have been at least part of Zared's motivation."

"Probably it was his whole motivation."

Danny reached over and ruffled my hair. "If it was, then at best the man's altogether blind."

"You don't need to console me. I didn't mean to sound sorry for myself."

"It wasn't meant to console you. I was merely stating a fact. Tell me more about this last will and testament you made. Was it Fraser's idea?"

"He said everybody should have a will."

"True enough, but whose idea was it to name him your sole beneficiary?"

"I don't know. He just suggested it would be easiest that way. He didn't make me do it. He didn't insist on it. Besides, who else did I have to leave it to?"

"You'd maybe better find somebody. Get on with your story."

"That seemed to take hours. Afterward, we went to lunch."

"Fraser House again?"

"No. The restaurant on the top floor of the office building. Zared has permanent access to one of their private rooms for all his business luncheons."

"Business luncheons. The man's obsessed by business. Was it just you and Fraser?"

"Nona and the twins met us there. Zared wanted to announce our engagement to them and make it official."

"Funny place to do that, wasn't it? I'd have pictured a quiet, cozy moment at home before a roaring fire."

I shivered, remembering how cold and sick I had felt. "A fire would have been a nice touch," I said. "The lunch did have something of the atmosphere of a board meeting, I must admit."

"What did they do? Vote on the merger?"

"Not quite, although there was considerable discussion. Romney thinks I'm not a suitable addition to that branch of the house of Fraser."

"Not suitable."

"He had his reasons all prepared. Typed out. In a folder."

"You heard his presentation?"

"Oh, yes."

"What were his reasons?"

"Mostly things I couldn't deny. I'm a social dunce. I've been in trouble with the law."

Danny snorted.

"I'm plain and clumsy. I may be mentally unstable. There were a few more. He almost convinced me."

"I wish he had," Danny muttered.

"What?"

"You're not mentally unstable, Constancy, unless your sitting there quietly and letting him say such things is proof of it. The very hearing of it sickens me. They were treating you like a property. Can you really love a man who would put you through such a thing? You must or you'd have thrown his fancy ring back in his face that very instant. Unless you're as mercenary as he is."

"I didn't have his ring at that very instant and that, Danny Egan, was a rotten thing to say."

He rubbed a hand across his reddened eyes and his shoulders slumped. "It was. Constancy, I'm sorry. I truly am. It was entirely out of line."

"Apology accepted."

He gave me a half smile.

"It was sickening," I conceded. "I went to the ladies' room and threw up, in fact. When I got back, Zared put this ring on my finger."

"You didn't choose the ring?"

"No. I did not choose this ring. It nearly blinded me when he brought it out. It actually hurt my eyes."

"Then I stand by my first impression of it. Tell me about the food at lunch. Although if you were throwing up before the lunch, and the brightness of the ring hurt you that much, you'd probably had the drug earlier."

"I don't remember tasting anything strange. I couldn't tell you how any of it tasted, really. I'm not sure it did. I didn't eat more than a bite or two. The awful thing was that the food was just so arranged. Everything was perfectly placed, like a photography session for a gourmet magazine. The servings were very posh, very small, very individual, and very, very weird. Unrecognizable shapes. Impossible, jarring colors."

He nodded. "Noisy colors. Like Stuart's car."

"Exactly."

"By that time you must have been well into your trip."

"Well, I hope I never see anything like it again. That pizza tonight was beautiful by comparison. All jumbled together like it ought to be, with the colors behaving themselves."

Danny gurgled into the remains of his tea, inhaled at the wrong time and came up fighting for air.

"I wasn't trying to be funny," I said.

"It was you complaining about greasy pizza a while ago."

"Maybe so, but at least it's good, honest grease. It's not putting on airs like Fraser food."

"Long life to the plain and homely pizza eaten pure dead sober," he said solemnly, with cup upraised. "Did you eat anything at all between the breakfast and the lunch?"

"There were drinks while Romney was having his say. I asked for something non-alcoholic. They brought me tomato juice. At least that's what I thought it was. It tasted like liquid salad, but I didn't think it was worth complaining about."

"It had a bit of hashish all blended in, maybe. That'd be one way to do it, if that's what they gave you. Any of them could have set it up, and made sure you were served more at lunch. What happened when you finished?"

"I went home."

"On the way you wandered out into the street and were nearly run down. Did you leave the restaurant alone?"

"I think so."

Danny got up to put more wood on the fire. "Think hard, Constancy. Did you step out in front of the car on your own or could you have been pushed?"

"I remember thinking I had plenty of time to get across."

"Odd that it should have been Stuart's car. I don't see how they managed that at all. If he had hit you, they could have got him more or less out of the way without the gunman. There's another thing. How long did this lunch last?"

"With all of the discussion and me taking time outs to go be sick, a couple of hours, I suppose."

"Unfeeling bunch. If you were that obviously ill and they weren't aware you were drugged, they should have taken you home right off. Or to a doctor. All right, when did lunch start?"

"That I do know. One hour past high noon. I thought it should have been straight up twelve. Show-down time."

"Going western in honor of Cousin Stuart now, are we?"

"I didn't know about Stuart then. It was a show-down. With Romney."

"Fine. Three o'clock when you left the restaurant. That can maybe be checked. If you did leave then."

"What are you talking about?"

"This is one of those discrepancies. You realize you told me it was almost dark when Stuart nearly hit you?"

"It was almost dark. I don't remember much, but I do remember that."

The new logs were burning to his satisfaction and he returned to the table. "Stuart confirms it."

"What's the problem, then?"

"You finished lunch about three. You stepped into Stuart's path just outside the restaurant. The sun sets early this time of year, but not that early. Some drugs can cause time distortion. Did your lunch last much longer than the two hours? Or did you leave the restaurant and come back later? If that's the way of it, where were you between the end of your lunch and the incident with Stuart?"

I shivered. "Is that why they call it a trip? 'My, how time flies when you're having fun'. Only I don't know if I was or not, do I? Danny, I am so scared."

Chapter 12

"We'll get it worked out eventually. I know this is difficult, darlin', frightening. That's why we're going over it. Patient persistence is the better part of detective work. Can you stand it a wee while longer?"

"For as long as it takes, I guess."

"Good lass. Now. Do you remember finishing lunch?"

"Yes. I was still feeling funny. Nauseated, but sort of floaty and vacant, too."

"Besides your being sick to your stomach, surely it was obvious you weren't your normal self otherwise."

"Must have been. Romney congratulated me on taking his advice about the tranquilizers."

"But you hadn't."

"Not to my knowledge."

"They let you walk out by yourself?"

"I seem to remember somebody, I don't know who, offering to take me home, but I don't think anybody did. The next thing I remember after that is stepping out to cross the street. Then there was the car's squealing brakes and Stuart trembling."

"After that?"

"Nothing. Stuart's face is the last thing I remember before waking up with an awful headache and a corpse in my kitchen." I shoved my chair away from the table and moved to the fireplace, feeling cold to the depths of my bones. "Danny, why don't I remember?"

"One of the attractions of drug use is its ability to make the user forget, even if it's only short-term. I can fill in a bit more. Stuart said you wouldn't let him help you. He turned his head to answer somebody's question. When he looked back, you were gone. He thinks you were alone. Nobody was openly claiming you, though there were plenty people on the sidewalk."

"It's all a blur or a blank. Do people really take that stuff on purpose?"

"I've seen days that blurring or blotting out might have helped. I didn't take that path and I'd surely not recommend it to anybody, but I can sympathize a bit with the temptation to do it." He turned the lights out again and peered through a crack in the kitchen blinds.

"Maybe the drug made me hallucinate," I said. "Maybe there really wasn't a body, after all."

"Sorry. I've never known hallucinations to clean up after themselves, nor corpses. No, my love, the body was very real. We've established that. Remember Stuart had a close encounter with your visitor, too."

As I stood staring into the hot, dancing flames, another thought struck me, a thought so frightening that I wouldn't have said it to anybody else in the world. "Danny, while I was still drugged, could I have killed him myself?"

"No."

Bless him. He didn't hesitate even a fraction of a second.

"Don't be worrying over that. It's just not possible."

"Why not?"

"You're not a murderer."

"Even drugged out of my mind? Maybe I got paranoid."

"You didn't. There's no evidence the murder was done in your apartment. If the man was even average size and weight, you'd not be physically capable of murdering him elsewhere, then getting him up the stairs, let alone down again, and away. Why would you? For that matter, if you had killed him in the apartment or elsewhere why would you have phoned me at all? You wouldn't have. You know I'm good at my job. You'd not have made up a thing like that merely to—"

He bit off the end of the sentence, but I knew what he had almost said.

"That's what you thought at first, wasn't it? That I'd made him up just so I would have an excuse to try and see you again? Was it ego or wishful thinking?"

He smiled. "That's what I thought at first, but I was wrong. There was no ego involved in it. It never would have occurred to me if I'd not been so tired when the phone rang."

"Danny, you've only got my word for it that he was ever there."

"Your word, which I would trust against all odds when I'm in my right mind, and a few other things. Tell me, darlin', would you have thought to clean the chair, table and floor if you'd invented him?"

"Not in a million years."

"Of course you wouldn't. Besides all that, my experience as a cop tells me your horror and disorientation weren't faked."

I was almost reassured.

Danny settled onto the couch again. "Cheer up. We're almost finished with the inquisition."

"Almost?"

"Sit down here, please, and roll up your sleeves."

"Why?"

"Whatever you had at lunch or just before shouldn't have knocked you out until morning. Especially if you were walking about at dusk. You had to have something else as well. The question is how and when and who gave it to you?"

"Why? Again."

"And why again. No recent needle marks. At least not on your arms."

"That's the only place you're going to inspect," I snapped, "and the old ones are from giving blood."

He smiled. "They probably fed you more tomato juice, possibly with a few more additives."

"Do you and Stuart really think Zared is behind all this?"

That time he did hesitate. "Constancy, do you believe absolutely that Zared Fraser could never be involved in criminal activity? Do you know him that well or love him that much?"

Looking into Danny's earnest face, I couldn't answer him. I didn't know Zared, or his family, well enough. Nona hadn't helped with her not-so-veiled innuendos. "How do we know that about anybody?"

"I know it about you."

It wasn't an idle claim. He'd backed those words with actions in plenty.

"Thank you, Danny."

"You may not be thanking me by the time I finish this thought. I was going to say that one doesn't reach such heights as the Frasers have reached by being either sentimental or squeamish. I'm not accusing," he added quickly. "I'm merely stating the facts as we have them now. Caleb Fraser came here. Caleb was to have met with Zared. Caleb vanished. The airport was his last known location, Fraser House his last known destination, and he was not sounding at all himself when last they heard from him. Stuart came looking for Caleb. Stuart had a near-fatal brush with a blessedly inept assassin who finished up dead in your kitchen, and you too stoned to know how. Never forget you're another link with the Frasers."

"Why don't you just get a search warrant and go looking?"

"If Caleb is alive and being held on Fraser property, even an application for a warrant could be dangerous for him. We don't know who's involved. As Stuart guessed, neither law enforcement nor the judiciary in this town is immune to corruption."

"I can't believe Meg Ferguson is corrupt. Or that she would let such things go on under her watch."

"I didn't say they all were. They're not. Not by any stretch of the imagination. But there is something that's not quite right going on somewhere in the system here. We've not found the source yet. Meg, by the way, is on extended leave." He smiled. "Maternity leave. She and Rob are expecting twins.

"So, if we go looking for Caleb, it'll have to be undercover."

"How will you do that?"

"I did say 'we'. You could get in. Nona's asked you to stay."

The shiver hit me again. "If there's any other way, I don't want to go stay there. I don't even want to go in there for a short visit. I don't much like Nona."

"I don't much blame you." He lifted my face with a warm finger under my chin. "Constancy, we'll look for alternatives, believe me. I don't want you in there, but if it comes to that, and there's no other way, will you go?"

"I'll go."

"I was sure you would. Just remember you won't be alone."

I had never felt so alone in my life. "Anything else?"

He yawned and stretched. "Not tonight, darlin'. You could do with some rest."

"So could you. I'll sleep upstairs in my old room. You can have Gram's bed if you get tired of the couch. There are already clean sheets on it, I think. I'll check before I go up."

But I didn't move. I could feel the darkness waiting for me up there and I was afraid.

"What's bothering you, love?"

"Nothing. Everything. The dark at the top of the stairs."

"I wish I could make it easier."

"You have. I never said thanks for not holding grudges."

"You've more of a right to a grudge than I have. Thanks, yourself." He slid his arm around me and squeezed, a quick, friendly hug. "Stay here a bit longer, if you like. I did offer protective custody." He still had his arm around me and he didn't seem to be in any hurry to move it.

It was more than I could resist, that offer of momentary shelter. I relaxed against him, taking comfort from his nearness and wishing I dared rest my head on his shoulder. I told myself it must be only for a moment. Then I would go up even if I didn't want to. Especially if I didn't want to. For my own peace, I didn't dare read more into Danny's friendship than what he was offering. If only I were sure what that was. One minute more and I would go.

Danny's head drooped against mine and his breath came warm and evenly, sending a gentle little breeze across my face. He'd gone to sleep again. If I moved now, I would wake him. He needed every bit of sleep he could get, whether he admitted it or not.

And that, a Heather-like voice in my head informed me, was as good a rationalization as any for staying with him just a little longer.

A log settled in the fire with a crack and a hiss. Flame flared, then burned lower. My own eyes began to close.

"Constancy?" Danny's whisper was soft, urgent.

Such a beautiful dream.

"Constancy!"

Not a dream! My eyes snapped open. The fire was dark and dead. How long did it take a fire to die? I sat up abruptly. "Danny, I'm sorry."

"Hush!" His hand shot over my mouth and he pulled me back

against him so that his lips were brushing my ear. "Don't apologize," he whispered. "I enjoyed sleeping with you. I wouldn't wake you now, but— Hold still! That was maybe less than tactful, but I need you awake. We have company. Listen."

I heard it instantly. Footsteps. Whoever was out there moved slowly across the back porch, paused at each window.

"He's been going round the house checking all the windows," Danny said. "Sooner or later, I expect he'll be making his way inside. As innocent as our wee nap was, I didn't think you'd want him finding us asleep in each other's arms. Or asleep at all, for that matter. Okay now?"

I nodded and took a deep, painful breath. "Is it somebody looking for Stuart?"

"We'll assume it is."

The footsteps were moving on toward the front.

"What are we going to do?"

"You'll go upstairs. I'll be waiting."

The sharp knock on the front door startled us both. "Constancy Stafford? Police. I need to talk to you."

"Danny, that's Lon Tirso."

"I thought it might be." He sounded almost pleased.

"Now what?"

"Open the door for the nice policeman and listen to whatever he has to say."

"He may be a policeman, but he's never been nice a minute of his life. What if he wants in?"

"He will, on some pretext or other. If he begins to make noises about searching the house, ask to see a warrant. He won't have one. We'll go from there."

"I'm scared."

He grinned. "Any lass who can face down Nona Fraser should have no trouble with Tirso." He gave me a thumbs-up gesture and slipped into the unlit library.

I unlocked the front door and opened it a crack. I also kept one foot firmly behind it. "What do you want, Lon?"

"Are you going to let me in?"

"No."

He shrugged. "You're paying the gas bill. Somebody reported a prowler in the neighborhood. Have you seen anybody around who shouldn't be?"

"Not unless I get to count a guy in uniform who's been creeping around outside my house messing with the windows. I hope you haven't been doing that at every house. One of my neighbors is a very nervous lady who keeps a loaded shotgun handy. Could be hazardous to your health. But maybe it's just me you're harassing. Again."

"You haven't got any smarter since the last time, have you?"

"Is that all you have to say about your alleged prowler?"

"He may be wounded and he's probably dangerous."

"Who reported him? Who wounded him?"

"Anonymous tip." Lon leaned his weight against the door. "I'd better look around inside for you."

"You're welcome to. If you can show me a search warrant."

He backed off a little. "Who said anything about a search? I thought you might want to be sure the prowler's not hiding in your house."

"I'm already sure. Even if I weren't, I'd rather take my chances with him than with you."

He grinned. "Same old Constancy. Standing in my way and obstructing justice."

"If you represented justice, I wouldn't be obstructive."

"Well, since you won't cooperate and let me in to do it myself, you'll have to deliver a little message for me." Lon was fond of ordering people to deliver messages for him.

"I don't do deliveries. Besides, I told you the prowler wasn't hiding here."

"You'll deliver this one. It's not for the prowler. It's for that boyfriend of yours. Tell him I'm watching him."

"Zared Fraser? You've got the wrong address."

"Oh, I'm not talking about Fraser and you know it. I'm talking about the guy who's probably in your bed right now. Everybody, including Fraser, knows all about you and Egan."

If I ever could be provoked to serious violence, it would be Lon Tirso who triggered it.

"Mr. Pure-and-righteous Danny Egan," he said, gloatingly. "It's easy to slip up when you play the kind of game he's playing. It's just a matter of time before I get him. I'll be back."

I took great care not to slam the door.

Chapter 13

"Good work," Danny said, easing past me to lock the dead bolt he had installed. "Constancy, you're trembling."

I was trembling so hard that I didn't dare move away from the wall. "Could you h-hear him?"

"I could."

"The game you're playing? What did he mean? "

"Who knows? The man sees evil in everything but his own actions."

"He was threatening you. What can he do? What are you doing that he can even say that?"

"Nothing." Danny looked too innocent for that to be true.

"Danny, I don't want him hurting you."

He shrugged. "Being intimidating is what Lon Tirso does best, remember? Don't be worrying about me. Come on, now. It's time you got some sleep."

"Sleep! How can I sleep?"

Danny took my hand and led me to the foot of the stairs. "Tirso knows I'm here. He'll not be back tonight. But if he should make that mistake, I'll have a message to deliver to him. Personally and with great emphasis."

"It's not just Lon. It's everything. Nona and Heather and all those lies about me, about us. All the gossip that's been going on since May. The whole town's buzzing with it. You heard what Lon said. Oh, never mind. You can't help it anymore than I can. I'm sorry I brought it up." I turned my back on him and started up the stairs.

"Shall I marry you and redeem our good names?"

Running smack into a brick wall couldn't have stopped me more jarringly. But I didn't look back. I didn't dare. "Don't! Don't laugh at me, Danny. Please."

He clattered up the stairs behind me, grasped my arm and turned me to face him. "Look at me, Constancy. I haven't the faintest idea what I am doing, but I do know I'm not laughing. Do I look as if I am?"

The green eyes were like burning points of fire in his haggard face. "No. No, you aren't laughing."

He dropped onto the step and rested his head on his arms so that I couldn't see his expression at all.

"Danny, if you're not making fun of me, what did you mean by that? Why did you even say it?"

"I don't know. Heaven help me, I don't know what I mean anymore. I only know what I want this very minute. I know it's taking me all my strength of will just now not to ask you to let me make those lies they're telling truth."

"Danny!"

He lifted a fierce, bewildered face. "You're no child, Constancy. Don't stand there gaping at me all wide-eyed and shocked as if you never imagined such a thing. I thought you wanted me to admit I'm in love with you."

"Is that what you're doing?"

"I've no answer for that, either. Do you not understand? I've never before in my life been in this place. I don't know what I should be doing or saying. I don't know myself anymore."

"Danny, I am shocked. Why shouldn't I be? You kept telling me your job was the most important thing in your life. You kept warning me off. You were horrible when I tried to tell you how I felt."

A bitter smile. "The bit about wanting never to see you again? I was, God forgive me, lying to both of us when I said that. Do you think I'm not human?"

He'd spent considerable effort convincing me he wasn't. "Sometimes I don't have a clue what you are. Every time I think I've got you figured out, you throw something different at me. All I know for sure is that you're the most impossible man in the world. I have no idea how I could ever have thought you were loveable."

"Nor do I. You're right. I am impossible. I am altogether the most impossible man on the face of this earth. Ironic, isn't it, that I see it all too late?"

"Miss Irma said you were afraid of me." I sat down a couple of steps above him. "I wouldn't believe it, except the first time you kissed me I saw fear in your eyes. Terror, almost. I couldn't imagine why it was there."

"I was afraid of you then. I'm afraid of you still. I've never been as frightened of anything as I am of you. I was so sure about my life, about what I was meant to do with it. Falling in love was never part of the plan. Nor marriage. I had work to do which needed all my concentration and energy. I didn't expect you, Constancy Grace. You shattered my well-scripted, self-righteous world. You made me want everything I had renounced. For my own sanity, I had to convince you, and myself, that there was nothing between us."

"But you came when I needed you."

"How could I have stayed away knowing you might be in trouble again? It never works, lying to one's self. I'm sorry,

Constancy. I'm so desperately sorry." He caught my hand and held it to his hot face, but he wouldn't look at me. "I hurt you last summer. I did it intentionally, hoping to get you out of my life once and for all. It wasn't right and it's not something I was ever proud of, but I'll tell you straight out that I had no idea of the enormity of what I'd done to both of us. Not until you tucked the blankets round me and kissed me good night earlier this evening as if I were the dearest thing in all the world to you."

"I thought you were asleep."

"That made it worse, don't you see. I couldn't think why you were doing it. I didn't understand how you could do it at all after the way I'd treated you. Then you were taking refuge in my arms, trusting me to keep the darkness away, trusting me not to hurt you again. I knew then that you'd meant absolutely what you said in May. That I had been dead wrong about everything. That I haven't the moral strength to run from you anymore. Or from what I feel. I don't even want to try.

"That's the irony of it. I've discovered I need you as much as I need my music, and air to breathe, and the earth beneath my feet." His cold fingers touched the diamond, shied away. He dropped my hand.

"But I'm wearing Zared's ring, and you still haven't reconciled yourself to breaking that vow you made when you decided to fight the darkness with a badge."

"How did you know about that?"

"It doesn't matter. Danny, you'll have to wage your personal battle on your own, but whatever you decide, you should know that the ring's on my finger only because I haven't seen Zared to give it back to him. I'm likely to lose it if I take it off before then. I couldn't afford that. For what it's worth, that's something I decided before this conversation. It's something I think I would have decided even if all this mess about Gram's diamonds hadn't happened and I hadn't had to phone you. I wanted to believe you were out of my life, too. And I did, until I saw you again. You weren't the only one lying to yourself."

"Then you're not in love with Zared Fraser."

"I never was, but I couldn't tell you that when you asked. I couldn't have taken another verbal bashing just then."

"Whatever happens, I'll never again do that to you. Ah, Constancy, I wish I could say—"

"Danny, you're exhausted. Don't say anything now that you'll be sorry for tomorrow."

He grinned a little. "I already have, but I"ll add this: What you told Nona goes for me as well. It'll be marriage or nothing. However strong the temptation, I will never ask you to go against your principles."

"If you ever do, the answer will be a definite, non-negotiable no."

I half expected him to be perversely offended. Instead, he looked pleased, and much less frightened.

I got up off the step, wondering if somewhere Gram was smiling at this conversation. She had Danny pegged very early. An old fashioned boy, she said. One who would keep things in their proper place.

"It wouldn't be easy denying you anything else you truly wanted, Brendan Conor Aengus Egan. Let that be a warning to mind your tongue."

His response was something between a chuckle and a yawn. "What a comfort and a blessing you are, darlin'. Where did you fetch up the names?"

"Somebody mentioned them. Never mind who or where or why. I like your names. All of them together. Good night, Danny."

"Constancy, don't let the Frasers make you feel inferior. You aren't. Forget Nona's designer fashions and Hugo and the diamonds. You've no need of them. You are, as my solemn Scots step-dad would say, 'a right stunner' in antique garnet silk."

"Thanks." I felt suddenly old and tired. Was Gram smiling? After a good night's rest, when Danny wasn't so exhausted and vulnerable, he would no doubt regret his confession and conclude that he could get along fine without me in his life. As an exercise in self defense, I should keep my emotional distance until he fought his battle and made his decisions. I should, but it was already far, far too late.

"Still worried about meeting the darkness up there?"

"Among other things."

He retrieved a small book from his back pocket and held it out to me. "Here, take this. It can be a great help."

The book was a Bible. I clutched it tightly, like the sword and shield it was meant to be. "Miss Irma calls you Brendan."

Danny smiled a little wistfully. "Ah. Those names. All heroes of Irish history or myth. Brendan was said to be a saint; Conor, a prince; Aengus, a warrior. In more recent time, they were my father's names. He was all three, and a hero entirely on his own. I'd better stick with plain Danny."

"Not necessarily. What is it they say—*Like father, like son?* I think your mother named you perfectly. Every one of those names seems to fit you."

Chapter 14

"Wake up, Sleeping Beauty."

Something cold and wet dripped onto the bridge of my nose. The kiss of a Prince Charming, it wasn't.

I squinted into the sad face of a wet, bedraggled chrysanthemum. Beyond it, Danny looked almost as bad, his nose red, his eyes watery. Another droplet from the flower hit the corner of my mouth. "You're drowning me." I pulled my quilt over my head, still half asleep. "What are you doing in here, anyway?"

"I knocked. You didn't answer. Besides, they say the morning dew's just the thing for a perfect complexion." His voice, raspy with congestion, sounded awful.

"Who says? My complexion's fine and that's not morning dew. For one thing, it can't possibly be morning yet, and I heard thunder. It's rain, probably acid rain. Take that thing away and don't wake me up until it really is morning."

"Constancy, come out of there. We have barriers enough to overcome as it is. An intelligible conversation's next to impossible with you submerged in the bedding." He barely got the words out before a gigantic sneeze shook him.

"Bless you." I cautiously pulled the quilt down to my nose. "Will you please put that drippy flower somewhere else?"

Danny carried the poor flower to the bathroom and left it. "The flower's by way of being a peace offering," he said. "It was the best I could do on short notice."

"Why a peace offering?"

"I wanted to be sure you had no hard feelings about last night."

"Why should I?"

A faint, sad smile. Nobody could do gloom and despair like the Irish.

"Is another unnecessary apology the only reason you're waking me at the crack of dawn?"

"There is no dawn. It's pouring cold, wretched rain and the only crack you're likely to hear is more thunder."

He sounded so theatrically dismal it was almost all I could do not to laugh. "Danny, I'm tired. Go away and let me sleep longer."

"Sorry, no. I've brought you a cup of tea."

"You and your hot drinks. What time is it?"

"Ten forty-five. Listen, Constancy. I woke you because Stuart needs to see a doctor. He's having some chest pain. I doubt it's his heart. It could be only the bruise from the bullet, but more likely he has a cracked rib or two." His mouth quirked upward a little at one corner. "I remember how it feels, but my sparse medical training doesn't run to a definite diagnosis."

"Why didn't you just say so? Do you want me to take him?"

"I'd better. There's a considerable amount of red tape when a man's been involved with a bullet, but I know a doctor who takes such things in stride. I'm only wondering if we should be taking you with us, to be sure you stay out of trouble."

"I have other things to do."

Instant alarm. "What?"

"I've got to see Zared this morning."

"Didn't I just say? Into the jaws of death?"

"Oh, stop being so morbid. Even if Zared is involved in this, he's not likely to murder me for awhile yet. He's got my will, but I haven't given him any clue about where the diamonds are. Why make things hard on himself? If he lets me live a few more days and is really nice to me, maybe I'll hand them over and he won't have to bother."

"That's not a thing to be joking about." Another violent sneeze.

"Danny, that was meant to be a joke, but I'm serious about talking to Zared today, whether you like it or not. I have to do it for my own peace of mind."

"I don't like it," he said, "but you're as stubborn as I am myself and I've thrown away any right to be helping you direct your life. How soon can you be ready?"

"If you'll get out of my room, I'll be ready in twenty-eight minutes."

I heard him blowing his nose as he went down.

Stuart was undeniably in pain, but he managed a smile and short greeting when I appeared.

"Constancy, a word with you." Danny was looking in even worse condition than Stuart as I followed him silently to the library.

"I want to know exactly where you expect to be," he said. "and when. Don't argue, just tell me."

"I wasn't planning to argue. Danny, have you caught a cold?"

"I have, and colds make me unendurably short-tempered, so I want no lectures from you about nutrition and sufficient sleep."

"Fine. I don't have time to give lectures, anyway. I'll arrange to pick up Zared at the front door of the office building. That way I don't have to get out of the car or even drive it into the parking garage. Then I'll take him to lunch at the burger place on the corner of 12th and Grand, and I won't tell him where we're going until I get him in the car. How am I doing so far?"

"Not bad. So far. You should be safe enough in public places.

Don't leave your food alone with him. Nor with anyone else. What if he refuses to see you?"

"If we're right about his motivation, he won't, will he? He wouldn't want to risk fatally offending me until I produce the diamonds."

"I sincerely hope your use of the word fatal is not prophetic."

"I've never spouted a prophecy in my life. I'm not likely to start today."

"All right, but if Fraser or anybody else should make a grab for you, scream first, apologize later if necessary."

"Yes, sir."

"I'm serious, Constancy."

"I know. Danny, don't worry. I'll be fine. I'll take little Brandon's pepper spray with me." Brandon had been my favorite kindergarten student. He once kicked Lon Tirso in my behalf and gave me the spray as an end-of-year gift.

Danny almost smiled. "The lad wanted to buy you a shot gun."

"His mother told me. Here. Have another tissue."

He used it to good advantage, and stuffed a few clean ones into his pocket. "All right. See you use the spray if you need it."

"I will."

"Any other errands?"

"Before I see Zared, I'm going to visit Gram's lawyer."

"To inquire about the diamonds?"

"To inquire whether anybody else has been inquiring about the diamonds."

"Good thought. While you're there why don't you have a different will drawn up?"

"I'd already planned to do that."

"Grand. Constancy, it might be best if you didn't broadcast the news when you've done it."

"I'd like to tell Zared. I'd like to see his reaction."

"His reaction might be more than you could handle without backup." He looked sincerely worried.

"Okay. I'll keep quiet. After I've seen the lawyer and Zared,

I'll come straight home and keep all the doors and windows locked. How about you?"

"It depends on what the doctor says about Stuart. Don't come back into the house until you see my car in the drive, will you? Do you carry a cell phone?"

"No."

"You should. All right. If we're going to be delayed, I'll leave word with, oh, Miss Irma."

"Okay."

He eyed me skeptically. "You're being much too agreeable this morning."

"Just trying to keep peace between friends."

He melted a little. "Is it permissible to ask what you'll be discussing with Fraser?"

"Still suspicious?"

"That mindset comes with the job."

"I need to get a few things straight with him, that's all."

He frowned. "Take care, love. Be sure you don't mention Caleb or Stuart."

"I'm not stupid." But I didn't make any promises. One of the things I intended to do was give Zared an opening for admitting to me that he had seen Caleb Fraser.

"Whatever you say, for all our sakes, don't break off your engagement to him."

Danny Egan still had the power to wound. Maybe it wasn't intentional. Maybe it was. Maybe he had already recovered from last night's momentary weakness. "Don't worry," I said, not caring that the words sounded bitter. "Even if one of us does break it off, you don't have to worry. I won't let my gratitude overwhelm my good sense this time."

He looked away for a moment and when his eyes met mine again, all the life seemed to have died out of them. There was only dull, dark pain, and then he closed even that down, so I could see no more than the careful, expressionless face of the impartial law enforcer.

"This has nothing to do with what happened before," he said. "Or what might be between us in future. I'm not wanting you to marry Zared Fraser, but we need this engagement because of Caleb. We may yet need you to help us get into Fraser House Friday night during the party. It could be our only chance of finding Caleb alive, if he is still alive. If the engagement is broken off before then, so will the party be. We'll have very little chance of getting in at all if that happens."

I peered into that stone-like countenance, thinking of what I had seen there last night. Even though he refused to show it now, Danny was as befuddled and frightened and distracted as I was, and every bit as much in need of reassurance.

"You know I'll do whatever I can to help find Caleb," I said. "Hadn't you better get Stuart to the doctor? Maybe he can give you something for that cold, too."

He turned to leave and I caught his hand. It was much too warm. "Danny, I'm sorry I snapped at you and I'm really sorry you're sick. Take care of yourself, will you?"

For a moment he looked at our clasped hands, then squeezed my fingers tightly and went back to Stuart.

Parnell Vanek gave me as gracious a welcome as a busy lawyer was capable of. His mother, Elaina, had been Gram's attorney, but she had retired several years ago, leaving the practice to her son. Mr. Vanek already looked near retirement age himself. Gram had liked both Vaneks equally well. "They're honest," she told me. "They appreciate clarity and brevity. You can't say that about all lawyers."

Keeping that in mind, I got right to the point of my visit. "I need two things, Mr. Vanek. First, I want to make a new will."

"You don't have an old one on file with us."

"No. My, uh, fiancé's lawyer took care of it, but I've decided it isn't what I want."

"I see." He was looking at Zared's ring. "What else?"

"The Soillse Flann diamonds."

He frowned. "Diamond fever hit you at last, has it?"

"Not me, but it seems to be hitting somebody. What do you know about that set?"

"Nothing that's going to be any help. I know Amanda had it, but I sure don't know where it is now except that it's never been put on the open market. If she'd sold it, her estate would have been worth many millions more. According to the inventory list, you own it now. I thought Amanda would tell you where those diamonds were before she went."

"She didn't. I didn't know they existed until yesterday, and that discovery was more or less accidental."

"Other people remember them."

"I wanted to ask you about that, too. Has anybody else brought up the subject lately?"

"One of the Fraser legal advisors was over here snooping for clues. It was my great pleasure to tell her again that the Frasers had no claim and that what I knew, if anything, was none of their business." He sat silent for a moment, absently juggling through a stack of papers. "Constancy, I was going to get in touch with you later today."

"Why?"

"I have a letter you should see."

"About the diamonds?"

"No. It was from, well, we both knew her as Lauren Stafford."

"M-my mother?"

The room hadn't changed in the least with that pronouncement. Mr. Vanek was still his calm, quiet self. I felt as if I'd been bombed.

"She doesn't call herself Stafford now," he said, "but, yes. Your mother."

For a few minutes I could find nothing to say. All I could do was sit there while waves of feeling washed over me. Rejection. Desolation. The sinking despair of abandonment. All the emotions that had overwhelmed me when I was six years old and realizing that my own mother didn't want me. Now, because of the nightmares I'd had since May about what might happen if I saw her again, a good amount of fear was added to that mix. "What does she want?"

"I guess it's hard for you not to be angry with her, even after all these years, but leaving you with Amanda was the best thing she could have done, for you and for Amanda," Mr. Vanek said gently.

"For herself, you mean. She didn't even try to be a good mother."

"She was barely sixteen when you were born. How much of the story did Amanda tell you?"

"Nothing about that." But it was more my fault than Gram's. Gram seemed to have forgiven Lauren entirely. Gram found it easy to forgive. She had occasionally tried to talk to me about my mother, but I had refused to listen. I didn't want to hear it. When I finally did want to, it was too late.

"Lauren wants the diamonds, too, now that Gram's gone. Is that it?"

"That wasn't the purpose of the letter."

"I wonder if she'd want them badly enough to kill for them."

I suppose lawyers aren't easily shocked, but I think I shocked Mr. Vanek with that. In fact, I shocked myself. The young Lauren Stafford had been hot-tempered, even violent at times, though she was never violent toward me. I remembered her being bitter and full of resentment. She was barely more than a child herself when I knew her. Maybe she had good reason for the bitterness. Who was I to judge? I'd never bothered to learn the facts. I had no proof she might be what Danny called criminal-minded. In fact, Gram had assured me that Lauren, though she made mistakes, knew how to learn from them and move on. Gram was convinced that Lauren had loved me from the beginning and still did.

"I'm sorry," I said. "I'm getting paranoid about Frasers."

Another whiplash glance at the ring.

"Yes, even those Frasers. Is Lauren here? In town?"

"You haven't asked what she wanted."

"I'm not sure I want to know."

"She wants to see you, that's all. She wants to see you and talk with you as soon as possible. A matter of great importance, the letter says."

"Like asking me where those diamonds are. No, thanks."

"Constancy, the letter doesn't say what she wants to talk about, but I believe she honestly wants to get to know you, and she wants you to know her. She regrets having lost her daughter."

"Then she shouldn't have dumped me."

"Think about it." He sounded tired.

"I can't right now. It'll have to wait."

"Do you want to tell me what's going on?"

"Another time, maybe."

Mr. Vanek sighed. "Then let me get Mrs. Raymond in here and we'll get that will written up for you."

"Make it very simple. Everything, including those diamonds, if they're still part of the estate, everything goes to Gram's church." I shivered. "I don't think I have any enemies there."

Chapter 15

I had been face to face with a murderer once. Zared, waiting in the shelter of his office building's elegant canopy, didn't look like a murderer. He looked like a spoiled child who couldn't have his own way.

He got into the car with a sulky frown and not a word of greeting.

"Hello, Constancy, darling," I prompted. "It's a beautiful day and I'm thrilled to see my intended bride on this bright and sunny day."

"It's raining cats and dogs," he muttered.

"I thought in the Fraser universe it would rain no less than Persians and Poodles."

He didn't smile. "What's the deal? You sounded like an irate kindergarten teacher on the phone."

"I am a kindergarten teacher, remember? Or I was, back when I could still get work, and it's been an irritating week."

"You reminded me of Mrs. West and her paddle."

Did he know about my talk with Irma? "If Miss Irma paddled you, you deserved it."

He began to thaw a little. "I probably did. I was a brat. I don't know that I've grown out of it yet. What have I done? Are you still mad about what happened in the office yesterday? Why are you calling me on the carpet?"

"I'm not mad. Aren't engaged couples supposed to want each other's company?"

"Where are we going?"

"Probably a new experience for you. Fast food."

The worst of the lunch rush was over. We had a fairly private table, but there were enough other people around to please Danny. I ordered our food and brought it back to Zared. "Here. Try this. You might even like it."

He prodded the paper wrapping. "I doubt it. All right. Let's start again. Why this meeting? Why here?"

"I wanted a neutral place, without the twins listening to every word. We need to discuss a couple of things."

"Like what?"

"Like I think you must have hypnotized me into this engagement."

He went very still. "Are you saying you want out?"

I badly wanted to say it. Someday soon I was going to say it. I could hardly wait for that moment. "I'm saying I don't know you. The things I thought I knew are mostly assumptions I've made, and you aren't giving me many chances to find out more. During the short time between the funeral and the engagement ring, we never talked about you or about 'us'. Only about me. I was so much in shock over Gram and so flattered by your attention that I didn't notice the omissions. And now that I've agreed to marry you, you're too busy for further discussion. Tell me why I shouldn't want out."

On the surface, his face was contrite. "I've been neglecting you," he said. "I admit I'm a workaholic. I assumed you'd understand my being tied up in the business, maybe take an interest in it yourself."

"This has nothing to do with the business. Zared, I don't even know why you want to marry me."

Zared's courtship, to use an out-dated term, had been highly unusual for our day, and much to my liking. It had been romantic in an old-fashioned sense. Lots of roses and hand-holding, a few chaste kisses and sweet words. Lingering looks that promised to be the beginning of something very special. He convinced me, or I convinced myself, that I could grow to love him. I could not recall his ever actually saying he loved me. He hadn't given any reason for his sudden, intense interest, either.

"I assumed it was obvious," he said. "You're attractive and it's time there were more Fraser children."

"You don't even know if I want any kids. We haven't discussed anything about after the wedding. Not children, not where we'll be living. Not how we'll spend our retirement years."

"Retirement years?" He laughed. "That is planning ahead."

"When I marry, I intend to marry for life. Do we have enough in common to make it last that long?"

"'Until death do us part'? You're really serious about the forever thing?"

"Don't you want a lifetime commitment?"

He gave me an odd look. "I assumed you agreed to marry me for the same reason several other women have thought I'd make a good husband. Then, if it didn't work out, you'd take your cut and go happily."

"You thought I wanted a cut of the Fraser millions, you mean? Hey, you sent the first rose, remember. Why? Why did you swoop in with your roses and sympathy at that particular moment, when you'd never bothered with any of our family before? You can't make me believe I'm physically irresistible to you. You could have any woman you want."

"I won't lie to you and tell you I'm madly, irrevocably in love with you at this moment." A glance that made me a little uneasy. "You don't feel that way, either. Not about me. I do want you, Constancy. Maybe because you weren't throwing yourself at me from the moment you were old enough." Zared watched me a moment. "Has some busybody been telling you that I want you for your millions?"

"If you do, you've wasted your time and a lot of roses. I can't even get a job in my chosen profession anymore. I certainly don't have millions."

He pushed his uneaten hamburger aside and nibbled at a french fry. "You might have."

"You mean the Soillse Flann diamonds?"

"Then you do know about them."

"The lost sheep of the pet rock flock. I found out about them just recently."

"From whom?"

"Does it matter?"

"I was wondering if you'd read about them in some of Amanda's papers."

"She never mentioned them to me before or after her death. For the record, I've never seen the things except in that wedding portrait. I have no idea where they've gone. Gram hated diamonds."

Another long look that told me nothing. "Did she? Why?"

"Maybe because of the greed she saw connected with them. Especially on Bartholomew's part."

"Good old Grandpa Bart."

"I've never heard much good about him."

"I never liked him myself, but he was a sharp business man. He greatly increased the Fraser fortune and kept what was left of the collection, post-Amanda, intact. The Soillse Flann diamonds are the only ones he ever lost. We have him to thank for our wealth."

Perfect opening. *Sorry, Danny.* "He stole it from his own brother." Zared smiled. "That's one theory."

"According to Gram, it was more than a theory. Even Lucian believed it in the end."

He shrugged. "All right, maybe Bart did frame George. Maybe he was a thief and a liar and supremely lacking in brotherly love. That's the distant past."

"Is it? What about George? He should have inherited some of Lucian's wealth, maybe all of it. What if he's still alive or had a family? Would the Fraser wealth revert to them if any of them appeared?"

Zared was neither too quick nor too slow with his answer. Nor was he the least bit rattled. "I doubt it," he said after a moment's thought. "I mean I doubt if he's alive or if he had a family. If he did, surely one of them would have made a claim by now. No, I think it's likely that George died without issue, as the genealogists say."

I think I kept my face as calm and collected as Zared's. Inside I was seething. What would Zared say if I told him I knew that one of George's family had recently vanished in Fraserton, supposedly after a meeting with Zared, himself? What if I told him that another twig from that branch of the family tree was suffering from a vicious attack on his life. Zared had met Stuart, even if he hadn't seen Caleb. He couldn't have failed to take in Stuart's family resemblance. Stuart had legal proof of his heritage, besides.

So that was one lie told deliberately and expertly. What would Zared do if I called him on it? How would he react if I told him I knew I was George's great-granddaughter? Did he know? Did any of them? "I really think we should try to trace George and find out for sure."

"Not for awhile."

"Why not?"

"Because, my dear, in just a few days the thirty-year provision on Lucian's will expires. After that, it won't matter."

"What provision?"

"The one Amanda convinced him to put in. Didn't she tell you that, either?"

"I have no idea what you're talking about."

Quick calculation in his eyes. "Well, it isn't important, but believe me, if George had family they would have made their claims by now. How did we get off on this? I was about to tell you the story of the Soillse Flann diamonds."

"I can hardly wait." Pity he hadn't been as eager to tell it to me before I signed my first will. Just what sort of provision had Gram asked Lucian to put into his will?

"The Soillse Flann diamonds came into the family in 1899," Zared said. "They were a fabulous set. You have the portrait and the garnets. They're both pale imitations of the real thing. The pendant stone in the necklace weighed eight carats. It was, as far as I've been able to learn, the largest red diamond ever found. What made the set especially valuable was that all of the stones, all five of them over a carat, matched almost perfectly in color. It was the very rarest of colors. There's not been more than a handful of red diamonds documented in the whole history of the diamond trade, and for awhile we held five of the very finest."

He went on to tell me much the same story that Irma had told, only he spoke of the diamonds lovingly and with great sorrow.

"Lucian gave the Soillse Flann set to Amanda as a wedding gift. He put it exclusively in her name. Shortly afterward it vanished. She said she had put it away some place safe for her children, but she wouldn't tell anybody where, not even Lucian. They say when anybody asked him about it, he gave an evil little chuckle and proclaimed it was Amanda's business what she did with her own property. Crazy old man. It's the only set of his original collection that's ever left the family. If it has left. It was never brought to market. If it had been, it would have made news all over the world. It's not in Fraser House, either.

Bart had the place thoroughly searched after Amanda moved out."

I gazed at him a moment. "Which of you had my apartment thoroughly searched the day of Gram's funeral, and several times before that? Did you expect to find them there?"

"Your apartment?"

His apparent surprise put another thought into my head. What if it was my loving mother who had done the searching? I pushed that aside to think about later. "Somebody searched Gram's house, too. The trespasser wasn't as cautious there. He left a super mess, some of it sheer vandalism. Did you authorize it?"

"What do you think I am, Constancy?"

"That's what I'm trying to find out."

"Why didn't you tell me about all this earlier?"

"Maybe because I was afraid you would react like you did when I told you about the body in my kitchen. It would have been good fuel for Romney's campaign against me. But since I'm telling you some of it, I may as well tell the rest. The day I signed the will, somebody drugged me. Is that news to you, too?"

He looked grim. "Are you accusing me?"

"It happened. I don't know who did it or how, but the only people I was with that day were Frasers and their employees. That afternoon outside the restaurant a car almost hit me because I was too much under the influence to see the danger of crossing a street. I'm also missing a few hours of that day, out cold, I suppose, while somebody did a more thorough search for a clue to the whereabouts of those over-rated pieces of sparkly carbon."

"That sounds like an accusation of attempted murder. I didn't drug you, Constancy. Why should I? I don't want you dead. I want to marry you."

"Would you still want to marry me if I had refused to name you beneficiary in my will? Would you have bothered with me at all if you knew for a fact that I never would be able to produce that set of missing diamonds for you?"

"The possibility of returning those diamonds to the collection was attractive. I don't deny that. But it wasn't the only attraction." There was a sudden watchfulness in him. As if he didn't quite trust me. "How's that for honesty?"

"Since you're being honest, tell me one more thing. Did the Triumvirate have a meeting and vote on which of you was going to propose to me?"

"Marrying you was entirely my own idea."

"But you didn't get that idea until Gram died."

"Wrong, Constancy. I've had my eye on you a long time. I've always thought you'd be quite an asset to this branch of the Fraser family, even without the diamonds, believe it or not."

"Then why wait so long?"

"In one word, Amanda. She would've called out the cavalry, the marines and the local SWAT team if any of us had come within ten yards of you. She as much as said so. Several times."

It made a certain amount of sense. Gram probably had warned them off. But I was convinced now that Zared, despite his protests, had never seen any charm in me except a diamond-shaped one.

"Zared, what if I changed my will before the wedding?"

His mouth took on a sudden cynical twist. He laughed, but I heard no trace of humor in it. "What is this? One of those old-fashioned, how-much-do-you-love-me questions? What if you did change it? Who would you leave your estate to? Your beloved Danny? He spent the night with you last night. Again."

His quick change from defense to offense didn't hide the fact that he hadn't answered my question. That, in itself, told me what I wanted to know. No sense pressing him further about it. "Who spread the gossip about Danny? Your mother?"

"Several people mentioned it. Are you denying the fact that he was with you?"

Nona's warnings about Zared re-echoed through my head. "Danny spent the night in my house, but not with me in the way Heather would like you to believe. Like I told Nona, Danny is concerned for my safety."

"Oh, of course."

"I can't make you believe it."

"I don't want you seeing him again."

Only the thought of Stuart's battered body and his missing father kept me from telling Zared exactly what I thought of him, his ring and our farce of an engagement.

"Danny's my friend, Zared. I can't, I won't promise I'll never see him again, but I promise you there is no affair in progress between us. Never has been. Never will be."

Zared (for the sake of the diamonds?) backed off. "Sorry. I didn't mean to play the jealous boyfriend. This whole business is ridiculous," he said. "I'm going somewhere and have a decent lunch. Coming?"

"No."

"I wish you would."

We both stood at the same time, but he moved more quickly. It was almost a lunge. I never had time to scream. I never even thought about the pepper spray.

Chapter 16

At least it wasn't kidnapping he had in mind.

Zared's embrace was pretty fancy stuff for a weekday in a fast food dining room.

We exited the place, hand-in-hand, to scattered applause and laughter and stood in front of the car, in the rain, staring at each other. "Well," he said, "that was something of a revelation."

Maybe it revealed something to him. For me it only raised more questions. Behind the blatant passion had been a touch of tenderness that momentarily knocked me right off-guard. Could the man be that good an actor? Did he really care about me? Or was it the thought of the missing diamonds he loved? Was he merely turning up the heat to convince me not to walk out of the engagement?

"Want some lunch?" Zared asked, his voice not quite steady.

"I'm not hungry, thanks, but I'll drop you wherever you say."

"I'd settle for just getting into the car right now. How about unlocking it before we wash down the gutter? I hate this rain."

"Sorry." I let us into the car. "Where to?"

"Fraser House, please. I'll need to change before I go back to the office. Come in and we'll find something dry for you, too."

A perfectly innocent offer? Or kidnapping by consent?

I considered going in and maybe creating some excuse to nose around. If I could find Caleb myself, I wouldn't have to go to that party and announce an engagement I no longer intended to honor. No. It wouldn't work. The place probably had forty rooms, not counting closets and attics and cellars and crawl spaces and, for all I knew, priests holes and secret passages and dungeons. Besides, even if none of the Frasers had any skeletons, present or prospective, in residence, they wouldn't leave me to explore every possible hiding place on my own. Worse yet, Nona might be there.

"Are you coming in?" Zared asked.

"Maybe another day," I told him.

He didn't insist. As I drove away, I saw him reflected in my rear-view mirror. A generic Fraser. He was Zared, but he might have been Romney or Timon, or even the ghost of a young Lucian. Irma had once entertained Gram and me with stories about how the boys subbed for one another while they were in high school.

Were they still playing that game? Caleb had been scheduled to meet with Zared. Stuart thought it was Zared he'd spoken to.

There was no guarantee it was actually the oldest Fraser brother in either case. Zared could be innocent on all counts. Was nothing ever simple?

The first thing I heard when I opened the back door was fiddle music. The first thing I saw was another stranger. This one stepped out of the kitchen just as I walked into the hall. At least I had a name for this one, and I was thrilled to have her in my house. "Hello. I wondered if I would ever get to meet you."

She smiled at me with a smile I had already learned to love. "You recognize me then?"

"How could I not? Danny looks so much like you." Even to the mischief in the green eyes.

"In my opinion, it's taken entirely too long for Danny to get around to bringing you to us. So I came to you."

"I'm glad you did."

"But look at you, darlin'. You're near drowned with the rain. You need to change. I've got soup warming on the stove and cornbread in the oven. I hope you'll forgive me for making myself at home in your kitchen, but those two in there are the next thing to helpless just now and both of them are needing to be fed."

"Me, too. That soup smells fantastic! Anytime you want to cook over here, you're welcome to. The only stipulation is that I get to eat some of the product."

"That goes without saying. You're equally welcome at our house, with or without Danny."

"Thanks." I kicked off my drenched shoes. "I have just one question," I said, as she took my coat and hung it to drip in the bathroom. "We haven't exactly been introduced. What do I call you?"

"Rose, of course. It's what they all call me. My name's Rosamond, but when Gavin and I joined ranks, poor young Cameron couldn't bear to call me Mum. I couldn't blame him. They're very touchy when they're just into their teens, aren't they? I didn't like to push him about it. Then one day, he came up with Rosamum, which got shortened to Rose and immediately adopted by Danny, who thought it very daring to call his maternal parent by her first name, and there you have it. Now, if I don't stir that soup, it'll be cinders and inedible altogether." She rushed into the kitchen.

I went upstairs and changed into dry clothing.

Danny's mother: I had expected to like her. Certainly I had

wanted to like her. I hadn't expected her to be one of those rare people with whom I felt instantly at ease, instantly sure that we could be best friends with no trouble at all.

I didn't think my reaction to her had anything to do with her relationship to Danny Egan. If I had met her without knowing Danny, I would have felt the same.

Rose was frantically stirring the soup when I got to the kitchen.

The fiddle music, unfortunately, wasn't live. It was coming from a tape player on the mantel. Danny was slumped in a chair by the fireplace. His eyes were fixed on the crackling fire, but he seemed to be listening intently to the music. He neither spoke nor turned around when I came in.

Stuart, sitting at the kitchen table with a newspaper, glanced up and smiled. "Howdy, cousin."

"How did it go?"

"All the doctor found was one cracked rib and some bad bruises. I'll survive."

"That's a relief. Rose, how can I help?"

"Bowls? Spoons? I was scared to do too much rummaging in another woman's kitchen. Some folk are offended by it."

"It won't offend me, but I'll set the table to save you the trouble this time."

"Use paper and plastic if you have them. No need to be fancy on my account," she added, and consolidated her claim on my heart entirely and forever.

The piece of music ended. Danny looked at me for the first time since I'd come in. "Your hair's soaked, Constancy. What on earth have you been doing with that fiancé of yours?" The room was almost uncomfortably warm, but Danny had on a flannel shirt and a wool pullover and was still shivering.

"We got drenched going from the burger place to the car. It's still raining outside, in case you hadn't noticed." The next tune on the tape began and again he lost himself in the music.

I put the proper equipment on the table as quickly as possible My appetite was back full force. "Rose, it's awfully sweet of you to bring this."

"I second that," Stuart said.

She smiled. "As I was coming into town anyway to pick up a part Gavin needs for the tractor, I thought I would bring this by. It gave me an excellent excuse to meet you, to see about Danny." She frowned and lowered her voice a little. "When I talked with him this morning, he sounded ill. I believe in letting my grown-up children live their own lives, but when one of them's sick I can't help but worry."

"I understand perfectly. Danny acts like he's miserable."

"He is miserable and he's not above letting it show."

"He reminds me of my kindergarten kids when they have a cold, all grumpy and self-absorbed."

"That's exactly the age he acts when he has a cold."

"Well, I know how to manage miserable five-year-olds."

She laughed. "I daresay you do. You'll have my blessing and my full cooperation if you care to try your methods on my miserable son. I'll be highly interested in seeing how that experiment turns out."

"No guarantees."

"It's worth trying, nonetheless." Rose waited until the music paused again, then turned off the tape player. "Lunch is hot," she announced. "You lads wash your hands and see you eat it before it's gone cold." She went into the hall and got her coat.

"Rose, aren't you staying to eat with us?"

"I would love to, darlin', but I have to get this thing for the tractor home to Gavin. I'll have to leave you to get it on the table for them, if you don't mind."

"I can do that. I'm just sorry we don't have more time to get acquainted."

"I'll phone you another time, if I may, and we'll have lunch together. Neither of us will need to cook."

"I'll look forward to that."

She stepped back into the kitchen, kissed Danny, patted Stuart gently on the shoulder.

I opened the door for her. "I'm glad you came, Rose."

"So am I. I have a feeling we're going to be great friends."

"I hope you won't think this is too presumptuous, but I have a feeling we already are."

She smiled and kissed me, too.

"I thought you'd had lunch with your fiancé," Danny grumbled, as I put the soup and cornbread on the table.

"We never got around to eating. Was that you playing fiddle on the tape?"

He didn't answer, but Stuart did. "I found that tape in his car, untitled as to fiddler. The names of the tunes were intriguing and the music was great, but he kept criticizing it so much that I knew it had to be his. Uncle Noah does the same thing. He records his playing and criticizes it unmercifully."

"I didn't hear anything to criticize on this tape. It's brilliant. Sounds professional to me."

Danny gave me an impatient glance. He was obviously sick. I reached over and touched my wrist to his flushed face. "Danny, you're burning up. You should be in bed."

He jerked away from my hand.

"All right. Did your mother make you take anything?"

"She knows better than to try."

"Well I don't," I said, ignoring the warning glare. "You two go on and eat. I'll get some aspirin."

* * *

"No use—" Danny interrupted himself with an evil-sounding cough. "No use putting it off. Did you learn anything helpful from the lawyer or from Fraser, Constancy?"

Still wrapped in the glow of Rose's acceptance and warmth, I didn't want to think about Zared. The soup was comforting and delicious and it was a shame Rose couldn't have stayed. I didn't want to talk business while eating it, either, but that couldn't be helped.

"Zared lied to me, I think. He said he believed George had no family. Stuart, you said you saw Zared in the office."

"Yep."

"You might have seen one of the twins. They all look alike."

"You were not to mention George's family to Zared!"

"I didn't, except in an abstract way. I didn't come right out and ask him if he'd kidnapped Caleb, for goodness' sake. Give me some credit. If I hadn't done what I did, I wouldn't have found out about the provision."

"What's that?"

"Some kind of provision in Lucian's will that'll expire in a few days. Zared called it the thirty-year provision. He wouldn't tell me any more, but I thought it might be important."

Danny looked at Stuart. "You mentioned something about George wanting to wait before contacting the Frasers here."

"That's why," Stuart said. "Amanda told us about the will. Basically, it says that if any of George's family is found within thirty years of Lucian's death, the diamond collection and Fraser House go to them. That's one reason Amanda came to us when she did. She thought Grandad ought to know about his chance to reclaim what should have been his."

"Could Lucian make that kind of provision legally?"

"Could and did and there wasn't a thing in the world Bart could do to change it."

Danny pushed away his bowl of soup. He'd eaten very little. "Well, that gives the present occupants of Fraser House motive in plenty for denying they'd seen Caleb."

Stuart was grim. "Grandad tried to tell us Bart's obsession might have been passed on to the younger generation. I wish Dad had listened."

"So what do we do now? Wait until the expiration date? Won't they release Caleb after that?"

"One way or another."

Stuart shook his head. "I don't have much hope that he's still alive. I almost wasn't. Why should they risk keeping him alive and then releasing him?"

"Why shouldn't they?" I said. "They *are* Frasers."

"What's that supposed to mean?"

"Keeping him alive and then releasing him is less risky than murder, surely. It shouldn't be any problem for them, no matter what story Caleb tells. As far as I know, the Frasers have a perfect reputation in this town, except for Bart, and nobody ever proved anything bad about him. Caleb, on the other hand, is the son of a man who was either a thief or was cheated out of his inheritance. He won't show up until after the provision expires and then he's somebody who has a motive to try and get revenge on our upstanding Frasers, even if he and his son have to manufacture ways and means. Why, they might even make up some weird story about kidnapping and attempted murder. Who are the citizens of Fraserton going to believe?"

Danny looked at me with disgust. "No wonder the bungling hit-man died and vanished. He would have lent credence to Stuart's part of the story. Constancy, the criminal element has missed a brilliant opportunity by not recruiting you."

"Haven't they."

Stuart was gripping the table edge hard enough to turn his knuckles white. "Could that really work?"

"I'd not like to have it put to a test," Danny answered.

"It's a good thing Gram never told anybody except Lucian that her baby was George's," I said. "They probably would have done away with her in some neat little accident. That must have been the real reason Gram left Fraser House when Lucian died."

Danny was absent-mindedly crumbling his cornbread. "I wonder when Bartholomew and his brood learned the secret."

"Do you think they did?"

"Oh, yes. Your grandmother did die in an accident, didn't she? Maybe that was coincidence, maybe not. What about your mother? Do you know why she left you or where she went?"

"No."

"With her gone, there was only you to deal with here in Fraserton. First as a mere child, now as the heir's fiancée. All very tidy, very clever. If you should hear of the provision, you'd not bother making a claim, since you'll be in the family anyway. Your being one of them insures our Frasers have at least one share in the family estate if the worst happens. They have only interference from the rest of George's family to fear. Did you change your will?"

"Yes, and I haven't told them yet."

"See you don't. Don't break off that insane engagement yet, either for your own safety."

"For my safety? I thought you didn't want me telling them because of Caleb."

"Both reasons are valid. Granted, for now they have you under their control with the engagement, but if you break that engagement, it might very well be the end of you. You could do them no good then, you see, and you might very well do some real harm. As one of George's family, you have it in your power to take away everything they own."

"I don't want it."

"You think they would believe that for a minute? I doubt it. There's altogether too much greed somewhere there for them to believe you wouldn't be interested. Look what's happened with Caleb and Stuart. When those two arrived, the Frasers here must have decided there were getting to be entirely too many claimants. Your mother could be in danger now as well. If she's still alive. Do you know?"

"She's alive. When I saw Mr. Vanek this morning, he told me he'd had a letter from her. She wants to see me. I thought maybe she wanted those diamonds, too. The letter said she had something important to discuss with me."

"Is she here in town?" Danny asked.

"I haven't seen her, but I don't even know that I would recognize her if I did. I have no proof, but she might have been responsible for some of the damage in this house. She's probably the only person besides me who knew those books were Gram's favorites. She could have thought the diamonds were hidden in them somehow, but maybe it was just spite. A long time ago she would have been capable of that."

"And now?"

"Now, I don't know. She hasn't been in touch with me for twenty years."

"Will you see her?"

"I haven't decided."

"I'll talk with Mr. Vanek, shall I? We'll need to get some kind of warning to her."

"Yes, please. Whatever she's like now, I don't want her hurt because of this."

He nodded and turned to Stuart. "How safe is your family?"

"Ordinarily, I'd say nothing could touch them. The ranch is in the middle of nowhere. There's not much crime in our area, barring a few fights in town at the tavern and a little cattle rustling. We haven't taken precautions against the extraordinary. Now, if you'll excuse me, I think I'll go make a phone call."

"While you've got them on the line, you might ask if they can give you the exact date that this provision expires," Danny said.

"You got it."

"Danny, why did they wait until now to start all this?"

"Maybe they didn't learn about George's other family until Amanda died. She might have had papers in the house. If they did know before, they must have been watching for any sign that George had decided to make a claim. His heart attack happened about the time Amanda died. Even if that was coincidental, it left the younger generation in control and would have made Bart's family nervous. Sure enough, George's family begins showing up on the Fraser doorstep. One or more of this lot decided it was time to be rid of the competition."

"I'm glad I changed my will. If something happens to me and the diamonds are found, they won't go to any Fraser. They'll go to Gram's church."

Danny rubbed at his forehead as if it ached and there was still a feverish flush across his cheekbones, despite the aspirin he'd impatiently swallowed for me. "Thank heaven you resisted the urge to tell Fraser about it," he said.

Stuart rejoined us. "Don't tell any of that bunch anything. Somebody inside Fraser House is involved for sure. Mom told me it was a secretary who arranged the meeting between Dad and Zared, not Zared himself. She didn't know the name, but I'd guess it's the same little beauty who assured me so convincingly that she'd never heard of Caleb Fraser. Young, blonde, an ego the size of Siberia and a heart with about the same mean winter temperature."

"Heather." It was a perfect description.

Danny glanced at me and frowned. "Is she up to something with one or more of the Triumvirate?"

"She would be if she thought she could profit by it, and she'd love to be wearing this ring, or an even bigger one, herself. She wouldn't look favorably on anybody who might be trying to part these Frasers from their diamonds."

"Something else to look into. What other news from South Dakota, Stuart?"

"Everything's fine as of now. Uncle Noah's going to upgrade security for the next few days." He grinned. "That means he'll let the Beast roam a little more freely and tell the ranch hands to be on the lookout for sneaking coyotes."

"The Beast?"

"The family dog. Capital D."

"Will that be enough protection?" Danny asked.

"You bet."

"What about the provision?"

"Expires the twenty-third of this month."

I must have made some little sound. Both of them looked at me. "No wonder Zared was in such a hurry to get married. It doesn't really matter now." I glared at Danny. "There's not going to be a wedding."

He glared right back at me. "There's certainly not going to be *that* wedding." He broke off in another fit of coughing.

"Here's a strange bit of news for you," he said, when he had his voice under control again. "Your Mrs. Jamison sold her house about sixteen months ago. She's moved two thousand miles away to a cottage in the woods of northern California and hasn't been back to town since."

I did a quick calculation. "I rented that apartment just about then. Did I rent it from her?"

"Oh, yes. A friend of mine traced her and I talked with her while you were out. She sold for about three times what the place was worth just after you signed the lease. The buyer put an interesting stipulation on the deal. Mrs. J. was to keep the fact of the sale strictly to herself. The new owner even arranged to have Mrs. J.'s property moved out at a time when few people would see it. The story was to be that Mrs. J. was away on extended holiday and the new person was managing the property for her during her absence."

"Who was this person?"

"Fern Maldin. Ever hear of her?"

"No. Nobody ever told me to change the way I made out the checks for the rent. I kept making them out to Mrs. Jamison."

"Were they cashed?"

"They were deducted from my checking account, anyway. Who's Fern Maldin?"

"As far as my sources can discover, she doesn't exist."

"Then how did she buy a house?"

"Paid cash. There are lawyers who aren't too particular."

"Why all the secrecy?" Stuart asked.

"Depends on who she is, doesn't it? Could be there's some altogether innocent reason, but my first thought is that it gave her access to Constancy."

"That was a long time before anything happened."

"Some people like planning ahead. There aren't that many people who have that kind of cash lying about."

Only the Frasers? I was tired of questions that had no answers. "Speaking of planning ahead, how are you going to manage tomorrow night? What am I supposed to do?"

"Your part's easy enough. You go and be the beautiful center of attention and get yourself officially engaged."

"For an encore, I can try to swim the Atlantic or flap my arms and fly?"

"It won't be that difficult, love. Just remember you're doing it for Caleb."

"Caleb's absolutely the only reason I'm still speaking to either of you. No. That's not true. What will you two be doing while I'm demonstrating to the upper class what a clumsy idiot I am?"

"I've a tux and a violin case. I can go in with the orchestra.

Stuart will come in with the caterers." Danny made a sad face. "It's not fool-proof, but it may work."

"I don't see it working at all. Stuart looks too much like a Fraser and you'll be sneezing all over your violin."

"I don't intend to have my violin in that case and Stuart won't be serving any food. Once we're inside, they'll not see much of us. We'll be off on our search. The excellent Miss Irma has provided us with a floor plan of Fraser House. It was stored in the library because the place is a historical building. Very convenient."

"I wish all this were over."

"It will be soon." Danny dragged himself up from his chair. "If you'll excuse me, I have a class."

"A class? Danny, you're too sick to go out in this awful weather. It's still pouring rain and the temperature's dropping. Why don't you just go to bed and let me bring you lots of liquids and periodic doses of aspirin?"

"Don't tempt me, love. There's nothing I'd like better, but I have to do this. Just keep out of trouble until I'm back, will you?"

"Well, of course."

"Never mind. It's a waste of breath to be asking such a thing." He scribbled a phone number on a scrap of paper. "You can reach me here if you need me, but I should be back before ten. Take care, Stuart. You'll maybe want to keep an eye on your cousin. She can be dangerous."

Chapter 17

Stuart was too tired to play watchdog. It didn't matter. I was determined not to cause Danny any more worry. Not until he was feeling better, anyway.

After an early supper, during which I had to explain that remark about my being dangerous, Stuart went up to bed. I headed straight for the silk dress in my closet. If I were going to be center stage at that horrible party, I needed to get my act ready.

It took some time and several trips to the attic to get everything assembled, but with the proper petticoats in place and all the hooks fastened, the dress fit as if it had been made for me. It wouldn't need any hemming after all, and the garnets were perfect with it. No fairy godmother could have provided better.

I dawdled for a couple of hours, experimenting with my hair and make-up and jewelry, pleased to see that I could be presentable, if not elegant by modern Fraser standards. Neither Heather nor Nona would be happy with the old-fashioned result, but I wasn't dressing to please them. I didn't care what they thought. I was sure Great-Grandad George would approve. That was considerable comfort.

Strange to think I had a family I'd never met. What were they like? Would they be willing to accept me as one of their own? I changed out of the dress and back into warm slacks and a sweater. If Danny decided his future shouldn't include me, I would take Stuart up on his invitation to visit South Dakota. Maybe I could find a teaching job there. I would be sorry not to have time to get better acquainted with Rose.

Assuming, of course, that we all survived the next few days.

Too morbid Constancy. Think about something else. *How about that dog?* Our neighborhood had a strict leash law. We didn't usually get dogs in our back yard. As I went to the window, the pitch of the barking changed, became louder, more frantic.

In the wet gloom, by the sickly orange glow of a street lamp, I saw the little dog. He was a sodden, pale mop of a thing, standing stiff and fierce with both his front feet braced at the edge of one of the new flowerbeds. Rain dripped from his chin, his ears and every clump of his bedraggled hair. He was barking as if to wake the dead.

If he kept it up, he would at least wake Stuart. I tapped on the glass. He shot one pained look up at me and redoubled his efforts. He didn't move from his position, but the barking became interspersed with anxious whines. It sounded almost like begging. Maybe he was trapped in some way I couldn't see. Maybe he was hurt.

I ran downstairs, grabbed my still-damp coat and an umbrella and went out to look.

The dog waggled his stump of a tail once, but kept right on barking. "Hush," I said. "What is wrong with you?"

He appeared to be free and well fed, even though he was thoroughly waterlogged. "Go home, dog!"

He darted a short distance, not at me, not away, but into the flower bed. He began digging furiously.

"Stop that! You'll dig up those bulbs. Stop." I pushed the

umbrella at him, not aiming to hit him, but hoping to urge him out of the mud. He ducked aside, then ran out of the yard at full speed.

Suddenly I lost all interest in the little dog.

His barking hadn't wakened the dead after all. Nothing short of resurrection day was going to waken whoever was attached to that grotesquely misshapen five-pronged thing that was reaching up out of the rain-sunken mud toward me.

It no longer much resembled a human hand, but I recognized it for what it had been. I had no doubt it was attached to the body that had once rested briefly at my kitchen table.

By now I ought to be used to seeing death where it shouldn't be. First at the school in May; then in my apartment yesterday. Now in Gram's flower bed. By now I ought to have learned how to cope. I hadn't. Each time was worse, like an inescapable noose tightening slowly, lethally around my throat.

"Constancy! What have you done?"

Heather. She was staring at me with something like gloating satisfaction distorting her pretty face. Where had she come from? Why had she come just at this moment?

"I've called the police," she said.

"Danny?"

"I said I called the police. Where have you been? Your precious Danny got fired from the FPD weeks ago. Everybody knows that. Everybody but you. Police business." She was laughing.

"Fired? He would've told me." But maybe he had told me in a hundred little ways and I hadn't caught on. That class, for instance. Lon's accusations and Danny's bitterness over possible corruption in the force. How could they fire him? He loved police work. He was good at his job. Surely Meg Ferguson wouldn't have fired him, not unless she had been corrupted, too. Wait. Danny had said Meg was on extended leave. How long had she been away? Maybe this had happened after she left.

"They fired him," Heather said, "because it never pays to be too good at a job. I wonder what the punishment is for impersonating a police officer. There's no way Danny Egan's going to get you, or himself, out of this one."

Even as she spoke, I heard the sirens coming down Broad Street, turning left on Elm. Heather had called them. Then it hit me. She had to have done it before I found the body.

The sirens turned onto West Lane, ever louder, ever closer, and the sound of them seemed suddenly to clear and focus my mind. I didn't know who was in the police cars, which of the officers, if any, I could trust. If I ran to the house, they would find Stuart as well as me. Better to get as far away as I could and as fast as possible. The sirens would alert Stuart. I would have to trust his instincts and Danny's God to keep him safe.

I pushed past Heather and ran. With any luck, she would be thrilled to point out to them the way I had run, and they would leave the inside of the house untouched long enough for Stuart either to hide or get away.

Through the back yard, through the hedge which ripped at me and tore the umbrella from my hand. Across the neighbor's yard. Across the street and into the shadows of West Park.

I paused under a stand of bare, dripping oaks to catch my breath. As I looked back, two squad cars stopped in front of Gram's house. They turned off the sirens, though the blue and red lights still pulsed through the cold, dreary night. That would wake up our sleepy neighborhood, and put paid to my trying to convince the town that I was an honest and law-abiding citizen.

I needed Danny. With or without his badge he would know what to do next. The phone number he'd written down was etched into my brain, but without money for a pay phone, it would do no good. The rain was dripping steadily down the back of my collar. The wind had risen, too, and my hands were already stiff with cold. There was no way I could evade any determined policemen for long.

Where could I go for shelter and a phone? I couldn't involve Irma or any of my other friends. I shoved my fingers into my coat pockets for whatever warmth might be there and touched metal. My keys, and on the ring was the key to my old apartment.

If I could get a warmer, more waterproof coat and get in touch with Danny before the police finished looking at the body in the flower bed, I just might keep myself out of jail.

The apartment wasn't far away. I'd chosen it, in part, because it was within easy walking distance of Gram. The icy rain and wind slowed me down. My shoes were sloshing inside already. At least the sidewalks were deserted; the streets almost were. With any luck, nobody would see me running from Gram's to my apartment.

Gasping for breath, I let myself in. It felt warm, but it was nearly cave-dark. I didn't dare turn on a lamp. I edged my way to the telephone and began to punch in the numbers before I realized there had been no dial tone. The phone was dead.

Why would it be? The weather? I hoped it was the weather!

Whatever the reason, the reality was that I couldn't use this phone I had counted on. There was a pay phone in front of the post office, if I could find some loose change in the apartment. If I could get to the post office.

While I was here I'd better get dry shoes and something more waterproof in the way of a coat.

Suddenly I realized I was shaking with an unreasonable terror. It wasn't just fear of the situation. It was the apartment. I had lived in that apartment for nearly sixteen months. It had been as familiar to me as any place I'd ever lived. Why did it feel so foreign now? So foreign and threatening. So absolutely terrifying.

Don't let your imagination run away with you, Constancy. Calm down. The closet where I kept the shoes was to my right. I could see its white doors in the tiny amount of light that filtered in around the window blinds. One step forward, and another. A sound of breathing.

Not my own breathing. Definitely not my imagination.

Something brushed against my neck.

So I could scream. Not that the effort lasted long. A rough hand over my mouth effectively stifled the noise; another around my waist, pinned my arms.

I thought my heart had stopped forever, but it did begin to beat again, painfully. Against my back, I could feel my attacker's heart beating in the same way. Hard and fast, as if he, too, were terrified. Belatedly, I tried to escape.

"Stand still." A hissing whisper. "You're not who I thought you were. I'm going to let you go. If you scream again, I'll shut you up. Nothing personal. I'd just like to get out of this alive."

Me, too. I nodded against his hand. Slowly he removed it and released me. "I'm sorry I scared you." He was still speaking barely above a whisper. "Who are you? I don't mean you any harm. What are you doing here?"

Since he seemed to be reasonable, honesty was maybe the best policy. "This is m-my apartment. My name's Constancy Stafford."

"Amanda's great-granddaughter? Thank goodness!"

"But who are you?"

No hesitation. "Caleb Fraser."

"Caleb!" Poor man. He suddenly had an armful of dripping Constancy clinging to him. But he was already dripping, too, so it wouldn't make much difference.

"Hey," he said. "I'm pleased to meet you, too, but you're about as wet a bundle as I've ever seen. You'll come down with something."

"Sorry. I'm just so glad to find you, I don't know what to do." I stepped away, but I didn't let him go. I didn't want to lose him now. "It's not like I'm going to get you any wetter," I said, halfway between laughter and tears.

"You're right about that. You people have some miserable weather down here, don't you?"

"It's miserable tonight." I stared at him, trying to see this new relative, but it was too dark to see his features.

"Caleb. Great-Uncle Caleb it would be, wouldn't it?"

"You can drop the great-uncle business. Makes me feel as old as dirt. Caleb'll do fine."

"Caleb, then. I just can't believe you're here, alive. Stuart was sure you must be dead. He's been worried sick. We all have, and now my phone's dead and I can't call Danny."

I felt his whole body stiffen.

"He told me Stuart was dead." Those few words held a universe of anguish.

"Well, whoever told you that got it wrong. Stuart isn't dead. He's got some bruises and cuts and a cracked rib, but he's sure not dead." At least he wasn't when I left the house.

Caleb made a small noise, almost a sob.

"Who told you he was?"

"The same guy who hijacked me at the airport. He didn't bother to introduce himself."

"How did you get here?"

"It took awhile, but I managed to get away from the guy. I came here looking for you. I didn't expect to find out that ornery kid of mine was still alive. Can you take me to him?"

"Yes. No. He's at Gram's house, or he was, but I can't go there. The police will be looking for me. Maybe you could go, though."

He gripped my arms. "Calm down a minute. You're running from the police? Why?"

"Somebody buried a body in Gram's back yard. Heather called the police. When I heard the sirens, I ran, hoping they would come after me instead of going in and finding Stuart."

"Whew. You lead a quiet life around here, don't you?"

"I used to. The problem is, we don't know who's involved in this mess. Danny's the only one who might have any idea which cops are okay and which aren't."

"Then maybe I'd better not get too close to them, either. Why did you come here?"

"I wanted the phone to tell Danny about the body and find out what I needed to do next."

"You need to carry a cell phone."

"That's what Danny says. Looks like both of you are right."

"Danny's a good guy, is he?"

"The best."

"Heather's not. I already know about Heather. This apartment's not the safest place for either of us. It won't take folks long to figure out I might have come here, and the police, if they're worth their salary, ought to check this place for you first thing."

"Do I have time to change shoes?"

"If you hurry. I'll keep a look-out in the kitchen."

It took me about two minutes. Caleb was waiting by the door when I finished. "Don't you have a coat?" I asked, as I pulled on my dryer, warmer one.

"Sure. Somewhere in Fraser House."

"You're sure you were in Fraser House?"

"Couldn't mistake it."

I had accepted the fact that the Frasers were involved some way. I still didn't know which ones. "I'm sorry I don't have a coat or anything you can use."

"Don't worry about that. This weather's mild compared to what I'm used to, wetter, but not nearly as cold. Besides, my sweater's wool. That'll keep some warmth even when it's wet. You don't happen to have a pistol around, do you?"

No, but I'm beginning to think I'd better invest in one and learn to use it."

"Even if you never need it for defense, you should learn to use one. Target practice is fun. Come on up to the ranch, and I'll teach you myself."

"I'll take you up on that. If we survive this."

"Have to believe we will, otherwise why bother trying?"

"Okay, then, what are we going to do? The police will probably be at Gram's house for hours."

"Let's discuss our destination after we get out of here. I don't like the idea of using your front stairs again, though. Too exposed. Is there any other way out of here?"

"I've got a couple of back windows, but if you can pick a lock, there's an easier way."

"Never did have too much trouble with locks."

The one on the door in the corner of my living room didn't give him any problem, either.

Chapter 18

Caleb and I stood for a moment looking out of Mrs. Jamison's back window. The rain was still coming down, not hard, but like it meant to go on in the same way for the next million years. "I guess it's too much to hope that you've got a car available?" he said.

"My car's parked at Gram's. No gun, no cell phone, no car. I'm a disaster as a rescuer."

He chuckled. "Is there anybody in this town you'd trust absolutely?"

"There are several people, but I don't want to involve them in something that might be dangerous."

"I can understand that. How about cops? Isn't there at least one you can be totally sure of?"

"None that I know how to get in touch with. Even Danny's out of town, but if I can get to a phone that works, I have a number that should reach him. If it doesn't, well, he's always raving about our State Troopers."

"I've heard some mighty good things about your troopers, myself. The only one I ever met personally was impressive. His friends call him Wolf. Calm, cool, about seven feet tall, and I wish he was here."

"Me, too."

"Look, Constancy, I want to get you to a safe place if you can think of one. Like you said, it might be dangerous and the longer we're out, the more dangerous it gets. If we do get into trouble on the way and you get a chance, any chance, you run like both our lives depended on it, because they just might."

"I couldn't run off and leave you by yourself."

"Okay. You want me to run for help while you fight off bad guys?"

"Well, if you put it that way, no."

"I'm putting it that way. I don't doubt your courage, kid. I just figure I'm better trained for the defense business than you are. I could be wrong. Tell me you've got a black belt in something and I'll eat my words."

I had to laugh. "You're not wrong. I'll do the running. If I'm lucky, I won't trip over my own feet, but where will I run to?"

"Any place with lights and people and a phone. Then call your Troopers and tell them they've got a brother fighting for his life. They may not get to me in time, but they'll give it everything they've got trying."

"You're scaring me."

"That's the worst case scenario, as they say. It won't happen, but we have to be prepared, anyway."

I thought it was very likely it would happen. He probably did, too, even if he was considerate enough not to say so.

"Okay. We've got to move. We can't stay in here the rest of the night."

"Why don't we go straight to somewhere with lights and people and call Danny and the Troopers right now?"

"That's what I want you to do, but you'll have to tell me where. I'll make sure you get there safely. Then, I'd kind of like to get back to Fraser House."

"Fraser House! Caleb, are you crazy?"

"Probably, but I sure would like to get my hands on my coat and my gun, not necessarily in that order. If some of them get a-hold of Stuart, they'll probably put him where they had me. They'll know I'm gone by now and they'll probably be out looking for me, so it ought to be fairly safe. They wouldn't expect me to go back there, and I know a way or two in that doesn't involve ringing the front door bell. So, where's the best place to go?"

"I don't know. Most of the businesses are closed now, except maybe for a couple of service stations or convenience stores. They're quite a distance from here. There's a phone outside the post office."

"We'd better start walking."

We stepped out into the raw, damp night. Maybe my ears were more attuned to the sound. "Caleb, listen."

"Sounds like a kid crying. Keep behind me."

As if I didn't know.

He edged around one corner of the house, then another. "On the porch swing," he whispered.

I peeked around him. A tiny shape on the swing was crying as if his heart would break. I recognized him instantly. "Brandon, what on earth?"

"Constancy, wait!"

I pushed past Caleb and headed for the swing. "Brandon. "

"Miss Constancy!" He gave a big gulp and launched himself into my arms. If it hadn't been for my uncle standing behind me, I would've toppled right over. The little boy was shaking so hard his teeth chattered. I held him close.

"Brandon, sweetheart, what are you doing here?"

"I can't find my house."

"Where were you? Where are your parents?"

"I don't know. They left me with Sally. She was having a party and I didn't like it. I tried to go home. When I saw your swing, I thought you or Officer Danny would help me, but it was d-d-dark up there." He was sobbing again.

"I'm here now, Brandon. I'm here now."

"Okay, Constancy," Caleb said, "Danger or not, you're going to have to call on a friend. We've got to get this kid somewhere warm and safe where his parents can find him. Where?"

I didn't have to think twice. "Irma West."

"Amanda's best friend? I didn't know she was still alive."

"She's living in an apartment in the retirement home. Lots of lights and people and a phone in every room. She knows Brandon's folks and it's not very far from here."

"Let's go, then. I'll take the kid."

But Brandon didn't want to be passed off to somebody he didn't know. "I can carry him for awhile," I said. "Walk. I'll try to explain."

We walked. "Brandon, this man is my Uncle Caleb. He's a policeman like Officer Danny. He's very nice and I'm very tired. Would you let him carry you? We'll go see Miss Irma and you can stay with her until your parents get home. Okay?"

"C-cookies."

"Cookies, definitely, and some warm milk."

"All right." He went meekly to Caleb, who grinned at me.

"I could do with some of those famous cookies, myself," he said. "I've heard stories about them that made my mouth water."

"Don't worry, there'll be plenty."

Irma took in the three of us without blinking an eye. "Looks like it's about time you got in out of the rain. What are you doing out in this, anyway? Is that Brandon?"

"Yes, and he'd like some cookies and milk, please, if it's no trouble."

"You know it's no trouble. I expect you big kids would be just as happy to have some. I'll make you some coffee to go with yours, though."

She led us into the kitchen, then peered up at Caleb. "Do I know you, young man?"

"No reason you should, ma'am. This is my first visit to Fraserton."

"Miss Irma, this is George Fraser's son, Caleb."

She gave him a long, hard look. So did I. It was my first chance to get a good look at my new-found uncle. He was the tallest Fraser I'd met yet. Tall and lanky. I had no trouble imagining him at work on a ranch.

His hair was probably more blond than Stuart's, although dripping wet as it was, it looked darker. I couldn't see many Fraser features in his face, except for his nose. He must be much more like his mother's side of the family.

"Well, well," Irma said. "That's why you look familiar. I'm pleased to meet you, Caleb Fraser. I can see George in you. You don't have his face, but you walk like he did and you have his kindness in your eyes. George was the best man the Fraser family ever produced, bar none. If he's still alive, you can tell him I said so."

"He is and I will."

"Glad to hear it. Now, let me get you some towels to dry off a little."

"Miss Irma, I need your phone before anything else. I have to get hold of Danny."

"Looks like that might be a good idea. Use the one in the bedroom. You know where it is."

The tones of the numbers I punched in seemed as loud as cathedral bells, the ringing at the other end ear piercing. It took forever before someone answered. The voice, when it came, sounded tight and angry. "Dunne College."

Was Danny taking a class or teaching one? "Danny Egan,

please. I'm sorry if you have to disturb him, but this is an emergency."

"You're too late," the woman said.

"T-too late? What do you mean?"

"I suppose it'll be common knowledge tomorrow. The Fraserton police had a warrant for his arrest. They took him right out of class."

I hung up gently.

I suppose the news showed on my face. Miss Irma, who kept a stash of child-sized clothes for the occasional visit from her great-grandchildren, was putting a dry shirt on Brandon. Caleb, mouth full of cookie, looked up at me and frowned.

"They arrested Danny," I said.

"Who did?"

"Fraserton police."

Irma threw Brandon's wet clothes in the dryer and slammed the door. "Well, of all the stupid tricks. I'll bet it was that Lonnie Tirso. He just takes the cake."

"My turn on the phone," Caleb said, grimly.

"I'll show you were it is. Get you a cup of that coffee, Constancy." Irma stalked out of the kitchen with him.

"What did Officer Danny do wrong?" Brandon asked.

I poured a cup of coffee and grabbed a cookie. "Absolutely nothing, sweetheart. Officer Danny is a wonderful man and he wouldn't do anything wrong on purpose."

"Then why did they arrest him?"

"Somebody's made a mistake, that's all. We'll get it straightened out. Will you stay here with Miss Irma until your folks can come for you?"

He nodded. "Miss Irma's nice."

"Yes, she is. She'll take good care of you."

A little grin that highlighted dimples in both cheeks. "With cookies."

"Exactly. Brandon, please don't ever run away again."

"I won't, Miss Constancy, I sure won't."

Caleb and Irma reappeared. "I'm going to head out now," he said.

"You take this coat." Irma handed it to him. "It was Mr. West's and I never could stand to get rid of it. Thought it might come in handy and sure enough it has."

"Miss Irma, you're a treasure. Dad'll be thrilled to know you're still baking cookies."

"I'll send some back with you."

"I'll take them. Nice to meet both of you."

"I'll walk out with you," I said.

The wind was whistling through the trees, blowing sodden leaves off the limbs and into our faces. "What couldn't you say in front of Miss Irma?" he asked.

"Not her so much as Brandon. Please be careful."

"It's part of the job."

"Caleb!"

Too late.

The man who seemed to have materialized behind him hit him hard. Caleb fell to his knees, not unconscious, but stunned.

"Howdy, cowboy. Howdy, Constancy." Bryce, of course. Something glinted in his hand and he hit Caleb again.

Only then did I remember I was supposed to run. I tried. Heather, who had stepped out behind us, merely stuck out her umbrella about shin height. When I looked up at her from the wet, wet sidewalk, she had a gun pointed at me.

"Well, well," Bryce said. "It's a nasty evening to be out for a walk. I think it'd be a real kindness to get you in out of the rain."

The fact that Bryce was a part of this didn't surprise me. The Frasers would be well above soiling their own hands with illegal activities. They did, however, have plenty of money to pay people who didn't suffer such scruples. It also explained who put the body in the flower bed. "You ought to stick to gardening," I said.

"Doesn't pay nearly enough, but it does have its moments. How'd you like the way I fertilized your flower bed?"

He stepped closer to Caleb and kicked him hard, just under the rib cage, for no reason that I could see. Caleb gasped at the blow, but he didn't cry out. Bryce looked disappointed.

"Leave him alone," I said. "You didn't need to do that."

"It could have been you, and may yet. Nobody makes me look stupid without paying for it. Your friend still has some paying to do."

"What do you want?"

"You've been invited to a party and they don't want you backing out of it. Heather, get the car."

Heather did so cheerfully.

"Now," Bryce said, "You both get in the back seat. Don't try anything stupid. Constancy, looks like you're going to have to help the old cowboy."

I didn't want to help Bryce do anything, but taking more abuse from him didn't seem like a wise idea, either. There was nobody else on the street. Nobody. Where were all those Fraserton eyes that saw everything they shouldn't see? Why couldn't they be watching when it would be helpful?

It wasn't easy getting Caleb into the car. He was groggy with the pain, not breathing well.

Bryce smiled when we finally accomplished it. "Very good. Now you get in."

Heather drove, Bryce kept the gun pointed at us. We went, of course, straight to Fraser House.

Bryce and Heather, too, knew ways in that didn't require ringing the front door bell. Heather led the way to a half-concealed door in the back. It opened on a narrow, dank, dimly lit flight of stairs.

"Down there," Bryce said.

After showing us the stairs, Heather vanished.

Caleb leaned heavily against me, his whole body trembling with the effort of walking. His nose and left cheek were already purple and swelling. One thin stream of blood trickled from his nose, another from an open cut just under his eye. We would be lucky if we didn't both tumble down the narrow staircase.

"You ought to be ashamed of yourself," I told Bryce when we reached the bottom. "At least go get some ice to put on Caleb's bruises."

I hated Bryce's laugh. "In a few minutes neither one of you will care," he said. "Keep going."

Eventually, we made it to his destination. It seemed to be the dumping place for old furniture the Frasers were tired of.

"Over there on that couch," Bryce said. I helped Caleb to the dusty couch and sat gingerly beside him.

Bryce put his gun on top of a little table by the door, tore the wrapper off a hypodermic syringe he'd pulled from his pocket and began to fill it from a nasty looking brown vial.

"What's that?"

"Let's say it's a sedative for that pain you were so worried about. In a few minutes, Caleb won't feel a thing."

"Are you going to kill him?"

"Not yet. Not with this. It'd be too easy."

Caleb sat very still, eyes half-closed, breathing harshly through his mouth. Bryce must have broken his nose and maybe several other bones. I had no idea what kind of internal injuries he might have. He needed medical help badly, but I had no clue how to help him or how to get out of this mess. There was no way the police would come looking for us here. Too bad. Even Tirso, rotten as he was, would be an improvement on Bryce.

"Just to ease your mind, I'll give Caleb his fix first," Bryce said. "But I'm warning you. You give me any trouble and you'll need it as bad as he does before you get yours."

The gun was much too far away. I couldn't possibly get past

Bryce and reach it. I wouldn't know how to use it if I could. What did it matter? I couldn't get past Bryce anyway.

He must have seen my glance at the gun, though. "Don't even try," he said. "Push up his sleeve."

"I'm not going to help you do anything else."

Bryce's violent back-handed response banged my skull into the couch. Had it not been well-padded, I think my neck would have snapped. As it was, I wasn't too sure my jaw hadn't.

Caleb had seen it coming and tried hard to intervene, but all it got him was more pain of his own.

Amazing how easy it was becoming to scream. "Stop it! Leave him alone! He can't hurt you now."

"But I can sure hurt him, and you. Now, push up that sleeve."

Caleb groaned. "Do it."

Feeling hopelessly outclassed and muttering apologies to Caleb through tears of pain and pure frustration, I pushed up his sleeve.

Bryce bent over him, needle in hand. I looked away.

This wasn't the way things were supposed to work. In a proper world somebody, preferably Danny, would burst through the door this very minute to rescue us, and evil Bryce would be quickly dispatched to some super-secure cell with no possibility of parole. In an ideal world, Caleb and I wouldn't be in this predicament in the first place, and Bryce wouldn't even exist.

Caleb sighed as the needle bit into his arm, almost as if he welcomed the coming oblivion. I wouldn't blame him if he did.

Bryce refilled the thing and it was my turn. He didn't bother being gentle.

Caleb tried to smile at me. "No communicable diseases," he said. "Sorry to get you into this."

"It's not your fault," I told him, then looked at Bryce.

Things were already beginning to get a little blurry. "Why did you put that dead man in my kitchen before you buried him?"

"It was supposed to be a favor for a friend of mine."

What friend? Zared?

Chapter 19

I woke to the silent scream of cramped muscles and the not-so-quiet complaint of an empty stomach. I was afraid to open my eyes. *Caleb?*

My voice didn't seem to be able to escape the pounding prison of my head, but my memory was working too well. Given the choice just then, I would rather have been without the memories than the voice. I tried again. "Caleb?"

"Right here, sweetheart."

Relief nearly swamped me. He was still with me and he was still alive.

"How are you feeling?" he asked.

"Awful. How about you?"

"Not bad, considering."

That had to be a lie. "Do you think if I open my eyes, my head will explode?"

"Mine didn't. Just take it slow." He sounded like he was trying to talk without moving his mouth. Or maybe he couldn't move it.

Did I really want to open my eyes? The air was dank and chilly, the bed cold and hard as rock. There was an annoying drip of water echoing in the distance. While we were unconscious, we had been moved. Judging by the way I felt, we hadn't been moved gently. Caleb had to be feeling worse than I did. He had certainly suffered more damage.

I pried my eyes open one at a time and found that our bed was rock, or at least concrete. There were a couple of thin, smelly blankets between us and the damp floor. Why couldn't they have left us on that dusty couch?

The only light came from a high window on a wall opposite. It wasn't strong light, but it hurt. Gradually, I could focus on Caleb's face, bloody and battered and swollen next to mine. As soon as I did, I wished I hadn't.

"Looks pretty bad, huh?" He sounded almost proud of it.

"You might get a part as a corpse in a gory horror movie."

"Don't make me laugh."

"I'm trying to keep myself from crying. It may not work. I hope you don't feel as bad as you look." Stupid thing to say. Nobody could look like that without feeling more awful than I wanted to try to imagine.

"I've felt better," he said. "I've also felt worse."

"When did you ever feel worse?"

"When I got trampled by stampeding buffalo a few years ago."

"Oh."

"Probably looked worse, too."

"I hope not. Any idea where we are?"

"Back where I started, more or less. It would be a good set for that horror movie you were talking about, wouldn't it?"

"Where are we?"

"Not far from where they brought us in last night. We're still in the Fraser House cellars, but this part looks considerably more secure than the first I was in. Can you move?"

"I don't know." It took a minute to figure out just where the outer perimeters of my body were. My arms and legs were so numb I couldn't feel them. "My hands are asleep, but I think they're tied in place. My feet, too." I wriggled until I felt the blood coming back into my fingers. "I hate pins and needles."

"Especially needles."

"Especially needles." Re-establishing circulation didn't re-establish freedom. "Bryce did a good job on these knots. How about yours?"

"I can't even stir up pins. Do you know this Bryce guy?"

"Only his first name and the fact that he sometimes works as a gardener. Caleb, if we're in Fraser House, Bryce must be working for one of them. Have you seen anybody else?"

"Bryce isn't one of Bart's clan?"

"As far as I know, Bart only had three grandsons and they all look like Lucian."

"I haven't seen anybody but Bryce and that girl, Heather. I thought you were her when you came sneaking into your apartment."

"Thanks a bunch."

"Well, I wish it had been her and you were out of this."

"Hey, then I wouldn't get credit for finding you."

He gave me a wry look.

"I guess finding you hasn't helped much, has it?"

"Not yet. Except it eases my burden to know that stubborn son of mine is still among the living."

"Stuart told me stubbornness runs in the family."

"Yeah? Well, he could be right."

"Have you ever been to Fraser House before?"

"Not in person, but Dad used to tell us stories about the place until I felt like I'd spent half my childhood here. He wasn't bitter about it. He loved this place and he wanted us to know all about it as a part of our heritage. I think talking about it eased his homesickness a little. Anyway, thanks to him I feel like I know every square inch of Fraser House, including these cellars. That knowledge is what got me out the first time. That, plus the fact that Bryce was a little late getting there with my next injection."

"They've been keeping you drugged?"

"Sound asleep most of the time. I'm less noisy that way. I haven't actually seen any Frasers, but one or more of them is definitely behind it."

"How did they get you in the first place?"

"I'll tell you, Constancy, I've made about every mistake in the book since I've been here. If I ever thought much of myself as a cop before, I sure don't now. Bryce picked me up at the airport in a limo. He was the perfect chauffeur. Polite, deferential, very correct. It had been a long flight and I was hungry. That limo was fully equipped. There was liquor, which didn't tempt me, and tomato juice and snacks which did."

"I'm acquainted with their tomato juice recipe. Very relaxing."

"Very. I should have known better, but you don't expect your relatives to be a bunch of criminals, even if you know their grandpa was. I just should have been more careful. Next thing I knew I was an inmate of the cellar. The message, brought to me by lovely Heather, was that I was going to be the Frasers' honored guest until the day after the provision on Lucian's will expired. After that, they would let me go."

"Why keep you drugged?"

"I'm claustrophobic and noisy when I know I'm locked in. Bryce prefers me quiet."

"Are you okay now?"

"It helps to have company." He sighed. "I wanted the family to know where I was, but I didn't want them involved in this. I told Heather if she didn't let me call home, Gwyn would be sending search parties. I wasn't thinking very well. If my brain hadn't been running on only about half its cylinders, I could have got help without alerting these guys. I thought I'd done a good job of convincing Gwyn nothing unusual was going on here. Why on earth did Stuart come after me?"

"Your story was fine, your consonants weren't. You slurred, and you talked too slow."

"Trust Gwyn to pick up on that. That woman knows too much for everybody's health."

"And Stuart wasn't going to sit back and let somebody mistreat his dad."

"Stubborn kid," he repeated fondly.

"Caleb, do you believe they were going to release you?"

"I don't see how they could. As soon as I'm out of here, I can hit them with all kinds of charges."

"It'd be your word against theirs, but who'd believe you? You're the disgruntled son of a man who missed out on his inheritance. They're THE Frasers. They're fine, upstanding citizens without a blot on their record. They'd have some good explanation for your injuries. Maybe you were trying to break into the collection and had a fight with a guard. They'd have plenty of witnesses, too. Your trying to accuse the Frasers of kidnapping might even convince some folks that George was the black sheep they said he was. They could let you go. Then they could get you arrested for trying to steal diamonds."

"Constancy, you have an evil mind."

"I'm part Fraser. No offense. Caleb, what are we going to do?"

"Wait." He sounded more resigned to that idea than I felt. "We can try to wriggle out of these ropes, but mostly we wait. Are your fingers alive now?"

"Yes."

"Mine are still numb. If we turn back to back, you might be able to work on the knots around my wrists."

"It's worth a try."

Bryce hadn't tied his ropes with our convenience in mind. Our positions were such that Caleb had to roll over onto his injured right side and he couldn't stay that way for long at a time. My stiff fingers could barely catch hold of the knots that held his arms so tightly, let alone untie them. I had made no headway at all when he groaned and sighed. "It's no use, Constancy."

"Rest awhile. We can't give up. Danny and Stuart were going to try to rescue you tonight. Now we may have to rescue them."

"You're right. Okay, kid. We'll try again."

So we did. Over and over. Caleb gritted his teeth against the pain in his side. I kept clawing at the knots until my nails were shredded and my fingers raw. Yes! It wasn't my imagination. "Caleb! It moved. The rope moved."

"Good girl! Keep at it."

Bryce, his timing impeccable, chose that minute to return.

He smiled. "Working hard, I see. Don't bother, *Miss* Constancy. I'll untie your ropes, myself. You and I are taking a little walk. You've been summoned into the royal presence."

"What about Caleb?"

"What about him? He stays here. For awhile. You're not planning to give me any trouble, are you?"

"No," Caleb said. "She's not."

Bryce looked at us approvingly. "Somebody's learning. Now, I'm going to untie your feet and you're going to walk out of here." He didn't untie the ropes. He sliced through them with one slash of a small, shiny knife. The sharp edge of the blade scraped my ankle. A thin red line appeared, but I felt nothing. He left my hands tied.

"Where are we going?"

"You'll see when we get there. Remember, no trouble. Any wrong move and Caleb gets his brains splattered on the far wall. I'm tired of messing with you two. I'd get rid of you both right now, except they want you awhile longer, Constancy. All right. Stand up."

"I can't."

He swung the gun toward Caleb.

"No! Listen to me! I can't. I physically can't. You've cut off the circulation with those ropes. It's going to take some time."

He jerked me up off the blankets by one arm and I promptly collapsed at his feet. His comment wasn't civil, but at least he didn't shoot Caleb or hit either of us again.

"The feeling's coming back now. Give me a couple more minutes."

"One more."

I was thankful that was all it took. The pins and needles were in full force, but I could stand up and even walk after the first few stumbling steps. As Bryce closed the door between us, I glanced back at Caleb. He tried to smile.

The door had been fitted with two modern, business-like bolts, but as Bryce was reaching toward them, he paused. "You know, they probably don't need him any more."

He reopened the door a crack, pointed his gun back into the room and fired. Then he calmly closed and bolted the door, all the while smiling.

I didn't see into the room. Didn't have to. Not seeing didn't erase the knowledge, didn't clear the choking stench of gun powder from the corridor or the ringing from my ears. This was nightmare of the worst kind. Too vivid. Too loud. Too, too real. Worst of all, I knew I wasn't going to wake up from it. Not ever.

"You killed him."

Bryce smiled. "Maybe. Or maybe he's lying there in agony bleeding to death. You may never know." He shoved me forward.

I tried hard to watch how we went, to concentrate on the twists and turns so that I could find that room again. So I could lead someone there to what was left of Caleb when, if, I ever had opportunity. But my sense of direction isn't terrific at the best of times and Fraser House is a first-class maze. It's also hard to see when the tears won't stop. What did it matter? Caleb was dead. I probably soon would be. Fraserton's police force was in league with murderers. Stuart was probably locked up or dead, and Danny, poor, sick Danny was worrying himself to death in some awful cell.

Oh, Father of Lights, please help Danny. Help us all.

Bryce and I turned and turned again, climbed stairs, went through long passageways, more turns, more stairs, another door. The last door led into a brighter part of the house. A piercing ray of sun through a window temporarily blinded me. Light in the midst of darkness?

Bryce caught my arm again and pulled me along. He was creating a nice crop of bruises on that arm. They would, no doubt, beautifully match the one from yesterday that I could feel throbbing on the side of my face. But that glimpse of the sun, painful as it was, burned a small opening through the hopelessness. Reminding and reassuring me. I wasn't alone. I still had light, physical and spiritual.

Bryce hauled me down another corridor, knocked at a door, then opened it. "Get in there."

With a little unnecessary help, I tumbled right in, and bumped my head on somebody's foot. Nona. She was seated like a queen in an ornate, gilded chair that could have been a throne if it had tried only a little harder. The royal presence? She reached down and helped me up, looking neither surprised nor alarmed.

"Nona, w-what's going on?"

She didn't answer directly. "Bryce," she said, "untie the girl. What are you thinking?"

Bryce, to my amazement, did as he was told. He was even a bit more careful with the knife than he had been in the cellar.

"Wait outside now."

Again, he obeyed instantly.

"Nona, what's happening?"

She touched my face very gently with an icy hand. "He hit you?"

I clutched at her arm. "Nona, he's done worse than that. He just killed a man downstairs. We have to call the police! Not the Fraserton Police. We'll call the State Troopers."

She pulled her arm away from me with a look of distaste hovering around her mouth. "He shouldn't have hit you," she said. Had she even heard what I'd told her?

"Listen to me! Bryce shot a man. It wasn't an accident or self-defense. It was cold, calculated murder. We have to do something!"

"Not until after the party, darling."

"What?"

"I'm sure you'll look absolutely beautiful tonight, but I could kill him for marking your face. It'll show in the photos. I'm sorry we couldn't get your own gown over for you, but the violet one should fit. If it doesn't, there are a few others in the closet. You'll find something that will do." She gestured toward a leather case on the table next to her chair. "I've taken a couple of the diamond sets out of the vault for you to try with them."

Maybe it was the only way she could survive, by retreating into her own little world of fashion and parties and diamonds.

I didn't argue. I turned my back on her and limped toward the telephone I saw in the corner.

"Don't bother, my dear," she said. "That phone won't get you outside Fraser House."

"Then show me one that will."

"Later. You have to get dressed now. There's not much time."

"Nona," I said gently. "How can I make you understand?"

"I understand perfectly. You're the one who's confused." She went and opened the door. "Bryce, darling, escort Constancy to the second guest room and see that she gets changed. Let's give her thirty minutes. No—forty-five. She'll need a bath. Her hair's filthy. If she won't cooperate in that time, you go in and help her."

Bryce grinned that slimy grin. "I'll look forward to it."

Nona was right. I was the one who hadn't been seeing reality. Nona was controlling Bryce. Was it Nona who had come up with this whole crazy plot? Did she think I would calmly attend her party as if nothing had happened, as if Caleb weren't lying dead in that cold, damp cellar beneath us?

"We've changed things around," she said. "Instead of announcing your engagement tonight, we're going to announce your marriage."

"What marriage?"

"That's why we have to hurry," she explained patiently. "First the wedding, then the party."

"I want to see Zared." Surely he wouldn't go along with this insanity.

"You will see him. As soon as you're dressed. He'll want you looking your best, so don't disappoint him." She shuddered delicately. "He gets so angry when he's disappointed. You've never seen him really angry."

The way she said it sent an extra sliver of ice skidding along my nerves. His mother was right. I'd never seen him really angry. Surely Zared, the hard-headed business man, the gentlemanly sender of roses, wasn't as mad with greed as his grandfather Bartholomew had been. Was he?

How could I say for sure? Nona had known him all his life. I didn't know him at all.

Chapter 20

I slammed the bedroom door in Bryce's leering face. Locking it probably wouldn't be much use, but it made me feel a little less than totally helpless. Then I looked around the room. Did I really want to be locked into it? The place was like a museum. Dark, massive furniture; oppressive, embossed wall paper; heavy velvet draperies hiding the windows. It was filled to overflowing with a smothering collection of depressing Victorian clutter, ragged Egyptian fans, dusty peacock feathers, tall dried grasses in a vase.

A glass-fronted box held scruffy, long-dead squirrels mounted in a library tableau. Three of them were seated in tiny wooden chairs around a little oak table. One of the squirrels had a Sherlock Holmes pipe in his mouth. Macabre.

Low wattage lamps, designed to look like early twentieth century gaslight, burned in several places around the room. They made the dark corners of the room even darker. Funereal. That was the word.

I pulled back a curtain. The windows were barred, but at least they let in a little natural light. It looked like late afternoon.

Friday, it would be, if this was the day of the party. How could they think I would go through with this?

In the bathroom, the gigantic claw-footed tub with gold-plated taps provided plenty of hot water. If I couldn't get out, at least I could get warm and clean. The water stung my various abrasions, but the heat eased some of the stiffness and aching out of my muscles. It felt good to get rid of the accumulated filth. If only I could get rid of the scum outside the door as easily, and the rest of the filth that was living in Fraser House. Maybe, if I survived this, I would file a claim on the property just to evict Nona and whoever else was involved, even if it included Zared.

Zared must be crazy if he were involved in this. How legal was a forced marriage? Surely it would never stand up in court.

But if the bride were dead shortly thereafter, who would know the ceremony was conducted over the barrel of a gun?

Was that why Zared had never mentioned life after the wedding? Because he wasn't planning marriage. Only a wedding ceremony.

And then a quick funeral.

How would they do it? Car accident? Too public. A fall down a steep staircase might work, maybe into a cellar where the body wouldn't be found for a day or two. Too complicated and they wouldn't want the smell. Most likely it would be a simple drug overdose. I could imagine Romney spouting off self-righteously about how he'd suspected me of addiction even before the wedding.

However it happened, I would probably be found with Caleb, the gun that had killed him in my dead hand. That would solve everybody's problems. Except mine and Caleb's.

So much for faith in locked doors. When I came out of the bathroom, a maid was waiting by the dressing table. She looked like a nanny stereotype left over from a Victorian novel. She was exactly right for the room, the type who would no doubt adore those squirrels.

"Who are you?"

"I'm here to help you dress."

"The people in this house are murderers. Did you know that?"

"Yes, my dear. I'm sure you're right."

They had already convinced her I was crazy. She was soothing, almost hypnotic, as if she dealt with mental patients all the time. Maybe she did.

"Come on, now," she said. "Let's find you a lovely gown and I'll help you with your hair and make-up. You'll be a beautiful bride. Everything will be all right then."

"If they told you I'm crazy, they're lying. Look at these bruises. The same man who bruised me killed my uncle downstairs."

"Mrs. Fraser told me you'd had an accident. Would you like a little pill to help you relax?"

Obey with a clear mind. Or without. "No. No pills."

One good thing came of this. If I needed any further proof of the existence of the being Danny called Satan and the hell that was made for him, I had the proof now. I saw the arrogant obscenity of his evil smirking in Bryce's eyes as the man beat and then murdered my Uncle Caleb. I saw it in the soul-consuming greed of Nona when she crooned on about her precious diamonds. If that destroying, sick darkness existed, how much more so the Light that kept it from completely overwhelming all of us?

Because, I was pleased to discover, I wasn't overwhelmed yet. I still had ways to fight and the determination to do it. I seemed to be the only player left to combat this particular nest of evil. If I had to, I would do it alone; but if prayer were the force Christians claimed, strength and help would come as I needed it. I could almost hear Danny's assurance. The Light does not forsake those who are His, or, I dared believe, those who want to be His.

"Here's your dress, now."

That awful purple dress. Why argue? I needed to save my strength for the real showdown. I put it on. It was too short, too tight, too low cut, but it did show all the lovely purple bruises to good advantage. Skin and dress were color coordinated. Nice touch.

"Ten minutes," Bryce said, rattling the doorknob.

"Almost ready," the maid called to him. "Let me do your hair now. Sit here. Such pretty hair."

I sat at the mirror and looked at my face while she braided my hair into some kind of chignon and fastened it with a diamond clasp. The face that stared back at me was pale and more badly bruised than I'd expected. The mark extended up my jaw to my temple. Even my eyes were black. I looked like a warmed-over zombie. Mine wouldn't be a beautiful face even without the bruise. No amount of make-up could fix that. But it was a determined face, a calm face. A face that looked almost peaceful. They would want me frightened. Well, I refused to be frightened. That showed, too. My face would do fine.

The maid, or whatever she was, clucked over the bruises, and covered them as best she could. I suppose Nona had told her they were a result of the "accident" that had also rattled my brain. Whatever she'd been told, I was sure, would be perfect background for the morning they found me dead.

Finally, the woman clasped an ornate collar of emerald-cut amethyst colored diamonds around my throat. "There," she said. "Beautiful." She was talking about the diamonds.

Bryce was less impressed. "You look like a corpse," he said, as I walked out of the room.

"Just practicing. Don't worry. I'm sure they won't bury me until they take off my diamond decorations." I swept past him and down the stairs, taking great care not to trip. Comic relief was all very well, but I didn't need that kind of an entrance.

Nona was waiting at the foot of the stairs. She, too, had changed into something more formal. She frowned. "Couldn't you do better than that?"

"Your beloved purple dress shows off the bruises very nicely, don't you think?"

She flashed a look of pure hatred at Bryce. "It'll have to do," she said. "Zared's waiting. Heather will be your maid of honor."

It must have made Heather's day when Nona ordered her to attend the wedding of the man she wanted for herself.

"Doesn't Zared have better sense than to get involved in this kind of stuff?" I asked Nona as she led me down another long corridor with Bryce trailing behind us. "He can't hope to get away with a fake wedding, and assault and kidnapping. And murder."

"He can get away with anything he likes. He always has. You don't know him very well yet, do you?"

"He made sure of that."

"Poor boy. He was worried about your great interest in that Egan man. Zared was afraid you would decide to call off the engagement because of it. We couldn't let that happen, could we?"

"Why kidnap Caleb? He told you they didn't want your house or your precious diamonds."

"Of course he'd say that, but who wouldn't want those beautiful, beautiful diamonds?"

"I'm beginning to think no sane person would."

"Hush, now. Zared's waiting." She swept me into a large, glittering room that looked like a miniature of the Hall of Mirrors in Versailles.

I glared at her son with all the scorn I could muster. For a moment, he almost fooled me, but the man standing with Heather was not Zared. His hair was combed like Zared's and he was smiling Zared's smile. He was also wearing Zared's clothes, but he was not Zared. I shot a quick glance at Heather. Whose idea was it to have Timon or Romney stand in for Zared? Surely Heather was smarter than that. She wanted Zared for herself, but even if Zared felt the same, did they honestly think they could fool his own mother?

Or was it Nona's idea in the first place? Maybe Zared wasn't behind all this. Maybe he had refused to take part in an instant wedding and the criminal activities, but if he had, why wasn't he stopping it?

I looked from Heather to Nona and back again. Heather seemed to have no idea that the Zared beside her was not authentic. She was giving me sullen you-stole-my-man glares and clutching his arm possessively. Nona either didn't know or didn't care. She was bubbly with excitement.

The twin disengaged Heather's arm and looked impatiently at his watch. "Hello, Constancy. I'm glad you don't mind rushing things."

Zared's voice and mannerisms, too. They must have given their poor teachers fits in school.

"Who says I don't mind? What do you think you're doing, arranging this farce of a wedding?"

"You agreed to marry me. What difference does it make when?"

"It makes a great deal of difference to me that I was drugged and beaten and brought here against my will. See all my beautiful bruises? It also makes a difference to me that there's a man lying dead in your cellar. He's your own cousin. What on earth makes you think I'll voluntarily marry into any family that uses criminal force to get what it wants?"

Nona was beginning to look dangerously angry.

"Calm down, Constancy." That from the twin, who didn't look at all calm himself.

"Why? Look at me. Look at my face and my arm and the knife cut on my ankle. Go look at what's left of Caleb. You're unspeakable, all of you."

I wanted to tell the twin what I thought of him personally, but something desperate in his eyes, as they held mine, stopped me. A warning, a plea. Pure, absolute terror.

"Mother," he said, "let me talk to Constancy a few minutes alone. I think I can convince her I love her enough to overcome any problems."

Nona pretended to go all misty-eyed. Who was the act for? Herself? "How sweet," she said. "You can talk in the library." Suddenly she laughed. "At least ours is in decent order. I should have ripped up a few more of Amanda's books when I went through hers."

"You tore up the books?"

"She used to read to the boys. I didn't like that. I waited a long time for that little bit of revenge, and enjoyed every moment of it." Nona smiled. "My only regret is that I had to wait until she was dead. Go and have your little talk."

The idea of Nona's murderous hands on Gram's precious books was enough to make me throw up, but, I remembered sadly, it had been a very long time since Miss Irma's cookies and coffee. There was nothing in my stomach to throw up. I was suddenly, ridiculously hungry, and mad, and ashamed of the way I'd misjudged my mother. Maybe, if I'd misjudged her on this, I might be wrong about other things. Maybe, if by some miracle, I did live through this, Mr. Vanek could arrange a meeting between us after all. My mother and I might have dinner together. A large and succulent dinner.

The twin put his arm around me and pulled me out to what passed as a library. It, like the rest of the house, was decorated in deep gloom and Victorian clutter. The leather-bound sets of books had probably never been touched, except maybe by George or Amanda. It was a dead room, stuffy and sad and depressing.

I turned to the twin. "I'm not going through with this," I whispered. "I know you're not Zared and I'm not marrying you, or him. Do you know what your mother's up to?"

"Some of it." He was holding me close because his mother was watching from the hall. He turned me a bit and leaned closer so that she couldn't see either of our faces.

"Do you know George Fraser's son is lying dead in your cellars and that one of his grandsons was very nearly shot to death practically on my doorstep because of Nona's obsession?"

"I'm not surprised."

"Listen to me! Understand this: I saw Bryce fire the shot that killed Caleb. They've got Danny and maybe Caleb's son. You can't let this go on."

"What more can I do? I've tried to protect you."

"How?"

"Shhh. Haven't I been trying to keep you out of this since the first day? Those diamonds. They're the curse of the Frasers, and the Fraser in-laws. I knew she was crazy, literally crazy. Zared didn't know, until t-today. I'm not sure about Timon. He may have played along with her on a couple of things. I only stumbled onto it accidentally when I found she'd bought Mrs. Jamison's house under an assumed name. When I confronted her, she told me the whole thing. She was so proud of herself. She wanted to be sure you had no contact with George's family. Your apartment was bugged and periodically searched. She even bribed the mailman to tell her if you ever got a letter from South Dakota."

"Why didn't you tell me instead of acting like such an idiot? Why didn't you warn me?"

"Would you have listened? Wouldn't you have thought I was just trying to make life difficult for you and Zared?"

"I don't know." It was too late to know. "Where's Zared?"

I felt a shudder run through him. "Zared wouldn't co-operate with her when he found out what she wanted."

"Well, good for Zared."

"Hardly." There were beads of perspiration on Romney's upper lip, though his face looked pinched and cold.

"What do you mean?"

"I was in the room when they were arguing about it. So was Bryce. When Zared refused to go along with it, Bryce hit him just once across the face. He dropped like a rock. I think—" Romney swallowed as if his throat hurt him. "Constancy, I think Zared's neck was broken."

Chapter 21

My hand went involuntarily to my bruised face. I didn't love Zared. I had never loved Zared. I never would, but he hadn't deserved that. "What about your mother?"

"My mother is the one who gave the order. When Zared fell, she didn't even look in his direction. She just turned to me and smiled and said, 'You've been promoted.' How can I be shocked by anything else? When she said I was to take Zared's place, I did it. Please don't tell her you know I'm not Zared. Even Heather doesn't know."

I shivered. "Does she think she can keep Zared's death a secret?"

"She's not going to bury Zared. She's going to bury Romney. I told you. She promoted me."

"How's she going to account for the death?"

"She'll find a way."

Crazy was too mild a word. "Rom, why didn't you go to the police a long time ago?"

"Wouldn't do any good. She has one or two of them in her pocket."

"Tirso?"

"Tirso's not above earning a little extra income. She owns a couple of commissioners and a judge, too. That's how she got your Danny out of the way tonight. He's lucky, and I don't intend to end up like the ones who weren't. I'll do exactly what she says. You'd better, too."

"Why make it easy for her? Help me fight her, Romney." I was clinging to him for real now, as he was to me.

"It's useless. She's obsessed."

"The minister's here," Nona called. "Come, children."

I would have no help from Romney, but I held close Danny's shining stars and the flash of sunlight I'd seen just as I needed it most. I pulled the engagement ring off my finger and dropped it into Romney's hand. "You'd better take this back to the collection. After today, I never want to see another member of Bartholomew's family. Or another diamond."

His lips were gray. "Listen to me, Constancy. If you don't do exactly what she says, there isn't going to be another day for you."

"There won't be, anyway. My will is worthless to her without a wedding. Once I'm married to Zared, any old Zared, I'll die. Then she gets Gram's diamonds, if they're ever found, and a claim to George's property." I smiled. "That's what she thinks. She's got one major part of it wrong, though."

"What do you mean?"

Nona came into the room. "Why did you take off your ring?"

"He can use it for a wedding ring." But not on me.

The glittering mirror room contained two entrances. Bryce stood where he had a clear shot at either of them. The gun was holstered, but it wouldn't take him half a second to retrieve it. A half second wasn't nearly enough time to escape.

Nona positioned the minister with his back to a great gilded fireplace. He was a plump, slick man with sculptured hair and a glittering diamond stick-pin. He'd probably never in his life practiced what he preached, if he preached at all. With a fake groom, why shouldn't Nona have a fake minister as well? Nobody was going to question a Fraser wedding.

"You stand there with Zared, Constancy. Heather, you and Bryce will be witnesses."

I glanced at the faces around me: Heather, dripping venom; the minister with his unctuous, unholy smile; Bryce looking bored, but watchful; Nona tense and excited. It was easy to read Romney's expression. He was convinced I was going to do something that would get us both killed.

The faux minister didn't waste much time getting to the will-you-take-this-man part of the ceremony. When he asked, I said no.

For a minute there was dead silence in the room. I thought he was going to faint. "You're supposed to say 'yes', or 'I do'. Something affirmative here, Constancy."

"But I don't. I won't. I'm not going to take this man as my husband. Not him, not anybody named Fraser. Not now, not ever. Is that clear enough to all of you? I said it before, I'll say it again: I was brought here against my will. Drugged and tied up and threatened with a gun, among other things. I watched Nona's pet murderer kill my uncle. I refuse absolutely to be a part of this degenerate, evil family."

Nona went white, then red. She was furious, breathing hard. "Bryce," she said harshly, "take her and convince her otherwise. Show her it's more pleasant if she obeys me. Do whatever you like, as long as she stays alive and conscious. Just don't bruise her face anymore."

Bryce smiled, happy to be of use.

"Mother, no."

Nona quelled her son's feeble protest with one glance.

Romney wouldn't meet my eyes. Heather was smiling, seeing

only that I didn't want to marry Zared and that I was going to suffer for it. I glared at that poor excuse for a minister. "Are you going to do anything to stop this?"

"It's not my problem."

"It will be. Do you believe in judgment day?"

He laughed.

"Nobody's going to help you now, Constancy," Nona said. "Bryce..."

Bryce advanced, but I was long past being scared of him. I turned, looked him in the eye, and said in my best kindergarten teacher, no-nonsense voice, "Stop right there. I'm not finished talking." To my surprise and delight, he stopped.

"Nona, it wouldn't do you any good at all, my marrying into your family. I went to Gram's lawyer and drew up a new will yesterday. When I die, nothing I own will go to any of the Fraser family."

Could a person explode from sheer fury? Nona looked like she was getting close. "I'm sure you think that's very clever."

"I think it was very necessary."

"When you signed that second will, you signed your death warrant, and several other people will die, too. Maybe all the rest of George's family. All because you're too selfish to give me what I want."

"You never needed my will. George doesn't want any of your precious possessions. His family doesn't. I don't. You've killed for no good reason. Caleb and Z-Zared. Your own son, Nona. Your first-born baby. Are you going to keep on killing for the sake of those horrid diamonds? Don't you have any humanity left?"

"I have to keep the diamonds," she said. "I will keep the diamonds, no matter what it takes."

She could see nothing but diamonds. No amount of logic or reason could reach her and I was out of ammunition. It was going to be up to Danny's forces of Light now and they were cutting it a little close.

"Bryce," Nona said, "she needs to change her mind about this latest will, too."

"Help," I whispered, as Bryce started toward me. "I really need that help now."

There was a flicker of movement in the mirrors. Neither Bryce nor Nona saw it soon enough. "Bryce, freeze. Nobody's leaving this room just yet."

The authoritative new voice was such a prompt and direct answer to my prayer that I almost expected to see some angel at the door. But if the woman standing there was an angel, she didn't look like any of the pictures I'd ever seen. There was no radiant, golden elegance. She was wiry and sun-browned, her auburn hair cut short and framing a cold, determined face. There were no white robes or shimmering wings. She wore rain-splattered jeans, a denim jacket and mud-caked running shoes.

The thing she held cradled so professionally in her arms was a far cry from the proverbial harp. It was also considerably more useful at the moment. The large, military-looking rifle made Bryce's 9mm pistol look like a toy, even to him.

She spoke to him again. "You, Bryce, you put your little gun on the floor in front of you and slide it toward me with your foot. Very carefully, very slowly. Constancy, move to your right so you'll be out of my line of fire if it comes to that.

Bryce had a look of deep respect on his face. Not for the woman, but for the weapon she wielded with such authority. He did exactly what she told him. So did I, my stomach doing little flip-flops of excitement. It worked. My prayers had been answered. *Oh, thank you, Father of Lights!*

"Now," the woman said. "All of you stand very still. We'll wait right here until backup comes along in a minute."

"But, lady," the minister whined, "you don't need me to stay, do you? I didn't know these people were criminals."

As he was speaking, I saw another movement in the mirrors, one the angel-warrior didn't see. From somewhere, Nona had pulled out a tiny gun of her own and was pointing it surreptitiously while my rescuer was being distracted by the minister. Even if I could have yelled a warning, it might have caused more problems than it solved. It all happened so quickly. My hand closed of its own volition on the only thing within reach, an ornamental vase that was probably worth a fortune. Good. I flung it with all my might toward Nona.

Against all odds it hit her arm and fell to the floor, shattered. Nona didn't drop the gun, but she did forget her original target. She swung the weapon toward me instead.

How very strange. I seemed to be not a part of earth time anymore. It was as if I had entered some placid, quiet dimension where everything was happening at an unbelievably slow pace. I no longer had power to move quickly enough. I knew I was probably going to die, but that didn't seem too important.

Absently, I watched three distinct little puffs erupt from Nona's gun, felt a tug inside my upper arm, another across my side. A little later, I realized I was falling. Only then did I hear the delayed reverberations of the gun's report echoing lazily through the room. I saw, as I fell ever so slowly, the angel-woman taking a swing at Nona with her rifle.

The mirrors were full of movement then, as measured and graceful as a stately ballet. I couldn't take it all in, but I saw Bryce limp on the floor with a blazing-eyed Stuart balanced over him. Saw the minister and Heather gliding out, right into the arms of some State Troopers. Saw Danny, white as angels' traditional garb, swaying on his feet, and another Trooper who seemed as tall as the ceiling, putting a steadying arm around him.

God bless the Missouri State Highway Patrol!

The floor and I met then, almost gently, and I felt a strange fire exploding in my side and my arm. The gaudy purple of Nona's precious dress was melting in the heat of that fire, changing to the color of the Soillse Flann diamonds, pulsing down my arm. Hot, steaming, liquid garnet splashed onto the beautiful polished wood of the floor, collected in a warm, growing puddle around me. The alien fire in my flesh burned on, leaving me weak and cold and ever more detached.

The faces above me were speaking. I recognized them, but I couldn't hear them, or feel the hands I saw frantically working to stop the fire. Caleb... Was I dying? Surely Caleb was dead, a walking corpse, all blood and bruises.

Maybe Danny was, too. Dead or dying. He was huddled close beside me now into the tiniest space possible for him, knees pulled up to his chin, arms locked around them as if he were rejecting us all, retreating deep, deep within himself. There was horror in his unfocused, unblinking eyes, and tears. Rivers of tears, crystal clear tributaries to the ocean of red between us. An ocean of blood. His father's and mine. I wanted to touch him, comfort him. I couldn't move.

My mother, kneeling there with us, had one arm around Danny, one hand on my wrist. My mother? The warrior-angel with the assault rifle? Her I could see best of all. Her face, her thoughts. It didn't seem at all odd to be looking into her mind like that. I was glad I could. I knew I was seeing things she wanted me to know and had no chance to tell me. She was afraid, full of an ancient, aching sorrow for what was between us, for what should have been, for what would never be. Then, wonder of wonders, I could see, shining with a brilliance that almost blinded me, a mother's true, never-ending love.

Yes. My mother. *Take care of Danny for me, Mama.* I couldn't have said it aloud, but she seemed to hear me. Her arm tightened around him almost convulsively and he leaned his head on her shoulder like a lost, frightened child. Smiling, I drifted toward peace.

Chapter 22

My mother was curled up in a chair beside my bed, her eyes closed, feet tucked under her, clothing rumpled as if she had been there for days. She seemed solid enough, but I watched her anxiously for a few minutes after I'd opened my eyes.

What if she weren't real? If I spoke, would she fade away into whatever dream world I had conjured her from? I had been having very odd and disturbing dreams. This wasn't my own room. Where was I?

As if she were feeling my thoughts, Lauren opened her eyes and looked at me. First that loving concern, then a wariness, like she was afraid.

"Hi." I smiled at her and my face felt stiff.

"Hi," she said, sitting up quickly. She pushed a button on the side of my bed.

A button? A hospital bed. Somehow that felt right. I had a feeling I ought to be in a hospital. Or in a coffin.

"Are you real?" I asked.

"As far as I can tell. Why?"

"I think I was dreaming some really weird dreams. Was I, or have we been having adventures?"

"Adventures. Oh, yeah. That's a good word for it."

"Where's Danny?"

"Probably right outside the door, unless they've found some way to pry him loose from there."

"He's okay?"

"Let's say he will be. He's recovering."

A nurse came in silently, smiled, checked my pulse, temperature, blood pressure. "Good," she said. "Are you hungry?"

I couldn't remember the last time I'd eaten. I did remember feeling totally starved. That hadn't changed. "When can I have dinner?"

"Just a little while."

"Can I have some water?" I asked.

"Let's go with some ice chips first."

When the nurse brought the ice, Lauren fed it to me. It helped some, but what I really wanted was a long, long drink of water. "When can I see Danny?"

Lauren grinned. "If you don't mind, I'd like to talk to you first."

"I want to talk to you, too. I didn't think I'd have the chance. For some reason, I expected to be dead." At the moment the reason eluded me.

"We all expected that and we're all very, very thankful we were wrong."

"How long have I been here?"

"Three days."

"I don't remember any of it. I don't even remember for sure why I'm here."

"You've been drifting in and out. I think they went pretty heavy on the sedative so you wouldn't mess up what they fixed. You're doing fine. They say they'll probably release you tomorrow. You're a tough kid. You always were. Do you know who I am?"

"Yes." One of my arms was immobilized, but I reached out with the other and she grasped my hand tightly. "I know you're my mother," I said. I watched her a moment. " I know you love me. Will you… Can you come home with me when I go? Only if you really want to, I mean."

Her eyes filled with tears. "Constancy, I do love you, but it's beyond me how you know. I sure didn't give much sign of it when you were little." She wiped her eyes impatiently. "For awhile there, I didn't think I was going to have the chance to make it up to you. Do you really want me?"

"I never gave up wanting you, but I was afraid. Mostly I was afraid you would never want me. It wasn't until I saw you kneeling there beside me with Danny that I knew I didn't have to be afraid anymore."

Suddenly the rest of the memory kicked in. "She shot me! That crazy Nona shot me."

My mother's face crinkled into sympathetic laughter. "Lie still, you'll tear something loose. You can't afford to start that wound bleeding again." She had beautiful, kind eyes, though they were tired and red-rimmed at the moment.

"She did shoot me? I wasn't just dreaming that?"

"Yes, she shot you. Twice."

"Is that all?"

"It was very nearly enough. Thank God, it was only a .22 and pulled a little off center. One bullet scraped your side with only minimal damage, but another one nicked an artery on its way through your arm. You nearly bled to death." She stopped for a deep breath. "You may yet need some therapy on that arm. The nerve is pretty close to the artery there. Still, it could have been a lot worse. If Nona's aim had been better, you could have died instantly."

"She fired three shots. I remember counting them."

My mother watched me a moment. "The third bullet didn't hit you."

I shifted carefully to what I hoped would be a more comfortable position and smiled at her again. I couldn't seem to keep from smiling. "You can't imagine how happy I was to have you appear just when I most needed you. How many girls have mothers who ride to their rescue toting a weapon like you were carrying? Is that monster yours?"

"No, but I did have permission to use it."

"Permission from whom?"

She shrugged. "It seemed the thing to do at the time. It's a flashy weapon. Impressive. Just holding it makes a pretty good point."

"It did with Bryce. Do you, uh, know how to use it?"

"I don't carry anything I'm not ready and able to use."

"But you didn't use it, unless I missed something."

"No. Don't think I didn't want to. I miscalculated. If I'd thought for a minute Nona was going to turn it into a shoot-out, I would have taken something else. But I couldn't risk firing that at her. Not even to save you. There were too many people in too confined a space, and all of them were moving. I wasn't sure which ones were on our side, and if I had fired, anybody not taken out by bullets was going to be sliced to pieces by all that glass. Something with less fire power would have been more practical. It was one of the worst moments of my life. I slugged her instead, but I couldn't get to her until after the damage was done. She'll probably try to have me charged with assault and battery."

I looked at her wide-eyed. "Are you a police officer, too?"

"Not exactly."

"Then where did you learn how to shoot that gun?"

"It's just something I picked up along the way," she said, with a quirky grin.

"You'd better come home with me. It's going to take you years to answer all the questions I have about you."

She had a delightful laugh, too. "We do have a lot of catching up to do."

"Was anybody else hurt?"

"None of the good guys except you ended up in intensive

care. Danny needed some heavy-duty antibiotic and a night's enforced sleep. Caleb spent a night here, too, for some earlier damage. Both of them are on their feet again now. It'll take awhile before everything's completely back to normal, but you're all going to be fine."

"I saw Caleb after I was shot. That's why I thought I might be dead. I thought Bryce killed him."

"Bryce didn't shoot to kill. Caleb said he just wanted you too scared to think. He didn't mind causing Caleb a little more mental anguish, either. He fired into a wooden beam. Caleb got splinters."

"I hope I never see Bryce again, except maybe to testify at his trial."

"You won't have to see him. Or testify against him. Nona's third bullet saved the taxpayers considerable expense. By then, she'd pretty well got her range. Hitting Bryce wasn't an accident."

"Oh. Oh! What about Zared? Romney told me he was dead."

"Calm down. Romney probably believed Zared was dead. So did Nona. Even Zared thought so for awhile. He was unconscious for some time, but Timon found him and managed to revive him. They figured it was time to get some help. At least they had sense enough not to get the local police. Zared called Danny's apartment. I was there and Danny and Stuart were just coming in. We called for backup and got here as quickly as we could. I happened to drive a little faster than Danny." A fleeting smile. "Zared sends his best, by the way. He says he doesn't think you'll want to see him, and to tell you he really was fond of you, but he's convinced Danny will make a better husband than he would. Especially for you."

"He's got that right, that I don't want to see him, I mean. I'll be happy if I never see another member of Bart's immediate family. Except for George."

"Any more questions?"

"Lots. Beginning at the beginning. Does anybody know who drugged me the day we got engaged and why?"

"Heather did, with a little help from Bryce. They gave you something in the tomato juice first. Then after the lunch, Heather volunteered to take you home. Instead, they took you to some quiet room in the office building. Heather had the bright idea that if they got you high enough, you'd tell them where you were keeping the red diamonds. She thought if she could get hold of those, Zared would drop you."

"I was a sad disappointment to them. Is that why they pushed me in front of Stuart's car?"

"Believe it or not, that had to be pure coincidence. You wandered away while they were both out of the room. You led them quite a chase, I understand, before they caught up with you and finally took you home. They knew Nona would be furious if anything happened to you before she decided the time was right. It obviously isn't wise to make Nona furious."

"I saw the Troopers grab Heather. Is she in jail?"

"She is, along with that so-called minister."

"One more question: How did you happen to be in the right place at the right time? Not that I'm complaining."

"I've been afraid you would be in trouble from the moment Gram died. I was also afraid you wouldn't want anything to do with me. That letter didn't get very good results, but why should it? I had no right to expect open arms."

"I'm sorry about that."

"I didn't blame you. I was sticking pretty close, anyway. I've been in town since the funeral, trying to keep an eye on things. Danny said you thought you were being followed." She grinned. "I'm slipping."

"It was you?"

"At least partly. Mr. Vanek knew what I was doing. I asked him not to tell you, if he could avoid it. But he did give Danny my address. Danny and I exchanged references and decided to join forces. He picked me up before his class and I rode out to Dunne with him so he could finish briefing me on what had been happening, and what he expected to happen next. That man's magic with a fiddle."

"So I've been told."

"You've never heard him play?"

"Not live. I've never even seen the fiddle. What happened?"

"They arrested him right in the middle of a good, fast reel. It was ridiculous, but there wasn't anything he could do. The cop had a warrant."

"Lon Tirso?"

"Yeah. He was having the time of his life."

I moved impatiently, trying to ease the relentless aching.

"Are you still hurting?" Lauren asked.

"More or less. Mostly I'm thirsty. Ice chips. Bah! I'm hungry, too. This drippy stuff going into my arm isn't very filling. How much blood did I lose?"

"Barely, just barely, short of too much. Do you mind if we don't talk too long about that part of it?"

"Okay, but will you help me with some more ice chips? They're better than nothing, I guess. Dracula must have felt like this about sunset."

When I'd nearly frozen my tongue on the ice, Lauren put the cup back onto the table. "I owe you my life," she said. "If you hadn't acted, it'd be me in that bed instead of you, or we'd both be in the morgue. I thought I was handling everything pretty well, but even with all those mirrors I didn't see her gun until you threw the vase at her."

"You couldn't watch them all at once."

"I meant to ask you, did you know who I was then?"

"I didn't recognize you on a conscious level. You look different from the way I remember you."

"Creeping old age, I'm sorry to say. You've changed some yourself."

"I guess I have. Anyway, all I knew about you then was that you were the answer to prayer and I didn't want Nona hurting you."

A wisp of a smile touched her mouth. "An answer to prayer. I don't think I've ever been called that before. Constancy, that was a very stupid thing you did. But very brave. Thanks."

"Thank you for being there. I wasn't exactly winning the battle when you showed up."

"I would have saved us all some pain if I'd come back sooner. Like several years ago." She paced around the room for a couple of minutes, with a frown creasing her forehead.

"What's wrong?"

"There's something else I have to tell you. I don't quite know how to do it."

"M-more bad news?"

"No. Oh, honey, no. Nothing like that. I'm sorry. It's that pig planter."

"What?"

"I remember, as a kid, thinking that pig planter was the ugliest piece of pottery Gram ever made."

I wanted to laugh, but it didn't seem a wise thing to do at the moment. "He was her favorite creation," I said. "She made me promise solemnly that I would never give him away or sell him. If I got tired of him, I had to smash him to little bits no bigger than the opals in her wedding jewelry and give him a decent burial. Her words. She was serious."

Lauren had a funny glint in her eye. "I'm sure she was."

"She didn't need to worry. That pig's precious because she made him, but what's he got to do with anything?"

"Your pig was more precious than you knew. He had something for you. A final present from Gram."

"What are you talking about?"

"Here. Make a nest in the blanket. We don't want them

escaping again." She dug a tiny leather pouch out of her pocket, like one a kid might keep marbles in. From it she poured not marbles, but a little stream of blood-red sparkle onto the bed.

Chapter 23

"Ta-da," Lauren said. "Meet the long-lost Soillse Flann diamonds."

I wasn't sure I was ready to meet them. "Where did you find those things?"

"I told you. Gram baked them into that pig."

So the pig had been up to mischief. Gram, too. "She put diamonds in the kiln? They're pure carbon. They can burn like coal. The Frasers'll have heart attacks when they find out. If I remember my physics, diamonds can ignite at a lower temperature than what it takes to fire clay."

"That's right, but to burn anything, you've got to have oxygen as well as heat. Gram wrapped the diamonds in asbestos cloth, then she sealed them into the clay base, so they were nearly air tight. It was a risk, but it worked."

"Why did she take that kind of risk with something so valuable?"

"She knew Bart wasn't going to give up looking for them, but he would never think to look there. Only a clumsy accident would have revealed them."

My involuntary burst of laughter became a groan. It could hurt to laugh.

"Careful! What's so funny?"

"Sooner or later I would have found them, if she was counting on clumsy."

"The planter was fired years before you were born, Constancy. My mother was less than a month old when Gram made it. This is one of the things that prompted my letter to Mr. Vanek. I thought it might be better if the diamonds were in the open, so you wouldn't have fortune hunters forever searching for them, putting you in who-knows-what jeopardy. You'd just be safer if the mystery of the missing diamonds were officially solved. Constancy, you aren't that clumsy."

"Oh, yeah? Ask Danny about that." I picked up the eight carat stone that would have been the pendant in the necklace and inspected it. Definitely gaudy, even if it was the nicest color I'd ever seen in a diamond. "How come Gram didn't just put them in a bank vault?"

"She was dealing with Frasers, remember. She was afraid they might be able to find a way to finagle them out of a bank. But they sure couldn't get them if they couldn't find them."

"How did you know where the diamonds were?"

"Gram told me, of course. In case something happened to her. I think she told Grandad George, too."

"I didn't know you'd ever seen Gram again after you…"

"After I deserted you." Lauren looked away from me. "Gram and I were able to make our peace years ago, Constancy. She told me a lot of things that I want to pass on to you. I hoped when you were a little older, she would tell you some of my story."

"It wasn't her fault she didn't. It hurt so much when you left me. I can't pretend it didn't, and I can't pretend that I was all noble and forgiving about it. I wasn't. I was angry with you all those years. I didn't want to hear anything Gram or anybody else said about you. I didn't want to forgive."

"It's what I deserved."

"No, wait. I'm not done. When Nona shot me, and you were kneeling there holding my hand and holding Danny, I could see that you loved me, that you always had. I knew that whatever your reasons for going without me, they must have been compelling ones."

"How could you know all that?"

"I have no idea, but I'm right, aren't I?"

"You're right that I love you and always have. Someday when we're over all this, I want to tell you why I left you with Gram and why I didn't come back into your life until now. Then you can decide for yourself how compelling my reasons were."

"I already have decided. Maybe we'll have some rough spots to work out and maybe not, but I'm not angry anymore. I'm just thrilled that you're here."

She squeezed my hand. "Thank you, Constancy. That's more than I deserve, more than I ever thought possible."

Both of us wiped tears from our eyes. "Sorry," I said. "I don't usually get all weepy."

She laughed. "It's definitely more sentiment than I'm used to, I'll admit. I've never much gone in for that touchy-feely stuff."

"Me, either. Did you have to break up the pig?"

"No. We just removed the base. Gram told me how. He's all glued back together now and both he and the ivy plant are doing fine."

I almost wished the things had been left in the pig. Would they ignite that diamond fever in Lauren? Gram had trusted her with the knowledge of where they were, but as long as they were hidden, they were an abstract, theoretical treasure. Now she was seeing them, touching them. They were shiny and real and worth more money than I could imagine.

I watched my mother's face carefully as she sat looking at the stones. I didn't want to see that fatal Fraser curse in her eyes, but I had to know. She poked at them with one finger. "They're pretty, aren't they?" she said. "But they're too hard and too cold and way too much trouble." There was no greed at all in her expression, not even a liking for the diamonds.

"Do you want them? If you do, they're yours." The ultimate test.

She looked at me like I'd offered her a glass of cyanide with her supper. "You couldn't pay me to take them. I didn't want them when Gram offered them to me several years ago and I don't want them now."

"I think I know where we could get a hefty sum of money for them," I said.

"Zared and company?"

"Right. We could auction them, but the Frasers would get them back eventually, anyway. We may as well go the direct route and save all the middleman fees. Now that Bart's out of it, I don't think Gram or Lucian would mind if they went back to the collection."

"I think you're right. What will you do with your hefty sum, if you don't mind my asking? You sound like a woman with a purpose."

"Our hefty sum," I said. "Both of us are descendants of George and Amanda, so the money's as much yours as mine. But with your approval, I do have a use for some of it. These dark diamonds have inspired a lot of evil. I want to use them now, or the money from them, to spread as much light as possible. First, I want to start a fund to help families of police officers who've been killed on duty. We'll look around and see if we can't find some other ways to lighten the darkness. Maybe George's ranch needs a new barn or something, too."

"Constancy, Gram would be proud of you. She would want you to keep some of the proceeds though."

"Why?"

"To put in trust for your children's education. They'll be descendants of George's eldest child, too, and that is why the diamonds were given. Gram wanted you and your children to have everything you needed."

"Did she tell you that, too?"

"Yes."

"But she left me the house and most of the rest of her estate. I don't need any more. Besides, I don't have any children."

"You will. You'll be a great mother." She gathered up the diamonds. "I'll give these to Mr. Vanek, if that's okay with you. He'll know how to handle the sale."

"Yes. I don't want to think about them any more."

"I don't blame you. Sweetheart, I've been very selfish, talking to you for so long. I know you're hurting, but could you endure another visitor for just a few minutes?"

"Depends on who it is."

"How about the man who's going to give you the children you'll need to educate?"

"If you're talking about Danny, don't be too sure of that."

"We'll see. I should have let him in sooner. He's been lurking outside the door since they let him out of bed yesterday morning and nobody can get him to go home. The staff's sick of having him underfoot. If you'll talk to him a minute, maybe you'll put him out of their misery."

I was hurting. I could feel all my injuries acutely, the aching muscles, the dull throb of bruises, a sharp, burning sting in my arm. But remembering Danny's reaction to those injuries, I thought it was possible he might be hurting worse. "I want to see him."

"Alone?"

"Please. But don't order any wedding cake yet. Last I heard, he wasn't quite ready to rescind his ban on marriage. Why don't you go to the house and get some rest."

"I hate leaving you." She blushed and bit her lip. "I'm sorry I ever left you."

"Please don't agonize over it. I'm not. Besides, this time it's just for tonight. You need to go get some decent sleep. I don't want you too exhausted to answer the rest of my questions, like what do you do for a living?"

She grinned. "You're sure you don't mind staying by yourself?"

"I'm sure."

"I'll admit a shower and a real bed sound good, but if you need me again tonight, I can be here in ten minutes."

"I'll be fine."

"Then I'll come first thing tomorrow and take you home as soon as they'll let me. After that I'll give you all the time you need to ask your questions."

"Mama, thanks for being here. Thanks for everything."

It was the first time in twenty years I'd called her that to her face. She gave me a glorious smile as she left, her eyes sparkling with a light more precious to me than the sparkle of any diamond.

A minute later, Danny slipped into the room like a half-materialized wraith and stood gazing down on me from a spot just inches from the door. There was no emotion at all visible on his haggard, emaciated face. I might have been a total stranger. "How are you feeling?" he asked faintly.

"Glad to find us both alive. Glad to have my mother back. Determined not to get in front of any more bullets."

"That was an idiotic thing for you to do."

"I'm prone to that, remember? 'Into the jaws of death.'"

"It's nothing to joke about," he snapped.

"It is today. I had to do what I did, Danny."

"I know."

But knowing hadn't made it easier for him. Though he was fighting it, there was plenty of emotion showing now, none of it good. "You've forgotten to eat again, haven't you?" I said.

He was in no mood for teasing. He shivered like he had a

chill. "How could I eat, remembering you lying there so pale and so cold that I was sure every drop of blood must've drained away in that eternity before they could get it stopped. M-most of it did."

"But I didn't die. I'm still here to make life entertaining for you in that morbid way I have."

I kept hoping to make him smile, somehow to ease his awful, useless agony, to explode that mile-high barrier he had put up between us. Nothing was working. "Danny, don't look like that. The nightmare's over."

"I'll go now," he whispered, and did it before I could open my mouth to protest.

I lay staring at the closed door.

Was that it?

Was that the end? No acknowledgment of the feelings that had grown between us, the attraction he'd finally admitted to both of us? Not even a formal goodbye? Even if he'd decided he couldn't marry me, he should have said so. I could have accepted that more easily.

I might have known it would end this way. Past experience should have taught me that much. Hadn't I told myself over and over not to let Danny affect me again? But I'd done it anyway. I'd fallen, no, leapt, straight into it and sunk more deeply than ever. Now I was going to be suffering the consequences for a long, long time.

When the nurse came with my supper, I couldn't eat much of it after all. Every ache and pain seemed worse than before. I almost begged her for a sleeping pill. Like Danny said, there were some days that blotting out might improve.

Chapter 24

"**R**eady to go home?" Lauren, smiling, tossed a white department store box onto the foot of the bed.

I didn't have the heart to stifle her eager excitement. "What's in the box?" I asked.

"I went out and bought my daughter a dress." She frowned. "I missed a lot leaving you with Gram. I'll have to make up for it by buying dozens of those sweet little size 3T pinafores for my granddaughters."

"Don't count them before they're hatched."

A sharp glance. "All right. This is clearly not a good time to talk about grandchildren. What's wrong?"

"Danny didn't stay more than three minutes in here last night. When he left, he just left. He didn't smile at me. He didn't come near me. He didn't even say goodbye."

Lauren looked first confused, then incredulous and finally angry. "You mean he didn't tell you? Honestly! That man's got fluff where the little gray cells ought to be."

"More Winnie-the-Pooh than Poirot." I giggled despite

myself. "He likes teddy bears, but he wouldn't appreciate that. What was he supposed to tell me?"

"The idiot! He promised to explain and instead you've been worrying all this time."

"Explain what?"

"Your doctor ordered him not to set foot in this room. He had an awful cold and it settled in his lungs and went bacterial while they were holding him and Stuart in that damp cell. He was coming close to pneumonia. I've never seen such rotten facilities. I'd better start at the beginning."

"How could they arrest him?"

"They had a warrant on some trumped up charge of impersonating a police officer. That Tirso barged into his classroom, frisked and cuffed him, read him his rights—the whole business—with all his students looking on. He took great care to make it as public and as humiliating as possible for Danny."

"That's Lon. Couldn't you do anything?"

"I did. I slipped out and phoned Danny's boss."

"Danny's boss? Heather said he'd been fired."

"Not by his real employer. Danny was working undercover in Fraserton, helping to investigate charges of police corruption on the force there."

"He found it, didn't he?"

"Not as much as they'd figured. It was only Tirso and one other guy who were moonlighting for Nona, or anybody else who would pay them."

"Then what's Danny? FBI or something?"

"Missouri State Highway Patrol."

Of course he was. I'd had enough clues to guess that if I had thought about it.

"Well, even with my tip-off to Colonel McCann, Tirso managed to hold Danny and Stuart almost twenty-four hours without benefit of council or even a phone call. Danny was a real wreck before the Colonel finally got them released. He—Danny, I mean—had a broiling fever and a cough that sounded like death. His nerves were a disaster. He was imagining all sorts of horrible things happening to you, and him not there to stop it. They did put him in with Stuart, whom they'd collected when Heather reported the body. It's a good thing for Danny that they did. Stuart managed to provide a little bit of a calming influence."

"No wonder Danny wouldn't smile."

"The doctor didn't want him near you yesterday because of the risk of infection. You were pretty weak yourself after that massive blood loss. So we were breaking the rules letting him in at all, but he really needed to see with his own eyes that you were alive and recovering. He promised he wouldn't touch you. That was a medical necessity, but he was supposed to tell you why. He's had some good sleep now. His fever's gone and his mother's forced a couple of decent meals down him. He'll meet us at the house."

"Are you sure he wants to? He was acting awfully strange last night. It wasn't just being sick."

"Fluff!" Lauren repeated, then her face softened. "And shock, maybe. He deserves a little slack on that. Nothing he had imagined was as horrible as the reality that met him at Fraser House. He got there just in time to watch Nona fire those bullets into you and realize there wasn't a thing any of us could do about it. He was convinced he was watching you die. He fell apart. I've never seen anybody, any professional, react quite that way to a shooting."

"Oceans of blood," I said.

"What?"

"When he was ten-years-old, he saw his father shot and killed. Oceans of blood, he told me. Friday night must have brought that back pretty vividly."

"First his dad and then you. That would explain it. It took a long time and a lot of sedative to get him calmed down. By morning, he was mentally in control again, but he's not entirely over it. I'm not sure he ever will be." Lauren picked up the box. "Let's get you ready to go. This dress isn't going to make any fashion statement, but it'll go on easily over your bandages and your stiff arm and the color will be good with your hair."

"As long as it's not purple."

"It's bright shamrock green. In honor of Amanda Casey and Danny Egan. Come on. The nurse told me you'd had all your lectures and the paper work and everything was finished. We can leave any time you're ready."

On the way home, Lauren filled in a few more blanks.

"Did Zared know what Nona was doing?"

"They all say not, and I think it's true. Heather happened to intercept Caleb's letter and she took it straight to Nona. They arranged the meeting and the kidnapping and hired Bryce to take care of the strong-arm stuff. Neither Caleb nor Stuart ever met the real Zared. Stuart saw Timon, who thought it was a big joke to play the part of his older brother."

"Nona sent the gunman after Stuart so he wouldn't find out the difference, and the gunman blew it and ended up in our flower bed?"

"Not exactly. As well as I can piece it together, he wasn't a professional. He was one of Bryce's dimmer associates. Nona intended, she says, that the guy just bring Stuart back to Fraser House to be kept with Caleb until the deadline passed. If that's true, which I doubt, he didn't follow orders very well. He was an addict, taking his wages in his drug of choice. When he bragged to Bryce about killing Stuart, it looks like Bryce may have given him a little something extra. He intended it to be lethal. They haven't finished the lab tests yet."

"Why did they put him in my kitchen and take him out again?"

"That was another one of Heather's air-head plots. She was sure Zared wouldn't want to marry you after another murder investigation. She and Bryce set up their old friend in your kitchen. Then Nona found out. Having you arrested didn't suit Nona's plan at all. She had other things in mind for you. She ordered Bryce to get rid of the body. It was dark when he took it in, but he took some big chances getting it out of there in broad daylight. I'm not sure what would've happened if you hadn't gone outside to wait for Danny. I don't much want to think about that.

"Bryce was hedging his bets, so to speak, by putting the guy in your flower bed. At any time, he could phone in an anonymous tip and they'd have you. As it was, they used it to good advantage."

"Nice."

Lauren turned the car into the drive. "Good. Danny's here."

Judging by the vehicles in the yard, several other people were, too. Even before we opened the door, I could hear music.

"What's going on?"

"Celebration and thanksgiving."

"I hate parties."

"This isn't a party and you won't hate it. Full, money-back guarantee. It's a family reunion. The South Dakota branch of the family is represented by Caleb, his wife and his brother, Noah, along with Stuart and his intended, Fiona. Irma West promised to come, and some of the Mackinnons, too. Rose and Cam, for sure. Gavin thought he might keep the girls home. He was afraid they'd be a little too much for you right now."

"I'm longing to meet Danny's sisters. Have you seen them?"

"Briefly. They're sweet girls, but they can be a little overwhelming all at once. Anyway, I'm not sure who else is in there, but they're all family, more or less. We've fixed Gram's bedroom for you, so you won't have to climb the stairs. We'll go in the front. You don't have to see any of them yet."

"Let's go in the front, but I want to see what's going on."

Lauren kept a protective arm around me as we walked quietly down the hall to a spot where we could see into the kitchen. At first glance it seemed to be overflowing with people and warmth and sunlight and fiddle music. Nobody had noticed our arrival. All eyes were on the center of the room.

Danny and a wiry, Fraser-featured man who was dressed authentically western from his scuffed and worn cowboy boots to his dusty, battered, beige Stetson, were sitting knee-to-knee with fiddles under their chins. Danny, intense, unsmiling, was blazing away at some fantastic, triple-speed reel, his fingers and bow a blur on the strings. The other man was doing his best to add a wild, screaming harmony to the tune, and his best was very good. It was a fantastic performance. The fiddles were perfectly synchronized, each perfectly attuned to the other. Both men were lost in what they were doing, and they pulled everybody else into it with them.

It certainly wasn't a Fraser House-type production and if I hadn't been so exhausted and shaky, it was just the kind of thing I would enjoy. Or so I thought until I began really to hear what was happening.

The piece was almost beyond music. Danny's fiddle sang a dark howling wail, bleak and savage and as terrifying as anything I'd faced in the past few days. Then I realized, it was what I'd faced. What we'd both faced. Danny himself must be the source of the tune, his over-worked emotions the driving power behind it, and the fiddle in his hands merely a channel for all the black turbulence still seething inside him.

Irma had been understating the case considerably when she said he was better than good. Genius is an overused word, but this was genius: passionate, brilliant, and so devastating that I couldn't bear to hear more of it. I couldn't yet face reliving everything we'd just been through. Trembling, I tugged at Lauren's arm. She was looking as shaken as I felt.

That disturbing reel pursued us to the other side of the house and I could have sworn I heard Nona's gunshots in it, and Danny's anguished collapse as it came, mercifully, to a crashing, dramatic end.

Gram's bedroom, by contrast, was light and warm and blessedly tranquil. For a minute, neither Lauren nor I could speak. Then the fiddles began again. This time they were playing something entirely different. It was a whimsical little waltz, perfect harmony for the warm sunshine flowing through the window and a sweet reminder that real life could be gentle and lovely and full of peace. They were playing away the darkness.

"That's better," Lauren said. "Constancy, that man of yours is flat-out spooky."

"He's not my man."

"Oh? I've heard him play this waltz before. You know what he calls it?"

"I have no idea."

"He calls it 'Constancy's Waltz'. He played it in class that night before Tirso arrested him. He tells people it's a portrait of you."

The music tripped and tumbled and lilted on. *Constancy's Waltz*. I'd heard it back in May on tape. I told Danny then that I loved it. I didn't know then that he was the fiddler, or the tune's composer. He certainly hadn't mentioned its title. Just as well. He couldn't have convinced me I meant nothing to him if I'd known.

Lauren got me settled on the bed with pillows in all the most comfortable places. "He does love you, Constancy. You don't need to worry about that. You can't listen to that waltz he made for you and doubt it, can you?"

"There are varying degrees of love. Writing a song for somebody and agreeing to spend your life with them are two entirely different things."

She grinned. "I'll send him in."

"Only if he wants to come."

"He'll come. But, Constancy, even though he knows now that you're going to survive, he's still taking it hard, berating himself because he didn't get there just a little earlier, and because he'd let you get into the mess in the first place."

"He didn't let me."

"I know, but he's convinced the whole thing's his fault. Take it easy on him. He needs reassurance from you as much as you do from him."

Danny came, looking, to use one of his favorite similes, like a puppy who knew he was about to be punished. Once more he stopped just inside the door. He was still clutching his fiddle.

"You come away from that door, Brendan Conor Aengus Egan. I don't want you escaping again before we have a nice long talk. Come sit here."

He laid his fiddle and bow gently on the foot of the bed and perched there beside them, jaw clenched, saying nothing. He was still far too thin and pale and his beautiful hands were shaking.

"I heard your reel," I told him. "Last May when I asked you if you played, you told me you dabbled. That, my blarney-proficient friend, bordered on a lie. One of your names should have been Oisin."

Still he didn't speak. A speechless Danny was an unnatural thing and an unnerving one. "Well, if that Irish tongue of yours has finally failed you, help me rearrange these pillows. My arm hurts."

My arm did hurt, but the pillow business was pure and simple ambush. As he reached forward to help me, it put his face in exactly the position I had hoped for. If he complained, I would tell him that the kiss, like his awful coffee, was medicinal.

He didn't complain. In fact, he cooperated with considerable enthusiasm. When he broke it off a little later, the color had come back to his face, he was no longer trembling and his speech was once more in full working order.

"'Dark Diamond Reel,'" he said. "That's the title of it. I'm sorry you heard it, but it was play it out of my system or explode."

"Umm. That's more like the Danny I know and love."

The light died out of his eyes. He picked up the fiddle again, cradled it in his arms as if its presence comforted him. "I've no idea how you could say you love me after Friday night. Or even ever forgive me for it."

"Well, I do love you, and what's to forgive?"

He ignored my attempt at reassurance.

"A grand, brave show I was putting on, wasn't it? When the crisis came, what did I do but fall apart? All the training, all the experience, and Danny Egan comes altogether unglued. It's just as well I've decided not to go back."

"What?"

"Who's to say the same thing would not be happening again and again?"

"I say so, you maudlin Irishman."

"You're the great expert, are you?"

"Use the good brain God gave you, Danny. Here. Give me that fiddle before you crush it. Please. Let me hold it a minute. I've never had a fiddle in my hands before. I'll be careful."

"Don't be touching the strings."

"I won't."

He handed it to me reluctantly and I propped it in my lap and ran my fingers over the satiny, glowing wood. It was comforting.

"You were nearly out of your mind with fever Friday night. I don't care how much you deny it, you were sleep-deprived and malnourished, too. You'd already set yourself up for some kind of collapse."

A bleak look.

"Danny, what can I say? If there were anything to forgive, I already would have forgiven it. As a Christian, aren't you supposed to understand both forgiveness and trust, or at least believe they're possible?"

With fingers as gentle and cold as snow flakes, he touched my face where the bruises had turned blotchy, nauseating shades of citron and plum. "It's hard to believe you could trust me enough to marry me," he said.

"Are you asking me to marry you?"

He bowed his head. "I was, though it wasn't a much better effort than Fraser made, was it?"

"Was, too. The answer is a provisional yes."

A quick, worried glance. "What provisions?"

"Just one. You can't quit your job."

The anguish in his face stabbed deep. "You don't understand. I can't have both things, and if I can't, I'd rather have you."

"Now, maybe. But sooner or later you might begin to resent the fact that I took you away from the job you love. If I weren't in the picture at all, wouldn't you be working again at the first possible moment? Tell me the truth."

"The truth?" He ran a finger down the length of the wood of his fiddle bow, which he hadn't relinquished. "I believed in my work. I've not wanted any other job, ever. But, my father... Constancy, I've seen what that job can do to wives, and to children. I know how the darkness uses it to batter the innocent."

"You also know how the Light sustains and heals them," I said. "Danny, everybody takes some hits in this life. Whether you married me or not, you couldn't protect me from every hurt. As Gram was fond of saying, 'If it's not one thing, it's another.'"

He opened his mouth and I leaned forward and shoved my hand over it. "Will you just listen? If you give up this job because you're afraid for me, nobody wins but the darkness. You're good at what you do. We need you doing it."

Danny pushed me gently back against the pillows. "Lie still, now, or you'll reopen that wound."

"What about the job?"

"Colonel McCann isn't wanting my resignation, either." A fleeting grin. "At least not at the moment."

"There. You're outnumbered."

He sighed. "Before you agree to marry me, you need to understand that the nature of the job makes police officers notoriously hard to live with. Musicians are an even higher risk. There's not much hope for us, is there?"

He wasn't going to scare me away with that. "No, I suppose not."

It wasn't what he expected or wanted me to say. He looked like I'd kicked him.

"Still," I said, "kindergarten teachers are noted for their tact, their patience and their resilience, so who knows?" I echoed his sigh. "Maybe since I can't get a teaching job now and there's not much hope for a marriage, I should go into research."

"Research?"

"Your mother mentioned something about an experiment and that put the thought in my head."

"What kind of research?"

"I was thinking it might be an interesting scientific study to see how the two stereotypes of musician-policeman and kindergarten teacher interact in a long-term relationship. I believe they would balance each other perfectly."

"Rose proposed that?"

"Oh, no. She was talking about something entirely different. This experiment was my own idea. Of course it might take a lot of years to do it right, but I've always wanted a long-term career. Do you think it might be a worthwhile study?"

He was silent for a long moment, his eyes on the fiddle. I held my breath.

"It might be at that," he said slowly, and glanced up at me, his face carefully blank. "You'll need an assistant for the experiment," he added.

"I know. But it's so hard to get good help these days. I might advertise."

"You might."

"Or I might offer you the job. If you're interested."

Again, I thought he wasn't going to answer. Then the mischief flashed back into those green eyes. "It sounds a daunting job. I expect there'd be certain compensations with it, though."

"You never know with experiments. That's what makes them interesting. Do you want the job or don't you, Officer Egan?"

"Well then, Ms. Stafford, my darlin', I believe I do." He smiled. "I do, indeed. Who am I at all, at all to be standing in the way of a new career for you, to say nothing of a worthwhile scientific study? When shall we start?"

"As soon as possible, I'd say."

"I shall be ready at your convenience." He solemnly shook my hand as if to seal the pact. Then, with a smile that increased my heart rate considerably, took the fiddle from me and began to play what must have been the happiest little tune ever composed.

This time, I was absolutely sure I heard Gram laughing.

~END~

About the Author

Donna Parker was born in the rural Missouri Ozarks during an ice storm. Despite some circumstantial evidence to the contrary, she did not grow up in the 1800s.

The most important things in her life are her Christianity and her family. She loves books, both reading and writing them, old things and their histories, and music—especially Celtic and bluegrass fiddle music.

She and her husband of thirty-four years currently live in Alabama. They have two adult sons.